Praise for *Death and Croissants*

"A joyous read."

—Alan Carr

"A very funny page-turner. Fantastique!"

—Adam Kay

"A writer of immense wit and charm."

—Paul Sinha

"Beautifully done. Very funny indeed."

—Miles Jupp

"This is hilarious and a great mystery too."

—Janey Godley

"*Death and Croissants* is a far funnier book than a story about a bloody murder has any right to be."

—Josh Widdicombe

"A tricksy whodunit and a really, really funny story."

—Jason Manford

"Good food and a laugh-out-loud mystery. What more could anyone want in these dark times?"

—Mark Billingham

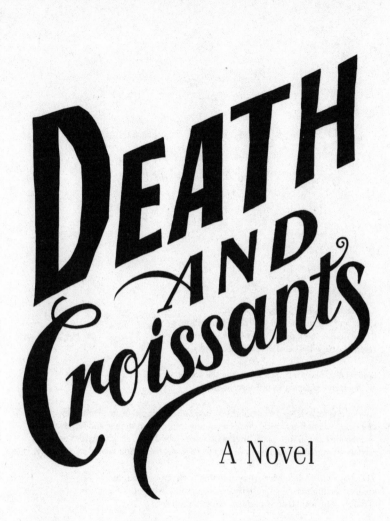

DEATH AND Croissants

A Novel

IAN MOORE

Poisoned Pen
PRESS

For Natalie and the boys

Published by Poisoned Pen Press, an imprint of Sourcebooks
P.O. Box 4410, Naperville, Illinois 60567-4410
(630) 961-3900
sourcebooks.com

Originally published as *Death and Croissants* in 2021 in Great Britain by Farrago, an
imprint of Duckworth Books Ltd. This edition issued based on the hardcover edition
published in 2021 in Great Britain by Farrago, an imprint of Duckworth Books Ltd.

Cataloging-in-Publication Data is on file with the Library of Congress.

Printed and bound in the United States of America.
WOZ 10 9 8 7 6 5 4 3 2 1

1

Is there anything in this world quite as joyless as muesli?

It wasn't that Richard Ainsworth was in a bad mood necessarily, just that he found mornings difficult. Trying would be a better word. He found mornings trying, something to be endured before reaching the slightly less trying afternoons and evenings. Mornings are the cold, filthy foot bath you're forced to step through before you're allowed into the warmth and relative cleanliness of the public swimming pool. He sighed with resignation. He was well aware that plenty of people had a problem with mornings, but plenty of people didn't also run a bed and breakfast. And a bed and breakfast in the bucolic Loire Valley, too, where things can *only* happen in the mornings.

Breakfast could be an awkward geography at the best of times; generally, Richard struggled to find that delicate balance between being on hand as a host while also leaving the guest to enjoy, if that was the right word, their morning meal in peace. The trick was to look approachable but disengaged. Attentive but standoffish. That way nobody could accuse you of not serving their needs but would hopefully think twice before actually asking for anything. It was less discreet customer service, more defense mechanism, and as usual, he was avoiding eye contact and trying to melt unobtrusively into the background.

He'd never actually tried muesli. It always reminded him of his nan's pet budgie, Vince, named after the singer Vince Hill, who his nan adored but who no one else had ever heard of, probably not even Mrs. Hill. Vince lived in a small cage, the budgie not the singer, which was positioned to overhang the right-hand side of a tired brown velour settee—everything was brown in the seventies—with a prime view of the television. His nan permanently occupied the left-hand side of the sofa, a large Rothmans International gripped in her bony, chopstick-like fingers, hovering, ash tip precariously long, between her narrow, pink-lipsticked mouth and an enormous glass ashtray. It was the bottom of Vince's cage, though, all half-eaten seeds and discarded grains and millets. That's what muesli reminded him of, rejected budgie food.

This memory, and with it a little dig at the modern world, a perennial pastime, cheered him a little. The thought that the twenty-first-century go-getter and fitness freak started the day not with a perceived "superfood" but with some 1970s discarded bird silage would carry him through the breakfast shift, most likely. And he needed it to. It was 8:45, and he was flagging already. In fact, he thought, retreating once more into the warmth of childhood memories, he felt a bit like Nan's old settee. Old and worn out, fraying at the edges a bit, put upon, though also slightly hungover, something he doubted many settees suffered from.

He was overdoing it with the hiding this morning, though, spending far too long gawking into the cereal jar, and far from melting into the background, he was actually now attracting the nervous "is he all right, do you think?" attentions of the Italian newlyweds in the corner. He assumed they were newlyweds anyway. Certainly, to his jaundiced eye, their constant need to grip one another with public displays of affection indicated that it wasn't, thus far, a long-term relationship. They were still at the excited, curious, physical stage of love. The novelty not having yet worn off. Ah well, good for them, he conceded, why not? He decided to make a show of trying to look busy and moved away from the muesli jar to adjust the old-style film camera that doubled as a light at the foot of the stairs. It was one of many ornamental nods to his former life as a film historian, the clapper board wall clock being another. He moved like it was urgent business, which in a way it was; Richard Ainsworth liked things just so, and the camera, though the light wasn't on, should be pointing up the staircase, as if waiting for the grand entrance of a star.

"Monsieur?" It was the young husband who spoke, raising his hand as he did so like a child in school or like every adult in a restaurant the world over. "Monsieur? Could you warm my milk up, please?" His French wasn't great, which gave Richard a little confidence boost. His own French was pretty good, though not fluent, meaning he lived in constant fear of reaching his language limit, of being found out like Gordon Jackson in *The Great Escape*, a simple bear-trap of a "good luck" away from disaster. It was a constant worry.

"Of course, Signor Rizzoli..." He picked up Signor Rizzoli's bowl. "And signora?"

"*Sì*, er, *s'il vous plaît*," she said, correcting herself, her pretty smile directed first at Richard, then quickly back at her husband, her hand searching out his on the small corner table.

Newlyweds always try too hard, he thought.

"Have you any plans for today?" Richard asked loudly and clearly as he moved away. Signor Rizzoli struggled with a stuttering response, but before Richard could helpfully ask again in English, a perfect translation of the question in Italian came from the stairs.

"*Hai qualche piano per oggi?*"

The Rizzolis were stunned into silence as Valérie d'Orçay glided elegantly down the staircase. Her poise was immaculate, as was the Louis Vuitton bag she carried in the crook of her arm, which contained a small, superior-looking chihuahua. Valérie d'Orçay dominated the room the way Cleopatra dominated Egypt, and as she reached the bottom step, she dismissively pushed the lens of the camera light aside so that it no longer pointed directly at her, as though shrugging off an impertinent paparazzo. *What an entrance*, thought Richard, who had met her only briefly, late in the evening before when she checked in. Norma Desmond had arrived, and this time it really was the pictures that had gotten small.

Dressed in a cream summer suit with enormous sunglasses perched on her head, she said a beguiling, non-specific "*bonjour*" to the room before placing the small dog on a chair and, with some words of comfort directed at the tiny creature, sitting down opposite. Again Richard's nan and Vince sprang to mind, though this was a world away from *Pebble Mill at One*, Rothmans cigarettes, and past-their-best sofas. The dog looked from its mistress to Richard, who stood still, slightly stunned by the entrance, and to the Rizzolis, whose cereal spoons hovered just short of their open mouths. It was only the pooch's head that showed, its jewel-studded collar glinting like a disco ball off the ceiling lights. It seemed to be waiting for something; they all did.

"Are you OK, monsieur?" Like a lot of French women in middle age, or possibly all women in middle age, or maybe just all French women, Valérie d'Orçay had a way of inquiring about a man's well-being that was both a form of expressing concern and utterly dismissive at the same time, like a policeman with a flaky witness. She looked at him directly, a hard, penetrating stare that would have floored many a man.

When arriving late the night before, she had been full of apologies for keeping him waiting and complaints about the traffic coming out of Paris. It had been dark, and he'd been a little tipsy by then, so he'd shown her to her room and left her to it. He hadn't noticed that she'd had a dog with her, and frankly, it went against the house rules. And though he didn't seem much bigger than Vince the budgie anyway, rules were rules and the "no pets" rule was clearly spelled out on all the websites. This would need some delicacy, he thought, sizing her up while dealing with the Rizzolis' warm milk.

She was classically elegant in that stereotypical French way: her hair in a short bob was dyed a dark brown and matched her eyes, which were warm yet distant at the same time, piercing and shrewd. There were lines around the side of her eyes, too, which suggested laughter and fun, but the dark irises, the core, said no nonsense. They missed little, Richard suspected, and felt quite self-conscious. He didn't consider himself a vain man; he was happy to look his age and, he'd convinced himself, measured up fairly well against other men at the same stage in life. His hair was evenly gray in all the right places, the hair at his temples perhaps receding a little as though the tide were going out. He had a slight paunch but nothing that breathing in and standing up straighter didn't hide, for now at least. Yes, there were a lot worse than him, he'd concluded, as though he was on the market and needing to write his own small ad. Something he might actually have to get around to doing very soon. Maybe. He wasn't entirely sure what his marital status was at the moment. His daughter had told him only last week that, "In Facebook terms, Dad, you and Mum are complicated," as if that was in itself satisfactory and not actually the trapdoor to a seething pit of uncertainty. But anyway, he'd resigned himself to bachelorhood for the foreseeable future, and if that was what unfolded, then, at fifty-three, he was ready for it. He may no longer have leading-man looks, but he could get away with charming character actor.

"Madame d'Orçay," he said in his best French accent while standing taller and breathing in slightly. "I'm afraid we need to talk about your dog."

"Passepartout?"

"Yes, er, Passepartout."

Passepartout, to his great credit, appeared to give Richard a "you're wasting your time, pal" look.

"Oh don't worry about Passepartout." She waved her hand elegantly. "Just a bowl of water will do." Her reply came dismissively in English, like a haughty Parisian waiter, bringing both annoyance and relief in equal measure. But with it came a friendly shrug, too, and all in an accent that in just one sentence veered from parody to femme fatale and back again. Richard breathed in a little more, which she noticed. "I, on the other hand, would also like some warm milk, please, for my hot chocolate. And perhaps a croissant."

"Yes, but..." Passepartout lay down in his bag, bedding himself in for the long haul.

"And please, call me Valérie, Richard. I'm going to be staying here a few days at least, so there is no need to be quite so formal, I think. I do so hate formalities." She said this to the Rizzolis, who looked like they were gripping each other even tighter.

Richard began to mouth something in response but had no idea where to start, what the middle might be, or whether there'd even be an end. His wine-slowed brain was trying to take stock of the situation; yes, she was attractive, yes, for the first time in what seemed like ages, an attractive woman had called him by his first name and not either "monsieur" or "oi," but also, in less than a minute, he'd been charmingly shoulder-barged out of his own rule book.

"So, it's bloody dogs now, is it? For Christ's sake!" came the hissing voice from the stairs where, in the same spot Valérie had recently descended, stood Madame Tablier. Her starch-white, pristine apron was in stark contrast to the filth of her mouth, her mop and bucket gripped tight in her oddly man-sized hands, and an enormous, incongruous 1980s-style cassette Walkman strapped to her belt with orange-colored foam headphones around her neck. Johnny Hallyday could be heard throwing the kitchen sink at a rock ballad.

"As if things aren't bloody difficult enough around here," she snarled loudly enough to be heard above full-flow Johnny, "what with people leaving their shit all over the place. Now it's dogs, is it?" She trudged down the last few steps and addressed the room. "As if I haven't got enough to do already what with cleaning blood off the sodding walls."

2

"Yes, OK, but I mean, it's...well, it's not *much* blood, is it?" An unconvincing Richard turned round to face Valérie and Madame Tablier, standing behind him in the doorway of one of the upstairs bedrooms. The two women couldn't have been more different, as far apart in almost every respect of their lives and appearance as could be, and as such, unlikely to be thrown together outside of a heavily contrived reality TV program. Right now, though, they were sharing an expression that made them look almost like sisters. The look was doubt bordering on disbelief, backed up with an "it's not really about the quantity of blood though, is it?" question in the eye.

In pure volume terms, Richard had a point. There really wasn't much blood. There was, however, a very clear, deep red handprint, like a child's school painting, to the right of the light switch outside the en suite bathroom. The fingers were extended, though slightly smudged at the tips; the palm was very clear, to the extent that the lines were visible, and the whole thing gave the impression of a mocking wave. Richard took a step back, without taking his eyes off the stain, tilting his head slightly to one side, as though he were an art critic unsure of modern trends. He let out a heavy breath, which was meant to sound dismissive, derisory even, certainly in control, but which sounded more like an out-of-depth whimper. *Typical*, was his summation of the morning so far.

"I don't like it," Madame Tablier snarled, and to add weight to her grievance shook her mop vigorously at the offending blemish. Richard had "inherited" Madame Tablier when he and his wife, Clare, had bought the business a couple of years before. She tottered permanently on the edge of outrage; swore relentlessly in front of the guests, whom she regarded en masse as an unnecessary, germ-infested, stain-creating evil; and appeared, on the face of things, to hate the world so much that "Sweet death, take me now" could have been the motto on her blemish-free apron instead of "*Je place le bonheur au-dessous de tout*," roughly translated as "I place happiness above all else," and surely bought in jest. "I've misplaced happiness and everything else" would have been nearer the mark. But she reminded Richard of an indomitable Irene Handl, and he was therefore willing to forgive almost anything. Plus how could you not employ a *femme de ménage* called Tablier? "*Tablier*" being French for "apron," and the sort of nominative determinism that kept Richard buoyant in times of strife. She stood there, poised for action, holding her mop up presumably in self-defense in case the bloodied hand leaped off the wall and pinched her on the bottom.

"It's quite interesting, don't you think?" Valérie d'Orçay was taking the colder, more intellectual approach. The others both looked at her quizzically. "No, really," Valérie continued, riding over their obvious skepticism in earnest fashion. "Look." And she lifted her own hand up to compare it with the bloodstain.

"Don't touch it!" Madame Tablier hissed. "It's evidence!"

"I'm not going to touch it!" Valérie shot back in a sibilant whisper, her hand still in front of her.

9

"Yes, well, make sure you don't," was the slightly stung response.

"Look." Valérie's hand hovered over the red hand on the wall. "You see?"

"Not anymore. Your hand's in the bloody way."

"Madame Tablier, I am trying to show you the size of the hand..."

"And what's that got to do with it?"

Richard, after a lifetime of experience, knew full well when not to get involved. He'd stumbled across two of his hens, Lana Turner and Joan Crawford, fighting over a dead mouse earlier in the week and he felt then just as he felt now: leave them to it and let nature take its course. Besides, arguments in French, in fact almost anything that required fluctuating emotion, he found more challenging linguistically, too demanding. Valérie slowly lowered her arm, put both hands on her waist, and turned deliberately toward Madame Tablier.

"I am trying to show you something. Now put your mop down and let me explain." He had never seen anyone get the better of Madame Tablier, though admittedly he'd never seen anyone try. But whether it was something in Valérie's eyes—from where Richard stood, he couldn't see—or just the slight tonal change in her voice, the older woman blinked first and lowered her mop. Their pecking order now established, Valérie continued. She raised her manicured right hand once more. "It was a man in this room, is that right?"

"Yes." Richard was slightly startled by his sudden involvement. "Monsieur Grandchamps. He's stayed here before."

"A small man?"

"Yes, I suppose so, he..."

"Well, he must be." She was emphatic. "I am not a large woman, but our hands are almost the same size."

Richard wasn't sure what relevance this might actually have to anything, but Valérie felt it was important and he wasn't one to argue. Madame Tablier, however, was even less convinced and, after finally putting her mop to one side, held up her own hand in comparison. The comparison made Valérie's hand look like a child's.

"My late husband, God rest his soul, used to say that with hands like these I could kill a horse the way I kill a hen!"

It was, under the circumstances, an awkward thing to have said, and both Richard and Valérie decided that the best course of action was to ignore it. Though neither could take their eyes off the older woman's astonishing, ham-like mitts.

"Well, he was knocking on, yes," Richard said. He was trying to remember, but the old man had had nothing remarkable about him, and he rarely hung around to chat to guests anyway. "Not a big man, no. Difficult to say really, he was quite, er..." He was struggling for the French word. "...stooped," he added apologetically in English.

"Stooped?" Valérie seemed cross, more at herself for not knowing the word rather than at a now panicky Richard.

"Yes, oh, what's the word?" He scratched the back of his head. "Erm..." He suddenly felt under a great deal of pressure, and bent forward to try and illustrate the posture. "*Courbé!*" he said triumphantly to the floor, and stood up straight, clicked his fingers and pointed, almost victoriously, at Valérie. "*Courbé!*" he repeated with relief. "Monsieur Grandchamps was *courbé.*"

"OK." Madame Tablier was dismissive. "We get it."

"This print tells us a lot, I think." Valérie was once again assuming command of the situation, and from somewhere produced a pencil and began to point it at the wall. "There is a lot of information here..."

"*Dio mio!*" The exclamation came from the doorway, where Signor Rizzoli stood and was now crossing himself vigorously.

"It's just a child's painting, signor," Valérie said in Italian, as quick as a flash, though the young Italian didn't seem convinced.

"Can I help you, signor?" Richard said loudly in English.

"*Più caffè, per favore, più caffè,*" he said without ever taking his eyes off the handprint.

"Madame Tablier, would you mind serving the gentleman, please?"

"Oh so that's it, is it? I'll go and do all the dirty work while you two cover up. Tch! I might've known it." She stomped past Signor Rizzoli and grumbled her way down the stairs.

"There goes my TripAdvisor average," Richard muttered sullenly as the nervous Italian followed her.

"What?"

"Nothing. What do you mean, 'information'? Information about what?"

"About who the gentleman is," Valérie said as if it were the most obvious thing in the world. "Look"—she raised her pencil again—"that is the lifeline, but there is a smaller line running parallel, you see?" Richard nodded. "The main lifeline swoops—it shows vigor and vitality, and the smaller line confirms that. Your Monsieur Grandchamps is very resistant to disease, it seems. Now, toward the base of the lifeline, here, is a split. That indicates a loner, split from their family. He was always alone, you say?" Richard had stopped following Valérie's pencil and was instead looking at his own palms. Depressingly, he had a split, too. "The headline here is long and straight, so he was a dedicated man, but stubborn, too." Again, Richard looked at his own palm, where there was barely a headline to be had. "This is interesting, though; there is no discernible heartline, or it has merged with the headline. This is good for a man, strong, successful."

"And a woman?"

"A woman? Not so good. Disruptive, harmful. Here, that is where a marriage line should be. But there isn't one. Again, he was a driven man. Not interested in marriage or the opposite sex, more himself."

"Or he wasn't married?" Richard ventured.

"No, more that he was too young to have developed a marriage line. But we know that cannot be right."

"I have no marriage line either," Richard said dolefully; this was turning into a really rotten morning. "Just wrinkles." Valérie looked at him sternly, then at his palm.

"No," she said, "you have many marriage lines, look, at least three."

"Three marriages!"

"Not necessarily. It can mean many marriages, one marriage and affairs, or even that you have one true love and you love her three times as much as one man can."

Richard closed his palm in disgust. "That's pretty bloody vague if you ask me!"

"Oh yes," Valérie said airily, "absolute mumbo jumbo"—he liked the way she said "mumbo jumbo"—"but some people believe it and that in itself makes it interesting."

Madame Tablier reappeared noisily at the top of the stairs. "That's got the Italians all excited," she said breathlessly. "Well? Found the body yet?"

"The body?!" Richard looked about him suddenly; the thought, oddly enough, hadn't even occurred to him. There was nowhere to hide a body, though. There was no wardrobe, just a wooden hanging rail. The bed was made as if it hadn't even been slept in, and there was clearly nothing under it. There was an ornamental trunk in the corner, which was open as usual and with lavender spilling out. There was no luggage. In fact, apart from the bloodied handprint, the room looked ready for the next arrival.

"This is all very well," Madame Tablier said, "but the longer that blood stays on the wall, the harder it is to shift. So if there's no body, then maybe it was just an accident and the bloke just cleared off without paying."

"Possibly something like that. A shaving cut." Valérie seemed deflated.

"He had a big beard," Richard said as he walked into the bathroom. "It can't be a shaving cut." He began opening and closing the drawers under the sink, checking to see if there was any sign of a stay at all.

"A nosebleed then?" Madame Tablier continued. "My late husband, God rest his soul, once had a nosebleed so bad it made the bathroom look like the floor of a slaughterhouse..."

"Was he a hemophiliac, your husband?" Valérie sighed; there was a detachment in her voice, a disappointment that the short adventure had come to such a mundane end.

"No. Communist till the day he died," was the proud response.

"No, I meant..."

"Or..." Richard emerged from the bathroom holding a small pedal bin. "He fell over and smashed his glasses and that caused the bleeding."

"Yes, well, there are many ways, I suppose." Valérie turned to go, but Richard flipped open the bin. In it were a pair of smashed and bloodied glasses.

3

The hens eyed Richard suspiciously, their heads cocked to one side in unison like synchronized swimmers, but without the fixed smile. Lana Turner and Joan Crawford had stopped fighting and were now wondering what was going on; why were they being fed at this time of day? They never got fed at this time of day. The third of their group, Ava Gardner, was in the coop loudly producing, more loudly than usual in fact, as though, despite always being the most enthusiastic layer, she was lamenting at missing out on something.

"Is this how you do your thinking, Richard?" It was Valérie, who had quietly, silently even, appeared at his shoulder. It was odd, he thought, how they had eased into some kind of conversational intimacy. From monsieur and madame to Richard and Valérie, from *vous* to *tu*, all in less than an hour. It usually took much longer than that to get over the minefield of French interaction etiquette. This, though, had been achieved in quick-smart time with Valérie, inevitably, choosing the moment. Richard felt flattered by it, bolstered, though he couldn't say why.

Of course, the prospect of violence, perhaps even the suggestion of murder, Madame Tablier's suggestion, had a way of breaking down barriers. Like in wartime, when extreme circumstances rushed things through because there was no time for standing on ceremony. But easier relationships aside, there *was* still blood on the walls *and* a missing guest. Richard was enjoying what his brain was telling him was a confidence boost, the newfound friendship of an attractive woman, but was also struggling with the bloodied catalyst.

He was about to respond with what he hoped would sound like typical English stoicism and insist that while he worked out the next step, life must go on.

"I would find it hard to deal with, too, I think, in your position," Valérie said, without really hinting at sympathy.

Dammit! She's in my head. Richard flounced internally, throwing some seed a little too harshly at the hens and getting a stern look from Joan Crawford in return. *The woman's a mind reader!*

"Life must go on," he said, "just wanted to gather my thoughts and the ladies needed feeding anyway." A loud squawk erupted from the coop, which sounded derisive, and Richard missed the slight smile that appeared briefly on Valérie's face.

"And what have you decided?" she asked, playing up to his role as taciturn male lead.

"Well..." He closed the seed box slowly.

"Had he stayed here before, this Monsieur..."

"Grandchamps? Yes." He turned round to face her but she was on her haunches, picking up some dropped seed and putting it into her open palm to feed the hens by hand, something he had often tried to do himself but had given up as an impossible task. He watched jealously as Lana, Joan, and a flushed Ava approached her without any caution whatsoever. "This was his third time, maybe fourth; I'd have to check my records." He couldn't hide his annoyance.

"You do not know for sure?" She stood up and clapped her hands to brush off the dust of the seed. The hens remained at her feet like disciples.

"Well, like I said, I'd have to check my records." Richard was avoiding eye contact.

"But if he was such a regular, you got to know a little about him, no?"

"No. No, I didn't." He wanted to add that he was running a B&B not a prison camp and that frankly *why* a guest booked was absolutely none of his bloody business. He decided against it.

"Well?" she said after a pause.

"Well..."

"Shall we go and look at your records?" She emphasized the last two words as though she wasn't expecting much.

"What...now?"

"Monsieur," she began, and the sudden formality set off alarm bells in Richard's head; like when a parent uses the full name of their child, what follows is never good. "You have a missing guest, an old man. There is blood on the walls and a broken pair of spectacles. I suggest we do something, don't you?"

She didn't wait for an answer, marching off instead. Behind her, Richard's shoulders slumped. This wasn't supposed to happen. Not to him. He was quite happy keeping the world at arm's length, not hiding exactly, just not pushing himself to the front. An extra, a background artist. But as he watched his client stomp off—without, it occurred to him, knowing where he even kept his records—he had a horrible, nagging feeling that Valérie d'Orçay wasn't going to allow that.

———

"If you want to wait here, I'll go and get my laptop."

Valérie surveyed Richard's front room, taking everything in. Richard was very proud of how clean and tidy he and Madame Tablier kept his B&B; they worked hard to do so, tutting at the slightest mark on the wall, or maniacally removing cobwebs. But that was the B&B. In the large main house, things were quite different. The lack of Tablier devotion to tidiness was clear. It was almost like his own habitat was the attic portrait to the *chambre d'hôte*'s Dorian Gray. There were books on every surface, half a dozen coffee cups left lying around, DVDs strewn about with no case, and two empty bottles of wine on the small dining table. You could argue that the room was that of a distracted intellectual, a professor working on a break-through. But actually the place just screamed "single man" and, for no good reason, Richard felt slightly ashamed of that. Valérie threw him a big smile, though, and cleared some space on the table before sitting down, placing Passepartout, whom she had collected from the salon, on the chair next to her still in his bag. The dog looked less than impressed by his surroundings. "I won't be a minute. I think it's up here somewhere." He disappeared from view. "I was watching a film on it late last night."

"OK," she replied, and Richard waited for the inevitable "What film?" question, which, disappointingly, never came.

He came back down a few minutes later having eventually found the thing under the left-hand pillow on his bed, turned it on, relieved to see that there was decent battery life left, and stood at Valérie's shoulder awkwardly typing in the details of his booking website.

Slowly, the site began to load. Richard's ancient MacBook, with penciled scribbled notes either side of the "mouse," whirred noisily, groaning like an old man getting up from his chair. For the first time there was an awkward silence between them; Valérie sat rigidly straight, wary almost, while Richard stood nervously behind her. Eventually, the full website loaded and Richard clicked into the "Reservations" page before Valérie, as though tired of their cumbersome geography, took over and scrolled through the list of names.

"Dupont, Faure, Favreau, Gosse, ah, Grandchamps." She double-clicked the name. "Vincent Grandchamps—well, he's stayed four times."

"That's what I said," Richard said, pleased with himself.

"You said three or four," she said, gently admonishing him. "He's actually stayed the last four Wednesday nights. Why?"

"It's not really..."

"I mean, that's very odd, no?"

"I don't think..."

"Why would an old man do that?"

"Well..."

"How old was he?" She whirled round to face him.

Richard scratched his head. "I have absolutely no idea."

She looked at him in disbelief. "Do you really have so little interest in people? Why is that?" she added more gently.

"It's not that I..."

"How old am I, do you think?"

Inside his head, his brain contorted roughly into something resembling Edvard Munch's *Scream* portrait.

"I'm not very good at ages," he said slowly, before adding quickly, "but he was old. Quite stooped. He didn't say much, but he always had to turn his head upward to talk to me."

"Why Wednesdays?" She turned back to the laptop.

"He had a walking stick, too. And a big coat and a hat. It always seems to be cold on market day."

"Thursday is market day?" She turned around again quickly.

"Yes," he said hesitatingly, not sure of what he had inadvertently discovered.

"So!" Suddenly she was full of enthusiasm, like a hunting dog discovering a scent, and then just as suddenly the fire went out, and she shook her head. "But why?"

"Maybe he has family in the area."

"So why not stay with them?"

"Maybe he doesn't like them."

She gave him a "this is no time for jokes" look over her glasses, which he felt was unfair as he wasn't actually joking.

"Will this thing have his home address?"

"People don't always supply that; it depends how they're paying," he said, reaching over her and taking control of the mouse pad thing once more. He sensed her tense up again. "Oh." He stepped back quickly. "There is a home address. I never look at these things normally."

"Where is Vauchelles? Do you know it?"

"It's just down the road, still here in the Val de Follet," Richard said, scratching his chin in confusion. "Only twenty minutes or so."

"It's on the number six bus route." Madame Tablier had appeared at the door, wearing a look on her face that said storms were approaching. She had her arms folded.

"What do you mean? The number six route? Is that important?" Richard was glad that Valérie was taking the lead on this; Madame Tablier didn't look like she'd put up with any fool questions from him.

"It's a special service," the stout woman said, though reluctantly as if it were against her will. "It runs on market day, so people from other towns can come and gossip."

"And do their shopping," Valérie added.

"Mainly to gossip."

"So this Vauchelles really isn't far then?"

"It's a fair way, twenty-five minutes I'd say. One of my sisters moved there, thirty years ago. Not seen her since." She made it sound like the Bermuda Triangle or a small village on a different continent, rather than actually in the same valley.

"But why did you not see your sister since then?"

"What, go all the way to Vauchelles? I'm not Jacques Cousteau. Only gossipers have time for that, not us workers. We write sometimes."

There was silence, and Richard caught Valérie's surprised expression. He wasn't at all surprised though. He remembered when they'd first moved to this quiet corner of the Loire Valley: they had been introduced to some neighbors who were fretting that their daughter was "moving away." They'd tried to show some sympathy until it turned out that "moving away" was actually only to the next village, and about three kilometers away. Some people are like that in the countryside; any change, however small, is always huge.

"Anyway"—Madame Tablier shrugged—"I have bad news and good news." She paused for effect. "That Italian couple have gone. Spooked, probably. Packed their bags and pissed off. Paid cash—two hundred euros, is that right?—anyway, here it is. Count it if you don't trust me." She moved forward and put four fifty-euro notes on the laptop keyboard with a flourish like a poker player throwing a winning hand.

"It's hardly surprising," said a deflated Richard. "Blood, violence, and a quiet break in the country aren't a good mix." He picked up the money and gave fifty euros to Madame Tablier, who took it silently. "That'll be another poor review."

"And the good news?" asked Valérie.

"That was the good news." Madame Tablier snorted. "One less room to clean tomorrow, and fifty euros in my pocket. If you think that's bad news, you've had it too easy, my girl!"

Richard decided to step in before this got out of hand. "So, the bad news, then?"

"Someone's stolen the sodding handprint. Cut it right out of the wallpaper."

"What?" Richard was on the verge of thinking *this* was the good news.

"And the glasses have gone, too. Strange goings-on if you ask me."

"The glasses have gone too?"

Valérie closed the laptop deliberately, as if a decision had been made. "I knew they were too good to be true," she said, unable to hide her annoyance.

"Yes, too obvious by a mile," agreed Madame Tablier immediately. "I've watched a lot of *Maigret*, you know?" She made it sound like a threat.

Richard hadn't the foggiest idea what they were talking about, so he stayed quiet, but tried to adopt a contemplative expression just in case.

Valérie stood up and picked up Passepartout's bag, and the three of them, Richard, Valérie and Madame Tablier, stood in silence for a moment.

"Well, Richard, what are you going to do about it?"

"I...er...well." Richard wasn't entirely sure if anything needed to be done about anything now that the clues, if that's what they were, had gone.

"Seems a fair question," Madame Tablier growled.

Richard, deciding that stoicism was no longer his friend, let his head slump down into his chest in defeat. He had no idea what he was "going to do about it," and he also knew damn well that that decision, bearing in mind the company he found himself in, was probably no longer his to take.

4

If there was one thing guaranteed to happen in a 1950s Technicolor Hollywood film caper, it was that at some point, the female lead, usually Grace Kelly, would drive the male lead, usually Cary Grant, in a sports car at terrific speed around dangerously winding roads, usually on the French Riviera. It was designed to give her the upper hand, and though the male lead would appear slightly uncomfortable, he would never actually lose his poise. Richard, not for the first time in his life, and much to his regret, realized that he was no Cary Grant.

"For the love of God will you slow down?!" he screamed, his face as gray as hospital bed linen.

"I am not going *that* fast," Valérie shouted back, the wind taking her words from just above the low windscreen, tossing them over the back of her roofless sports car and onto the retreating tarmac behind them.

Richard had offered to drive, but Valérie had bluntly decided that his battered old 2CV with "Les Vignes—Chambre d'hôte" emblazoned on each door was too conspicuous for the job. Richard hadn't yet worked out why the hell they shouldn't be conspicuous nor how a roof-down, canary-yellow classic sports "roadster" roaring over the horizon was apparently less so. He also wasn't sure what "the job" was, and he had a feeling that she might just be showing off. And to add to his confusion, he couldn't work out why she would do that either.

They had left a deeply suspicious and frankly none-too-happy Madame Tablier looking after the place, with strict instructions not to let anyone in. Though the instructions should have been "don't let anything else out," as so far that morning Richard had lost a guest, found a bloodied handprint, and broken and bloodied glasses, lost both handprint and glasses, and lost two more guests, which he put down to them being afraid, but which Valérie, the one guest he hadn't lost so far, feared was far more sinister. He'd also lost a slice of expensive wallpaper to which said handprint was indelibly attached. Thursdays were supposed to be quieter than this. Thursdays were normally bang out a couple of breakfasts, saunter into the market, nibble on a baguette, take some of the free saucisson on offer, and then knock back a pastis or two on the square. That was Thursdays. Not wild goose chases, femme fatales, or blood on the wallpaper.

His head was in a spin. And this wasn't helped by Valérie's seemingly reckless and determined attempts to kill them both in a traffic accident. He winced again as she overtook another hay-bale-laden tractor on a blind rise. Yes, determined was the word. Valérie d'Orçay was determined, and the empty space on the wall where the handprint had been had only made her more so. It had also caused her some indignation.

"Well!" she'd barked after rushing up the stairs to see for herself, arriving in advance of a puffing Richard with a smug Madame Tablier bringing up the rear. "That is quite absurd!" She'd scowled at the thing for what seemed like ages, almost trying to will the missing handprint back into place, while the other two exchanged quizzical glances. Valérie had then taken a big deep breath, shaken her head as if to clear it, and stomped off back down the stairs.

Richard and Madame Tablier peered around the doorframe, watching her go. Passepartout, his head sticking out of her shoulder bag, seemed to offer a facial warning. It said, "I'd leave it a few minutes, if I were you."

"Do you want me to clean their room?" Madame Tablier asked gruffly.

"What?" Richard was still looking down the stairwell. "Oh, yes, you may as well."

"Are you going down there?" She threw a dismissive hand in the direction of the dining room.

"Yes," said Richard decisively, "probably."

Madame Tablier tutted and went off to clean the Rizzolis' bedroom.

Should I go down? Richard was asking himself, hovering at the top of the stairs. What was to be achieved by it? The woman was obviously deranged. Why on earth was she so upset? OK, a bit of blood and broken glasses could, if interpreted in the darkest possible way, look a bit, well, dark. But it might also all be perfectly innocent. The old man had stumbled maybe, the fall had broken his glasses and cut his face, then he'd accidentally dripped blood on the walls, which left him mortified, so he ran away. Richard would probably have done the same. Most men would, he suspected. It was all perfectly innocent.

He straightened up and walked assertively down to the salon. Without catching Valérie's eye, he made for the coffee pot. "It might all be perfectly innocent." He affected diffidence. "He might just have cut himself and got a bit embarrassed by the mess." He turned to

Valérie, whose lips were pursed in what he knew was French woman shorthand for "I'm not buying it."

"No," she said quietly, leaving the word hanging there with Richard expecting an explanatory follow-up that never came.

"Well, I don't know what we can do really." He sat down opposite her. "The evidence of…of…whatever happened has gone. There's no point reporting it; what are we reporting? A guest running off without paying? We'd get short shrift with that on market day, I can tell you." Valérie stayed silent. "Anyway, it's only eighty-five euros and a bit of wallpaper. I can put a mirror over that." Again she'd said nothing, just stared into her black coffee. "I never liked that wallpaper anyway. My wife chose it. Too plain for wallpaper. I mean you may as well just paint the wall rather…"

"He asked me to help him." Her voice was very steady, and with a hint of anger running through it that left Richard in no doubt that she had every intention of doing just that, even if it might be a bit late.

"I thought you hadn't met," he replied warily.

"I'd forgotten all about it. It was very late and I came down to get some water for Passepartout. He was in the kitchen. I didn't know who he was obviously."

"And he asked for your help?"

"Yes. He said something about being hunted. *Chassé*. I couldn't really make it out."

It was the first time he'd seen any kind of doubt in her, or vulnerability, and she'd avoided eye contact as she quietly repeated the word *chassé*. No wonder she'd been angry upstairs or eager to find out exactly what was going on; she felt responsible for the missing Monsieur Grandchamps.

"I took the bowl back up to Passepartout and when I came back to the salon he had gone. To bed, I thought." She grabbed his hand.

"Now I am not so sure." Richard was unable to move, not that her grip on his hand was vise-like; quite the opposite, it was very gentle, but even though Richard had been living in France for a few years now, he still hadn't gotten used to continental tactility. Especially the touch of a very attractive woman who was now looking pleadingly into his eyes. "We must find him, Richard, we must. You will help me, won't you? Please."

And that was that. Every fiber in his body and every cell in his brain knew that it was against his nature to "get involved," but frankly they could go bugger off. If Valérie d'Orçay wanted help and she was prepared to get it by looking at him the way she just had, who was he to refuse? And though the voice in his head was screaming, *Wake up, man! Are you that desperate?* He instead heard himself say, in calm matinee idol fashion, "Of course."

She had immediately let go of his hand, stood up, scooped up Passepartout and said forcefully, "OK, let's go."

And going they were, at a frightening rate and dangerously around the few bends in the road between Richard's edge-of-town *chambre d'hôte* and the village of Vauchelles where secretly he hoped to find an embarrassed Monsieur Vincent Grandchamps.

Richard opened his eyes briefly enough to see the road sign, "VAUCHELLES 3km." Soon this would be over, he thought, while also wondering if he could get a bus back home and avoid this motorized death trap. Another kilometer down the road and Valérie slammed on the brakes and pulled the car over to the side of the road, throwing up so much dust in the process that it was a few seconds before Richard could make out the driver beside him.

"Why are we stopping here?" he asked, hoping she'd changed her mind about the whole venture and was about to suggest a spot of lunch instead.

"Maybe you were right," she said without actually turning to him. Richard was beginning to catch on and finally suspected that she was softening him up. Something he didn't object to in the slightest, though he couldn't remember suggesting anything, let alone something right. "This car will attract too much attention," she continued, "we'll leave it here and walk into the town."

"But that's three kilometers away!"

"Nearer two I would say now. I have two rucksacks in the boot; we can pretend that we are *randonneurs*, hikers."

"I think it will take more than rucksacks to convince people we're hiking," he said stiffly, a futile gesture but one that he thought he should make nonetheless.

"We are walking our dog." She beamed. "What could be nicer on a sunny Thursday?" And she leaped out of the car.

"*Our* bloody dog," he chuntered to himself. "I don't even know if the thing has legs."

"What did you say?" She was rustling about in the boot.

"Nothing."

"Ah, here they are." She appeared at his door with two of the most luminous rucksacks he had ever seen.

"And those are less conspicuous, are they? We'll look like we robbed a school trip!"

"They will do the job. That is all. Now, come on, it's not far and according to Google Maps"—she was holding her large smartphone like it was an ancient sextant—"Jules Ferry Street is this side of the village, so it won't take long."

The walk of about fifteen minutes or so was done largely in silence with Richard finding it difficult to keep up with Valérie, who again was like a bloodhound on a scent trail. Passepartout, on the other hand, his legs slightly smaller than Richard's fingers, had given up after a few hundred yards and been put back into his cocoon, which Richard was now carrying.

They passed the sign that said "VAUCHELLES" and saw the first signs of life, old rundown farm buildings mostly with the odd more modern house in amongst them. Valérie instructed Richard to put Passepartout back on his lead and that they should just stroll into town. To underline the "couple out for a pleasant walk" look, she slowed down herself and put her arm through Richard's, whereupon he immediately snapped into a rigid posture and could barely walk.

She smiled at him. "Don't worry, it won't be for too long!" Her tone was mocking and flirtatious and Richard felt literally hooked. They turned right at the next crossroads into Jules Ferry Street where, after a couple of hundred meters, two very large *maisons bourgeoise*, almost identical, stood opposite each other, solid and immovable and almost like they were in a staring competition, glowering at their opposite number.

Valérie skipped off to the house on the right while Richard leaned against the gatepost of the one on the left, watching her go and realizing that she was thoroughly enjoying herself. He bent down to take the rucksack off his shoulder, which even though it was empty was making his back sweat. As he did so he saw the name on the letterbox in front.

"This is it, Richard!" shouted an excited Valérie from across the road. "The letterbox, it says 'M. V Grandchamps.'"

Richard rolled his eyes and sighed heavily. *Is nothing ever easy?* He thought sullenly while also running his finger over the name of "his" letterbox, the letterbox also of a certain "M. V Grandchamps."

5

If only there was a way of pausing life, he thought. Just long enough to gather your thoughts, regroup, and plan your next move. Television adverts seemed to use the trick a lot, usually to push "cheap" loans or the claims of some dietary supplement that would protect you against the frenzy of the modern world. As Richard sensed Valérie crossing the road behind him, her energy like a force of nature, a fireball of curiosity about to engulf him, he wished he had that power. Just a short time-out. And then his phone rang. "Thank you, God," he whispered, before looking at the screen, which said, "Incoming Call—Clare." "Oh, thanks for nothing," he added, leaning his head heavily on the letterbox in defeat.

"Hi! How are you?" he said brightly, his false joviality at odds with his posture.

"Richard?" came the loud response. "What's the matter? Why are you so cheerful?"

"Can a man not be happy to hear from his wife?" The joviality disappeared quickly to be replaced by the easier to maintain world-weariness.

"Now I know there's something wrong!" Clare laughed; perhaps she was mocking, perhaps she wasn't, but Richard decided not to say anything anyway, not to rise to the bait, if that's what it was. Also, and Clare herself would have understood his difficulty here as "men can't multitask" was one of her favorite subjects, he was half concentrating on Valérie, watching her cross and re-cross the road, double checking the identical letterboxes, and shaking her head at the impertinence of it all. "I rang the house, Richard, but you're not there."

"Obviously. It's Thursday," he said automatically.

"Oh, of course. I forgot. Market day." She paused. "So you've had a few then?"

"No, I have not, as it happens!" His concentration snapped back to the phone conversation, leaving Valérie to tut away in the background, almost like one of his hens. "I thought I'd go for a walk instead. Vauchelles way."

"What on earth for?"

"Exercise."

Clare snorted at his unlikely response.

Again there was an awkward silence, and Richard caught Valérie's impatient eye; she had her arms crossed now and was tapping her foot like a prima ballerina who'd been let down by one of the junior dancers in the corps de ballet. "Anyway," Clare said; there was a slight hesitation in her voice, "how have you been?" There was another pause. "How's business?" she added hurriedly.

"Oh, you know. I've been very busy on the book..." He heard her sigh and guessed that she'd be rolling her eyes as well.

"Still on that, are you?" If she'd tried to hide her disappointment, and she'd never bothered to before, then she had failed miserably.

"It's going very well actually."

"Yes, dear."

"Look, can we talk later?" Valérie was now theatrically looking at her expensive watch. "I don't have much battery left," he added, offering a lie that he knew Clare would quite easily believe, and in fact, though he hadn't checked, might even be true.

"I can't later, Richard, I'm going out." Of course she was; well, he was out now—why was his time less important?

Valérie got out her phone and started taking pictures of the two grand houses, and of the names on the letterboxes. She was probably overcautious because of the disappearing handprint, though why she thought these two at least one-hundred-year-old houses would also disappear was a bit of a stretch.

"Are you listening to me, Richard? I said I can't later, I have an appointment." Something in her voice suggested something he hadn't seen in Clare for a couple of years. What was it—vulnerability? Anxiety? Her amateur dramatics evenings were paying off handsomely then, he thought unkindly. "I said, are you listening to me, Richard?"

"Yes, of course!" Valérie was now inches from him and quite clearly demanding the same level of attention as his wife. He gave what he hoped was a "I know, but what do you want me to do?" face and turned his back on her, walking away to give himself some privacy. "Sorry, Clare, look, I know we need to talk, I've been avoiding it, I know I have. We need to sort things out, but I don't want to do it on a mobile phone while I'm standing in the middle of a crowded street." A lizard ran over his shoe. "I think I'd be better off sitting down."

"With a drink?" she asked softly.

"It sounds to me that I'll almost certainly need one." He hadn't meant to come across as quite so pathetic, but what the hell? A touch of melodrama never hurt anyone.

"I don't know. I've made my mind up and I think we should talk about it. I'm coming out there. I'll be out in a few days and we can have a proper talk then, can't we?"

"Of course." His tone was suddenly a little too breezy for Clare's liking, but he was trying to keep up with Valérie, who'd gotten bored of waiting for him and was marching off in the direction of the town center, already a good twenty meters ahead of him.

"Oh, Richard!" Clare sounded on the verge of tears. "I know you're trying to be strong, like one of your bloody Hollywood heroes, but we have to do this. We have to have this conversation. Remember"—there was a nervous pause—"it was all your idea to start with."

"Yes, yes." He was now a little out of breath. "I think face to face is the way to go." He lost sight of Valérie as she disappeared around the corner.

"Good. So do I. So you'll pick me up then?"

"Yes, of course." Where was Valérie going? "Of course I will. Just send me the flight details." He took the phone away from his ear momentarily as he sped up. Guiltily, he realized that Clare had still been talking.

"So I'll see you then?"

"Yes. See you then," he parroted, racking his brains to think of something else to say. Something stoic? Something tart? "It'll be good to see you." He winced as he said it, realizing that it was neither stoic nor tart, more like a brush-off to a vague acquaintance you regret arranging to meet in the first place. He stopped walking, took a deep breath. "Sorry, Clare," he heard himself saying, "it really will be nice to see you."

This time there was a longer pause. "Thank you, Richard, that means a lot. Bye."

He turned the phone off, just as Valérie came back around the corner, her impatience not having dissipated in any way—quite the opposite.

"Well?" she demanded coolly. "Are you finished?"

"Yes," he answered sadly, "yes I think we are. Look, I'm parched. Can we go for a drink? I need to take stock of all this." He held up his phone, trying to show that "all this" wasn't just about identical letterboxes. Before she could answer, a shadow fell over them both, the hot sun suddenly hidden as an enormous man dressed in the dark-blue uniform of the *police municipale* came around the corner. He stopped and stood still, folding his arms in front of him so that his biceps, already the size of watermelons, were exaggerated against his bulletproof vest. His peaked cap was arrow straight on his head, his mirrored sunglasses giving nothing away. His gun gleamed in the holster on a belt so polished Richard could see himself in the buckle.

"Madame *et* monsieur." His voice was surprisingly quiet, almost gentle. "May I have a word, please?"

6

I 'll have a pastis, Bruno," the policeman said to the wiry, immaculately dressed waiter, their outside table overlooking the town square. The midday sun was beginning to get fierce, and they'd chosen a table shaded by a large, green parasol. The bistro, brasserie, whatever it was—Richard was never entirely sure there was a difference other than in the levels of pretension—was postcard pretty. It looked like one of those old-world bistros/brasseries that nowadays would be the face of a cheap, supposedly antique-looking wall clock. Its dark-green front, matching the parasols, looked slightly weathered, as it should, and the wrought-iron, marble-topped tables looked like they belonged to a different era. Even the stone ashtrays suggested a time gone by, and Richard immediately felt at ease with Chez Bruno. The eponymous Bruno bowed his head to acknowledge the policeman's order. The man's bright-white shirt, black tie, black trousers, and white apron were in keeping with the place, as was his air of toadying gratitude. "And my guests will have…?" The policeman, having taken off his cap to reveal a gray, almost white, crew cut, smiled warmly at his "guests."

"I'll take a pastis as well, please." Valérie's tone was cautious.

"Well, as we're in Vauchelles, I'll have a glass of whatever is local if I may?" Richard had no idea how to play this, but he may as well observe traditional Thursday routine and try an alcoholic drink he'd not had before, knowing very well that each small town in the Val de Follet proudly had its own hooch variation. He missed the twinkle in Bruno's eye at his request, though.

There was an awkward silence until the drinks arrived, which was thankfully very quickly. A pretty, young waitress placed them gently on the table, humming to herself as she did so, each glass placed on top of a crisp new coaster artfully designed to look old and featuring a vintage advertisement for a brand of absinthe. The only giveaway to its lack of authenticity was the small-print asterisk at the bottom reminding you to drink responsibly.

"*Santé!*" said the policeman cheerfully after diluting his pastis with ice-cold water. Both Richard and Valérie responded the same, Richard with genuine appreciation, looking forward to what- ever he was about to taste, and Valérie with a certain coolness, like Catherine Deneuve, he thought, not for the first time. They all took a sip of their drinks, Valérie only a little, the policeman nearly the whole glass, and Richard, whose small sherry glass was half full of a dark-amber-looking liquid, some way between the two.

"So, let me introduce—" The policeman began and was immedi- ately interrupted by a violent coughing fit as Richard was suddenly convulsed by the molten lava he'd just drunk. His face had turned deep red, and he could well imagine steam coming out of his ears as his forehead was instantly drenched in sweat. His throat burned like the morning after a teenage night on his dad's stolen Woodbines. The policeman finished the rest of his own drink in one gulp, poured water into the glass, and offered it to a grateful, puce Richard.

"Thank you," he croaked.

"Bruno!" the policeman called over his shoulder. "I thought I'd told you not to serve Old Remi's *gnôle*?" Bruno threw up his arms and made to admonish the waitress before thinking better of it, and disappeared inside, grumbling, "*Buon Dio!*" as he went.

"It's a local eau-de-vie," the policeman explained to Valérie as Richard gradually returned to his normal pallor. "The legend has it that on cold February mornings the *chasseurs*, mostly local farmers, would drink the same stuff as their tractors did; it was thought to be good luck. Only, few of the farmers or their machinery ever reached old age if they did so. It's more a ceremonial thing now." Valérie, while taking this in, was trying to suppress a smile at Richard's comic discomfort, while also not wanting to crack her own façade. "Two more pastis, Bruno, please! Madame? No? Ah, but you are driving of course." It was Bruno who appeared quickly with the drinks this time. "Bruno," the policeman said gently, "don't serve that stuff again."

"He said 'local,' we gave him 'local.'" The man's odd sing-song accent made him sound like a character in an operetta.

"Bruno," repeated the policeman softly, putting his enormous, bear-like hand on the man's wrist, "never again." Bruno withdrew quietly. "So, let's try again." His tone was jovial once more. "*Santé!*" The policeman took a smaller sip this time, Valérie the same and Richard, too, cautiously. He'd had pastis many times; he loved the stuff. The sharp aniseed flavors and the ice-cold water were a staple in the hot summer months, but he had visions of it acting as the spark to the rocket fuel he'd just drunk and them having to pick exploded bits of him out of the neatly trimmed plane trees that bordered the pristine square.

"*Santé*," he said, a little embarrassed.

"Well, I'll begin." The policeman delicately placed his glass on the table and pulled at his shirt to remove creases that weren't there anyway. "I am Brigadier-Chef Principal Philippe Bonneval."

Richard nearly choked on his drink again. *Blimey*, he thought, *that's some title for a village bobby! How do you address him? You can't say "Monsieur le Brigadier-Chef Principal" at the start of every sentence: this conversation would go on for hours.* Richard noticed again the enormous size of the man, the way his chair was hidden from view by his muscular bulk so that he looked like a hovering Buddha or a Cossack freeze-framed in mid-dance. How to address him was obvious then. "Sir" would do nicely.

"I'm Richard Ainsworth." He offered his hand in belated formality and immediately began to regret what would surely be a crushing handshake, though surprisingly it wasn't. "I run a *chambre d'hôte* in Saint-Sauveur." It was becoming very obvious that Valérie wasn't joining in.

"I know it well, obviously, monsieur." The officer smiled.

"Call me Richard," he replied, leaning forward to take some peanuts from a small, brown bowl brought this time by the young woman who was humming to herself as she worked. He noticed Valérie watch her, almost distractedly, as she went back indoors. Valérie then beamed a charming smile, which disarmed both men not only with its easy beauty, but because it just appeared from nowhere like a spectacular flash of lightning.

"I am Valérie d'Orçay." She held out her hand regally. "*Enchantée.*"

"And do you run the *chambre d'hôte* also, madame?" The subtext in the question was clear as their eyes locked, leaving Richard as eager to hear the answer as Officer Bonneval.

"I'm a guest," Valérie said coolly and with deliberate ambiguity.

"I see." Bonneval leaned back in his chair. "So what brings the English owner of a *chambre d'hôte*—your accent was a giveaway, monsieur, no offense—and his charming French guest to Vauchelles, I wonder?" He very deliberately took one solitary peanut from the bowl and waited for a response, crunching the nut loudly. There was a moment's pause, and then Richard and Valérie both started answering at the same time, stopping almost immediately, lapsing once more into a tense silence.

Eventually Valérie said, "You can explain, Richard."

"Oh really?" Richard said through clenched teeth.

"You do it so well." Valérie was urging him on as if she suspected he had something planned, which he very much did not.

"Thank you," he said. Though "thanks a bloody bunch" would have expressed it better. "Well, er, well, you see..." The others were watching him, the policeman lugubriously and Valérie with some alarm. Neither seemed wholly confident in the outcome. "Well, it's this place really, if not Vauchelles itself, then certainly around here." He stopped, as if that was enough, and took a few peanuts.

"What about *around here*?" the policeman asked, a serpent-like smile slowly spreading across his face.

"Yes," Richard said confidently, "I'm glad you asked me that. Well, I'm a film historian, was a film historian, and I'm trying to find the location of a film that was, er, filmed near here I think." Again, they both looked at him as if he'd be a fool to think that was even remotely enough by way of explanation. He took a sip of his drink. "Yes," he said, suddenly more confident, "*The Train*, 1964, Burt Lancaster. It's about the Resistance, you know?" They didn't look like they did and his attempt to change the topic by introducing the Resistance was clearly going to fail, too. "Also, Paul Scofield was in it, who of course won an Oscar a couple of years later playing Sir Thomas..."

"And you think it was made around here?" Bonneval sounded suspicious. "I think I'd know." He not only sounded skeptical but he was giving him a look that Richard knew all too well, one he'd been receiving since his film obsession first took hold as a teenager. It was a mix of incredulity, sympathy, and boredom. Richard had an encyclopedic knowledge of British and American film, from prewar to pre-video rental, and sometimes he couldn't help but show it. Clare called it his cinema Tourette's syndrome.

"Possibly before your time." Richard was trying not to name the full film credits and ooze flattery at the same time, but Bonneval now had a look on his face suggesting that what was oozing was more pungent than that.

"Our dear mayor, perhaps not the man he was, has served our small community for many decades, he has never mentioned a film, or Hollywood stars."

"Not even Jeanne Moreau?"

"Not even Jeanne Moreau."

"Pity. I thought there was a disused railway line near here, one that may have been used in some of the action scenes. I'd still like to have a look."

Bonneval weighed this. "And you, madame, you have an interest in trains also? Because if so, I don't understand why you would leave your car where you did, nor head straight for Jules Ferry Street and the house of Judge Grandchamps. Why not, instead, go to our excellent *office de tourisme*, for example."

They were both taken aback and Bonneval theatrically took another peanut, enjoying his moment once more.

"Monsieur," she began, clearly not wanting to waste time on his full title, "have you been following us?"

"Not at all."

"Good. Then how..."

"There was no need."

"Oh?"

"Your car, and it is exquisite, madame, a 1983 Renault Alpine, is it not?" He glanced briefly at Richard, a "this is the kind of knowledge the ladies go for, mate, not old films" glance. "Only fifty-one four-cylinder engines were ever made, I believe." He popped another peanut.

"No, it's a 1979 V6. It's an easy mistake to make." *That's right*, Richard thought, sinking into his seat, *antagonize the man*. "And what makes you think we were looking for Judge Grandchamps?"

Bonneval brushed the salt from his fingers, indicating it was now time for business. "Because he phoned me, madame. We have had a number of burglaries in the past few months so people are a little jittery, our distinguished judge especially. And it means that I'm a little under pressure not to let any more burglaries take place."

"I see," Valérie said sympathetically, "that's perfectly understandable. Do you work here alone?"

"Alas, yes. Government cuts. There is barely enough for my salary let alone a proper force. That's why I tend to tackle things before they occur, before there is any trouble." He paused, then added quickly, "Not that you are trouble!"

Richard started to relax. The man was just doing his job, and actually being quite charming with it. It can't be an easy place to police on your own, a small town, probably a few remote hamlets and cut-off farmhouses. Talk about stretched resources! He was glad he'd invented the train story then; that would be a weight off their minds and an easy cover story to get behind.

"You are right, of course," Valérie said coquettishly and Richard's heart sank, "it was the judge that I wanted to see. He and my mother knew each other in Algeria in the late 1950s. My mother died recently and though they had lost touch, I just wanted to pass on her affection for Vincent." She was taking a gamble and Richard couldn't help tensing up, which was the exact opposite, he noticed, of Bonneval's changing demeanor.

"Ah, I see, madame. Well, I'm sorry to hear about your mother, my sincere condolences, but that is why the judge is so nervous, you see? The judge's brother, your *Vincent* Grandchamps—an easy mistake to make—has disappeared." Richard and Valérie couldn't avoid catching each other's eye. "Yes," Bonneval continued, taking a whole fistful of nuts this time. "Vincent Grandchamps disappeared six weeks ago."

"Well, that can't be right!" Richard blurted out, immediately regretting it as Valérie kicked him sharply under the table.

7

Richard limped heavily as he tried to keep up with a marching Valérie. She was not best pleased but rather than communicate that personally, she'd delegated to the bag-bound Passepartout, who was shaking his head from side to side, partly as a result of Valérie's stomping but also, and Richard was sure about this, because he was tutting in admonishment.

"That really bloody hurt! What are they, Rosa Klebb shoes?"

"They are Jimmy Choo," Valérie responded, obviously thinking Rosa Klebb to be some high-end shoe brand, but not as high-end as the ones she was wearing.

"But what's the problem? I thought you wanted to help Monsieur Grandchamps? I don't see how telling the police what we know is a bloody problem?"

She turned on him, anger in her eyes, and Richard half expected Passepartout to go flying off, jettisoned as she spun round. "I thought Englishmen were tight-lipped and taciturn. Why tell him what we know?"

"Why *not* tell him what we know?"

"Because the old man asked me for help, that's why. And so it happens that he's been disappearing for a few weeks. That's a cry for help, no?"

"Maybe. But which is also a police matter, surely."

"If Monsieur Grandchamps wanted the police involved, if it was that kind of thing, he would have gone to the police himself, don't you think?" She jabbed her finger in his chest.

"Not necessarily," Richard sulked.

"Instead, now we have a meeting with Juge Grandchamps and Brigadier-Chef Principal Philippe Bonneval."

"Right. That'll be the missing man's concerned brother and an officer of the law, then?"

"Listen, Richard, please, just don't mention the blood or the glasses. Can you do that for me?"

"Why not, though? They are quite possibly the only people who *should* know!"

She sighed heavily and moved closer to him, looking into his eyes. "Because, one, we have no proof, none at all. And two..." She broke off.

"And two?" Richard thought he spotted some vulnerability and was trying to be more assertive.

"Honestly?"

"Honestly."

"I'm bored, Richard. Life is boring. I have been widowed now for nearly a year, and I am so bored! That man asked for my help, and maybe I need a little adventure." She spun around again, leaving Richard face to face with Passepartout.

"I didn't know," he said quietly. "I didn't know you had lost your husband. I am sorry."

"Don't be, really." They walked on a bit, approaching her car. "It was mercifully quick, not drawn out like some of these things. Jean-Pierre would have wanted it that way, I think."

"I suppose we all do really."

She put Passepartout on the backseat.

"What did he do, Jean-Pierre?"

"He had his own business, not very glamorous, pest control. Rats and moles mainly. But, even though he was much older than I, we had a lot of fun." She put the key in the ignition and started the engine. "I do miss him." She leaned dramatically on the steering wheel.

Richard was silent for a few seconds. He recognized bare-faced emotional blackmail when he saw it and knew full well he was being played. Played by a quite possibly crackpot woman who was thrill-seeking her way out of life's middle-aged boredom and possibly grief, or possibly not grief. He knew all that, and, surprisingly or maybe not, he didn't mind it one little bit. He wasn't exactly having his own laugh-a-minute time himself.

"OK," he said eventually, and affecting a big put-upon sigh for the sacrifice he was about to make, "let's go for the adventure."

She went to interrupt.

"But on one condition." He wasn't letting her in, with her doe eyes and her pleading ways. "If this is serious, if the poor man has been done away with, we get Principal-Chef Brigadier Philippe..."

"It's Brigadier-Chef Principal..."

"We get whatsisface involved, and involved *tout* bloody *suite*. Deal?"

"Bonneval. His name is..."

"Deal?"

She gave him a big smile and he went to shake her hand, but instead she gave him a kiss on the cheek, put the car in gear all in one move and roared off through the town back to Jules Ferry Street.

———

She glowered at him from across the road. It was a look that only really stubborn people can give. A look that comes naturally, without being forced, that says, "I'm quite clearly dealing with an idiot." Teachers specialize in it, Parisian waiters too and, thought Richard, who could be just as stubborn if he put his mind to it, every French woman he'd ever met. Valérie stood at the gate of one house belonging to Monsieur V. Grandchamps and Richard, no more than twenty feet away, stood at the other gate belonging to a Monsieur V. Grandchamps. Neither was willing to budge but neither had pressed the doorbell either, their certainty not quite certain enough to spread to proof or the possibility of error.

"He said the house on the right!" hissed Valérie. She was facing the direction in which they'd arrived and her arm was outstretched like a cyclist indicating a turn.

"I know!" Richard hissed back. He was looking the other way down Jules Ferry Street, and his right arm was also stretched out. He was aware of how ridiculous they both looked, and he was also aware of how little it actually bothered him whether he was right or wrong, but he was drawing lines in the sand here, and so not backing down. If he was going to take part in this "adventure"—an innocent word, he reckoned, more reminiscent of Enid Blyton than old blokes being possibly done in—then he was going to make damn sure that Valérie d'Orçay didn't just take him for granted. That she couldn't just use him as a...well, whatever he was being used as. He glowered back at her and then saw the imposing figure of Officer Bonneval appear behind her at "her" gate. "A lucky guess," he muttered to himself, scratching the back of his head with his arm as if that had been his intention all along, and sauntered, as nonchalantly as he could, over the road.

"It's an odd setup, isn't it?" he asked, nodding his head back to where he'd just come from. "Two brothers living opposite each other like that, identical houses."

"They can't share a house," Bonneval said, opening the gate. "They hate each other."

"Then why live near each other at all?" It was Valérie with the question.

"Because, madame, they hated each other so much they couldn't let the other have the luxury of independence. I'll explain more inside. The judge himself might explain it better. It depends."

"It depends on what?" Richard was getting a bit irritated with all the ambiguity.

"On how he's feeling today."

"Bonneval!" The cry, almost a demand like a master to servant, silenced them all. The voice was high and arch, more like an old woman's than an old man's. "BONNEVAL!" It came again and the huge policeman's shoulders visibly slumped.

"Is he feeling good or bad, do you think?" Richard asked, and Bonneval shot him a look as if to say that this was no time for levity, instead indicating sullenly that they should follow him inside.

The entrance hall was so dark it took time for their eyes to adjust to the dinginess after the bright sunshine outside. The place smelled musty, as though the air never circulated and the doors and windows always remained shut. Bonneval led them down the dark passage to a room at the back of the house. The shutters were closed here, too, just a narrow shaft of light penetrating the room like a laser, moodily showing a large dining table, row upon row of bookshelves, and in the corner sat a small man in a wheelchair, lizard-like, his malevolent eyes catching the gleam of the outside light and following them as they filed into the room.

"Monsieur *le juge*, these are the people I told you about. They have news of your brother."

"The only news I need of my brother is an announcement of his death," he spat. "Do you have that? Hmm, well, do you?" he badgered. *Quite the charmer*, thought Richard. "Ha! I thought not," the judge added with genuine disappointment.

"He was staying at my *chambre d'hôte*," Richard offered, "even though it's really not far away."

"And that surprises you, does it?" Every word the judge spoke was dripping with a mean-spirited edge. "Well, it doesn't surprise me. He does this all the time, just to embarrass me."

"How does that embarrass you exactly?" The tone in Valérie's voice showed she was unimpressed by monsieur *le juge*, and certainly not intimidated.

"Because he goes off, checks into places, pretends to be *me*, more often than not, and generally makes a nuisance of himself. It's a childish game he plays."

"Why?"

"I don't know! You'd have to ask him that. He's a nasty little man. Always has been. He's spent his entire life on the wrong side of the law."

"Yet you're a judge?"

"Was. The *right* side of the law."

Richard had had very few dealings with either the law or with crime. He'd once had to plead for leniency to a magistrate to avoid a driving ban and, on the other side, he'd once wandered into the wrong East End pub on the day of a gangland funeral. He'd found the experience with the magistrate far more intimidating. He was made to feel like a criminal for having exceeded a motorway speed limit at two in the morning driving through unmanned roadworks yet made to feel welcome like a member of the family by weeping London hoodlums. Richard wasn't a huge fan of certainty and didn't easily trust people who had no doubts, and the law, as far as he was concerned, required conviction and absolutism, the naked "I'm going to do this no matter what," like a drunk karaoke stalwart, plowing on regardless.

"Vincent and Victor fell out a long time ago," Bonneval said quietly, as if trying to hide the fact from the old judge.

"Nonsense!" the old man exclaimed. "We never fell in!"

"It's rare for twins to hate each other so much," mused Valérie, "yet your bond kept you close."

"Bond! Pah!" The old man leaned forward, his sharp chin almost used as a pointer. "The bond was in blood and in name only. We didn't even look much alike."

Richard wished he could confirm that but all he saw when he thought of *his* Grandchamps was the beard and the stoop.

"Well..." began Bonneval.

"Be quiet, man!"

"So why live as neighbors?" Valérie's very reasonable question was met with silence initially while Bonneval looked at his enormous boots and Grandchamps picked at some imaginary fluff on his gray trousers.

"I don't like that *femme de ménage* you found for me, Bonneval," he said eventually as if the brief pause had rendered the question irrelevant. "She's too proud of her tattoos, is that girl. If you can't keep your own body free of stains, how can you keep a house clean?"

This man is barking, thought Richard, though he had some sympathy with the whole tattoo issue.

Bonneval looked hurt. "As you know, Marie only works a few hours at the bar. She needs the extra money."

"And you've got your eye on her, too, no doubt," the judge said cruelly.

"Monsieur *le juge*," Valérie said sternly, interrupting the bullying, "you didn't answer my question. Why did you and your brother, your

twin brother, live as neighbors if you hated each other so much?"
Again there was a short pause, and then the judge broke out into a
hideous grin. It changed his demeanor entirely. Richard could have
sworn that the man hadn't cracked a smile in some thirty odd years,
probably not since some appalling miscarriage of justice that he'd
helped to perpetrate. But this sudden grin, unpleasant though it was,
revealing spiky yellow teeth, softened the eyes, showing a surprising
array of laughter lines and crow's feet.

"Why, madame, you ask why?" He cackled. "Pure. Spite."

"He moved here to make your life miserable?"

"No." The smile widened with difficulty. "*I* moved here to make
his life miserable!"

There was a stunned silence while Bonneval looked vaguely embarrassed, like a relative publicly apologizing for a flatulent uncle. "I could
have gone into politics." The judge continued staring into space. "Who
knows how far? But that worm, that snake in the grass, he held me
back. He didn't hide his criminality, his lawlessness. He was brazen. So
I retired a common or garden-circuit judge, respected, yes, feared, certainly. But worse, I was pitied. Pitied! 'If it hadn't been for his brother...'
they'd say. He ruined my career, and when I retired, I was determined
to ruin his. I would follow him wherever he went. People would be
less willing to do their business with him if they knew monsieur *le juge*
Victor Grandchamps was watching from across the street."

It was delivered with such conviction and certainty, thought
Richard, a crackpot scheme that sounded more like the statement of
a clichéd supervillain revealing their plan for world domination, usually just before they meet their complicated demise. Valérie leaned in
close and whispered in his ear. "This man is a lunatic," she said quietly.

"Why are you looking for him anyway?" The judge snapped back
from his spiteful reverie.

"He was friends with my mother in the Algerian war. She died recently and…"

"Was it a one-night stand? Probably. Because my brother deserted the army very quickly."

If Valérie was insulted by the remark, and that was surely the intention, then she didn't show it. "I made a promise to her that I would pass on her regards. I'd still like to do that."

"Well, I hope you do! He keeps disappearing, Bonneval will have told you that. I'd go out and look for him myself, but as you can see, I can't get around too easily these days. Find him, bring him back." He cackled again. "I'm bored without him! What do you say, Bonneval?"

The policeman shrugged. "You can do what you want. He's not reported as missing; in fact, it's the opposite. People keep reporting that he's turned up. You are not the first *chambre d'hôte* to come by saying he skipped off without paying."

"I'm not paying his bills!" the old man interrupted. "You'll get no money from me!" There was a knock at the door. "Oh, it's that painted woman. That's too many people in my house now, you'll have to go." And with that, he theatrically spun his wheelchair around, effectively turning his back on them. Bonneval nodded to them to start to leave.

"*Bonjour!*" came a cheery voice from the door. "And how's my poisonous reptile today?" It was the young waitress from the brasserie, and belatedly she saw the others in the room. "Oh, I'm so sorry," she said, turning bright red as she began taking in all the faces one by one, obviously startled to see visitors.

"Typical," spat the judge. "I blame the tattoos."

8

"onsieur?" An old woman coughed behind him.
"Monsieur?" She repeated herself, this time a little louder.
She turned to another old woman waiting behind her, and
rolled her eyes in time-honored "Men. They really are useless, aren't
they?" fashion. Richard just stared at the electronic weighing scales,
though, unaware of their annoyance. His mind was anywhere but on
the task at hand, namely weighing and pricing some Passe Crassane
pears for the following day's breakfasts. A late booking had come in,
and while Grandchamps's room was temporarily out of action, the
Rizzolis had vacated and paid, so he would get double for the same
room, which he regarded as a small victory in an increasingly confusing world. The machine in front of him noiselessly produced a sticky
label but Richard continued to stare, unfocused, into the distance.
The two ladies tutted loudly.

An arm reached around him, plucked the ticket from the
machine, slammed it onto the bag, and thrust the pears roughly into
Richard's distracted line of sight, waking him up. It was Valérie, and
her mood since the journey back from Vauchelles had not improved.

"I don't understand you at all!" she hissed at him, getting his attention and the attention of the two waiting old women. They turned to Richard for his response. He sighed and hung his head.

"For the last time," he said wearily, "I have enough excitement in my life."

The eyebrows of one of the old women shot up, while the other stood transfixed, popping an unweighted grape into her mouth.

"What does that even mean?" Valérie was rigid with frustration and anger. "Who has *enough* excitement?"

One of the old women turned to her friend and nodded; there was no way a mere man could come back from a question like that.

"Well, not excitement as such. Just, you know, things. Things going on." He was trying to talk quietly and calmly, and not cause the scene, the very public scene, that Valérie so very obviously craved.

"Argh!" she cried and practically threw the bag of pears into his chest, before stomping off. Richard looked at the old women, who shook their heads in unison at his pathetic maleness.

"Look," he said after catching up with Valérie at the cart, "I moved here for the quiet life and to finish my book. I have no interest in trying to find some petty criminal who just seems to want to wind his brother up. It's none of my business." Valérie said nothing. "Besides"—Richard laughed unconvincingly—"we don't even know what kind of 'criminal' old Vincent Grandchamps is, was, probably is. I'd say a few unpaid parking fines. Jumping a red light. It's the Loire Valley; maybe he was spotted drinking a heavy Burgundy with fish."

Valérie turned to him and gave him a stern look. "Vincent Grandchamps ran an illegal wine market for one of Sicily's biggest mafia families."

Richard dropped the pears. "The mafia? The Italian mafia?"

"Sicilian."

"The Sicilian mafia?" he whispered, looking about him to see if anybody was still listening in on their conversation. "The bloody Sicilian mafia!"

"Yes!" Valérie's eyes were wide open with excitement, also because she'd entirely misread Richard's reaction. "Exciting, isn't it?"

"No!" he shouted. "No, it bloody isn't! I'm a film historian who makes breakfasts! I'm not Eliot Ness!"

"Maybe it would do you good to actually *live* a life rather than just watch a load of silly old films about it!"

"Oh really? You know the advantage of watching silly old films, Madame d'Orçay? They don't kill you! They don't torture you; watching *Singin' in the Rain* of an evening isn't going to get me buried in the desert! The mafia. Honestly!"

She looked disappointed but put her hand gently on his arm. "I think also it would do us *both* good."

"What are you talking about?" Richard had the distinct impression that he had somehow managed to gain two wives and both were overtly, terminally disappointed in him. Or worse, trying to improve him. "What good? Are you kidding? I don't need that much 'good'! These people are killers. I don't want to sleep with—" But before he could get to the "the fishes" part, he was interrupted by an English voice behind him.

"Richard?"

His shoulders slumped again as soon as he recognized the voice. Valérie kept her hand on his arm. "Martin," he said, turning round and affecting joviality, "how are you?"

"Not as well as you are, obviously!" Martin offered his limp hand while keeping his eyes glued, rather lasciviously, on Valérie. His wife, Gennie, couldn't tear her eyes away from Valérie either, and was equally desirous. The uncomfortable feeling was of two predators sensing new blood. Richard had been here before and knew it was *exactly* like two predators sensing new blood. The damage these two had wrought with their "games" in the local expat community was legendary and one of the reasons why Richard and Clare, in her brief time here, had largely stayed out of its social whirl.

They were both in their late fifties, well-preserved, quite small in stature and always wore at least one item of matching leisurewear: one day trainers, the next day a tracksuit top. It was like they'd become separated from one of those Japanese tourist parties that always wear bright, matching clothing with a tour party logo emblazoned on it. They rarely stopped touching each other either, and there they stood in the fresh fruit aisle of the supermarket, arms round each other like kids at a school disco and practically dribbling on the floor.

"Aren't you going to introduce us, Richard?" asked Gennie, who had briefly let go of Martin to offer her hand.

"Erm, yes, of course, this is Valérie d'Orçay, she's a guest at the B&B." He didn't like using the words "B&B," he much preferred, to him, the classier "*chambre d'hôte*," but equally he had a problem using French words with fellow Brits, even if those Brits also owned a B&B or *chambre d'hôte*. The British are never good using foreign words in front of other Brits; it's just seen as showing off and Richard hated the idea of showing off.

"Are you a guest, really?" Martin winked at Richard, making no attempt to hide the supposed conspiracy from Valérie. "We are Martin..."

"And Gennie."

"Thompson. We're old friends of Richard and...and, well, just *everyone* around here. We run a *chambre d'hôte* as well."

"But we're not rivals!"

"Oh no, we cater for, well, a different clientele mostly."

"How nice," Valérie said cheerfully, either choosing to ignore the heavy inference, or more likely, thought Richard, not seeing it. "I was beginning to think Richard just stayed at home alone watching films; it's nice to know he has some excitement in his life!" She laughed; Martin and Gennie laughed, too. Richard smiled wanly and felt a Passe Crassane pear disintegrate in his hand.

"Well," Martin said after the hilarity was over, "of course Richard never *really* got involved in our little group..."

"It wasn't for a lack of us trying to persuade him though!" Gennie threw into the mix.

"I can imagine!" Valérie snorted loudly, and put her arm through Richard's. "But, he's how you say..."

"A stick-in-the-mud?" Gennie beamed, woman to woman.

"Yes, that's right, Richard, you *are* a stick-in-the-mud!" Martin slapped Richard heartily on the back, making Richard feel like taking his squashed pear and shoving it in Martin's face, Cagney style.

"It's so nice to meet you, Valérie, and so good to know that Richard isn't bored with Clare away so often."

"You must come round," Gennie said, fumbling in her pocket for something. She produced a business card; "Martin and Gennie Thompson" it read, their names either side of a goldfish bowl with some car keys in it, and at the bottom in calligraphy dripping with intent, "Helping Expats Get Together."

"Oh, perhaps." Richard was trying to edge away and had one hand on the cart. "I've got so much going on at the moment..."

"We can see that!" Martin and Gennie both laughed again, with Valérie joining in belatedly though not knowing why.

"No!" snapped Richard. "Not that. Valérie is a guest who needed a hand with something." He instantly regretted his choice of words. "She had a problem. Look, anyway. I have breakfasts to prepare for tomorrow and Clare arrives, erm..." He suddenly realized that he hadn't been listening when Clare told him when she would be arriving, or at which airport. "Anyway, must crack on. Swing by if you're..." He took a deep breath and turned his cart around, the *Carry On...* style double entendre of leaving the Thompsons and disappearing up the meat aisle weighing heavily on his mind.

"He seems quite stressed," said Gennie, with genuine concern.

"Yes, he does." Martin's concern was less genuine. "He needs to let his hair down a bit. Valérie, you must come round, the two of you; we'll have a high old time, won't we, Gennie?"

"Oh, yes. A high old time."

Valérie was watching Richard slumped over his cart, slowly making his way into the distance, concentrating on his shopping list. "Clare is his wife, is that right?"

"Why yes, you mean, you didn't know?" Martin's eyes widened at the prospect of twenty-four-karat-gold gossip and he also took a step closer to Valérie.

"No." Valérie turned to him and was surprised he was so close, stepping back. "I am a guest. We met this morning, that's all."

"Well, good for you," Gennie said, sensing Valérie's uneasiness. "Clare's never here anyway. Between you and me"—she looked about her as if they might be overheard—"I think they're having problems."

"Poor Richard," said Martin, his insincerity shining like the lamp on a miner's helmet.

"You may have come along just at the right time, Valérie." Gennie winked. "You can cheer him up!"

"Oh, like I say, I'm just a guest. I just helped him with some clients this morning, that's all." She started to edge away herself; the Thompsons were beginning to make her feel uncomfortable. "Just some translating with an Italian couple."

"Oh, you've got one, too, have you!" Martin made "Italian couple" sound like a breed of dog. "We had a couple arrive this afternoon, charming people and *sooo* attractive. Funny name, sounds like a pasta shape!" He laughed at his own joke.

"Oh, Martin." Gennie gently hit his arm. "The Farrolis, they're called. Lovely people. I speak a bit of Italian, though I don't let on. I heard them talk about family over in Vauchelles. Seems a long way to come."

"Yes it does," said Valérie, wondering at the chances of this coincidence.

"I wouldn't cross the road to see most of my family," huffed Martin, then like a snake added, "Friends you can choose, though. You must come and visit, Valérie."

"Yes, you must!" enthused Gennie.

"Yes." Valérie smiled. "I rather think I must."

9

⌒

Slowly letting the handbrake off and allowing the car to roll gently down the hill, Valérie quietly began her evening's work. About twenty meters from the house she sparked the engine up smoothly and drove toward town. There was no urgent need for such cloak-and-dagger tactics, of course, but why not add a little drama to life's humdrum journey?

"One has to live life to the full, my dear girl," one of her husbands had told her, though she couldn't quite picture his face. "Life is for the living!" he'd said, before a moment later disappearing over the side of their Corsican ferry, an unseasonal wave claiming him, never to be seen again.

She had made a solemn promise to Richard earlier that evening that she would not get involved with the "bloody mafia," as he'd called them. "Let's take stock," he'd said, "sleep on it." It was the most English thing she had ever heard, and when she told him that, he'd become quite sulky, which made her giggle.

She liked Richard. And it was clear that Passepartout liked Richard, too, and dogs are the best judges of character. Richard himself seemed a little like a dog. She smiled at how hurt he'd be by that description, but it was true. He was like an old hunting dog, too tired for the chase anymore but perhaps with one big hunt left in him. His big sad eyes and slightly too large ears fitted the image perfectly. Not that he wasn't good looking, she thought, he just needed to carry himself like a man who knew he was. He seemed to pad about with his tail between his legs, like a scolded hound. She preferred dogs to men in general, and was happy to have had more dogs than husbands, though admittedly the score was pretty tight. She'd never considered a combination of the two, however, and the idea amused her. *A house-trained husband,* she thought, *now that would be a novelty, one properly brought to heel.*

She drove through the sleepy town of Saint-Sauveur, its shops all shut, the two bars empty and even the Café des Tasses Cassées restaurant only half full. Market day seemed to have worn the place out, and it was getting ready for an early night. She passed the large supermarket where they'd met the Thompsons earlier and continued for three kilometers toward the even smaller town of Faurent. "We're about two hundred meters past the *boulangerie,*" Martin had said, even managing to make the word *boulangerie* sound suggestive, "big hedge, you can't miss it." They were right, too, she thought, as she parked the car in the shade of a nearby plane tree. The hedge was laurel and the densest she had ever seen, almost less of a boundary marker and more of a "we don't want you prying" kind of fortress. They didn't seem to be the type to hide anything when she'd met them earlier, though—far from it.

"Co-eee!" Gennie's head appeared just over the top of the hedge, hidden under an enormous straw hat. "You are punctual, aren't you?" she said cheerfully. "Are you sure you're French?"

"Ha! Just her little joke!" Martin's bald head appeared from nowhere. "If you want to come in, go a bit to your right; I'll show you my secret passage." Valérie had a feeling she was going to find it harder and harder to maintain her forced smile, but she did as she was told. A heavy wooden door swung inwards, revealing a beautifully manicured lawn and a croquet set. She stepped forward, a little nervously, and the door banged shut behind her. Martin and Gennie stood there, both grinning, each holding a croquet mallet and wearing, apart from Gennie's hat, not a shred of clothing.

Valérie was not a woman easily shocked, and if she was, she certainly wasn't the kind to show it, especially to strangers, especially to naked strangers. "Ah, well, I feel slightly overdressed," she said calmly and before Martin could get in the inevitable comeback, added, "What a lovely garden you have."

"I like to dig and prune," he said, winking as he did so.

"That's enough Martin," Gennie sighed. "Go and mix some drinks." Martin shrugged his shoulders in a "you can't win them all" way, and waddled off. His body was among the most unsexy things Valérie thought she had ever seen. A drooping middle-aged chest, resting on a protruding belly. His shape reminded her of a Volkswagen Beetle she'd once owned. Without obviously trying, she'd also noticed that there wasn't much under his hood either. She'd had a husband like that once; what *was* she thinking at the time. *Poor Gennie*, she thought, who actually looked pretty good for her age, but not good enough that Valérie felt entirely comfortable when Gennie put her arm through hers and led the way to a secluded pergola.

"This is just seasonal, no?" Valérie asked.

"What? Oh." Gennie giggled. "Well, we certainly couldn't live like this all year round here. Ha! We'd freeze our bits off! No, we have another B&B in Spain in the winter months; even that's pushing it at times, though. It doesn't upset you, does it? We like to be upfront about things, and naturism is very much what we're about at this time of our lives." Her tone had become oddly serious and yet hollow during the statement, almost like she was remembering the words from the jacket of a self-help book. *Poor woman*, thought Valérie again, *I bet it was all Martin's idea; surely he must be at least well off?*

"Not talking about me, I hope!" Martin was carrying a tray of drinks across the lawn. "I can feel my ears burning." Which, Valérie could see, was the least of his physical problems. He placed the tray down on the wooden table and sat next to Valérie, nudging her backside with his and saying, "Budge up, budge up." She did so, quite a long way, while looking around for a spare croquet mallet. "So what's the gossip, then, Val?" He really was a repulsive little man. "What's all this about you and Rich?"

"Well, that's really why I'm here," she began, noticing the other two lean in with interest. "I didn't want you to, what is it you English say, get the wrong end of the stick..." Martin made as if to interrupt but a sharp look from Gennie told him to save it. "I really only met Richard this morning, well, late last night when I checked in; there's no 'us.' I just wanted to make that clear. He has a wife, after all." She admonished herself; this wasn't the line she'd wanted to take at all and she didn't want to be here any longer than necessary, hemmed in the corner surrounded by sagging flesh.

"Yes, Clare, she's quite attractive," Gennie said, the compliment studiedly underwhelming.

"Very cold, too, though," Martin added, with a hint of bitterness.

"At first, yes." Gennie's eyes now suggested she was elsewhere before snapping back to the present. "She went back to England. I think there were problems with Richard." She barely said the last three words, just mouthing them. *There's something very peculiar about a naked woman affecting concern about being over-heard*, thought Valérie. *On the one hand, so false, on the other, hiding absolutely nothing.*

"That's a shame, he seems very nice."

"Not your type though, eh?" Martin asked; there was a pathetic tinge of hope in his voice. "What is your type, I wonder."

Valérie felt like saying "clothed," but stopped herself by breathing in loudly instead, as if to savor the place they were in. "It's very calm here; you must be very busy all the time?"

"Oh yes." Gennie smiled. "Rushed off our feet. It's two businesses, you see, and they have to be kept very much apart."

"Two businesses?"

"Yes, on the one hand we have your traditional French B&B." Martin was trying to sound professional and businesslike, a ludicrous attempt given his state of undress. "And the other..." He went strangely coy, looking to Gennie for help.

"The other is a, well I guess you'd call it an 'introductions' business. We introduce like-minded people..."

"Like-minded people," Martin repeated needlessly.

"Like-minded people"—Gennie took up the reins again—"to each other."

"It's a kind of agency," Martin said flatly.

"Swingers," Gennie explained with a hint of confrontation.

"Swingers?" Valérie asked. It wasn't a word she had come across before. "You mean like jive dancing?"

"Well, that's one way of putting it!" Martin snorted.

"*Échangistes.*" Gennie clearly took the whole thing very seriously indeed.

"Ah, I see." Valérie couldn't think of anything worse. "And that's successful, is it? There are a lot of these *swingers* in the Loire Valley?"

"People come from much further afield." It was Martin's turn to be slightly aggressive, while Valérie tried to hide her disbelief.

"Well, I think that's marvelous, I really do! Consenting adults should be allowed to play." Within the realms of reason and, to a certain extent, good taste, she might have added.

Gennie suddenly giggled. "The only difficult part is keeping the two businesses separate! Oh, Martin, do you remember that funny little man a couple of weeks ago?"

"Oh Lord, yes. Poor fella. He picked the wrong door when he came in late; I'm still not sure how, but that's what he did."

"We were, well, we were with guests and he just sort of stumbled in! Terribly embarrassing, of course! For him, I mean."

"He ran away pretty quickly!" Martin had tears in his eyes. "Which considering his stoop was quite good going! Then he just buggered off. Left without paying."

"He must have been in quite a state, though, poor man." Gennie was trying to control herself. "He must have fallen over in his panic; he cut himself on his glasses, left some blood on the bathroom wall even."

"Never saw him again! Of course we thought about finding him to give him his specs back, but, well, probably best left alone, we thought."

So Grandchamps had stayed here too and done exactly the same disappearing act, although at Richard's B&B it was without the *échangistes* part, obviously, unless he was keeping something back from her. She immediately dismissed the thought from her head. No, he was definitely not the kind.

"But the young Italians you have staying now, the Farrolis, they're not into all that, are they? Newlyweds, I mean." She was finding it harder and harder to hide her opinion of the whole thing.

"Ah," Martin said, "sadly not. And Gennie had the name wrong; it's Rizzoli, not Farroli. No, they don't seem the sort. You get a sixth sense for that kind of thing."

About half an hour later Valérie was standing outside Richard's window. She'd managed to extricate herself from the Thompsons quickly enough; hopefully Martin's sixth sense had picked up that if he tried anything she'd break his neck. She also wanted to get back and tell Richard everything: Grandchamps, the blood, the Rizzolis. But she stood there now in the dark and she watched him without being seen herself. There were no lights on, just the flickering images from an enormous television set. Ingrid Bergman was on screen saying goodbye to Humphrey Bogart; even Valérie knew that film. But the look on Richard's face was what stopped her: a look of childish wonderment and complete passive contentment. He looked so peaceful and happy. Her news could wait, she thought, let him dream first. Besides, after an evening spent in the cloying company of the Thompsons, she badly needed a shower.

10

Passepartout was the center of everyone's attention, and he seemed not in the least bit fazed by it. Madame Tablier stood glowering at the small dog from the corner of the room, a rolled-up cigarette tucked behind her ear, a bucket in hand and a look on her face that, if Passepartout had been sensitive to these things, he'd have known meant, "One false move, matey, and with a flick of the wrist you're casserole."

Monsieur Meyer sat opposite Passepartout. He didn't seem a happy man anyway, and the small dog was just adding to his woes. The family, consisting of a rather brusque wife and twin nine-year-old daughters, had arrived the evening before from Alsace, and life just looked a little too hard for poor Monsieur Meyer. Richard felt some empathy for him. They had turned up to breakfast on time, as people with German blood in them always do in his experience, but hadn't bargained for a chihuahua with a fine line in haughtiness to be dumped at their table. Madame Meyer was giving Monsieur Meyer a look that asked what, if anything, he was prepared to do about it, while Monsieur Meyer just stared at Passepartout as if he were the living embodiment of all his worldly disappointments.

Richard stood behind his breakfast bar, as usual trying to look inconspicuous, rather like a nervous Wild West sheriff waiting for someone to pull the trigger first. On the one hand Valérie had massively overstepped the mark in asking the Meyers to look after Passepartout "for a moment" as if she owned the place; but on the other he was trying to affect an air of "what can you do? She owns the place." It was the cowardly way forward, and one he was fully willing to exploit for now. The Meyers had booked for three nights; there would be plenty of time to iron things out. Maybe.

Valérie came rushing down the stairs, a long flowing cream dress adding to her not inconsiderable elegance, but also making her look something like a ghost, ephemeral. Richard suspected she'd gone back to her room just so that she could make a second entrance at breakfast, but after plucking Passepartout from the relieved Meyers she produced a notepad.

"I've been doing some thinking," she said, as if she and Richard were alone. "We'll talk after breakfast."

"OK," he replied meekly, catching Monsieur Meyer's eye, which plainly said, "You, too, eh?"

There was a brief lull, long enough for, ostensibly, the *patron* to draw breath, and then Valérie stood up again with another flourish. "No," she said, "it can't wait! Follow me, please." And left by the open patio doors.

"I'm in the middle of serving breakfast, I can't just..."

"I'm sure Madame Tablier can fill in for now," she shot back over her shoulder, to which Madame Tablier replied with another of her "casserole" looks. The Meyers, who had been patiently waiting for the coffee to be ready, all looked at each other, then the three females of the party all looked at the male. The male's heart sank; action would be required.

He raised his hand as Richard passed the table to try and get his attention. "Yes," Richard said distractedly, "sorry, the coffee will be ready in a second. Madame Tablier, would you...?" He hurried on past, avoiding eye contact.

"Coffee, is it?" Madame Tablier asked in a threatening manner of Monsieur Meyer.

"Er, yes please."

Madame Tablier snorted in response, watching Richard leave the room after Valérie while keeping her position in the corner like a guard. The coffee could wait.

Valérie was standing in the garden, Passepartout at her feet, looking every inch the accessory. "Look," Richard began, "I can't just keep dropping things for this nonsense. Those people have paid good—"

"Yes, yes." She dismissed his complaint with a wave of her hand. "So have I. Now, look. That nice Italian couple who left yesterday. What do you know of them?"

"Why? What does it matter?"

"What do you know of them?"

"Well, that they're a nice Italian couple, honeymooners they said, and they, quite reasonably in my book, have a problem with blood on the walls! So do I, come to that."

"They are staying at the Thompsons."

"So?" Richard couldn't help but be a little put out at this knowledge and if it came down to it and he was a guest, he'd prefer a bloodstain to the kind of antics that Martin and Gennie got up to. *That'll test their marriage early doors*, he thought.

"It doesn't concern you?" Valérie, exasperated, was in full "schoolteacher with a thick student" mode.

"Why should it concern me? Why does it concern you for that matter? They came to the Loire Valley on honeymoon, they left my place, fearing for their lives probably, and are still staying locally. I don't get why that bothers you."

"Because something is going on. I can feel it."

Hot flushes, Richard thought, though wisely didn't say it out loud. If he was having something of a midlife crisis it was perfectly feasible that Valérie was having some kind of menopausal upheaval of her own, surely?

"Excuse me"—Monsieur Meyer appeared—"but we have been waiting for coffee now for ten minutes."

"Yes, sorry. I'll be right there."

"They are following poor Monsieur Grandchamps. I know it."

"Your poor Monsieur Grandchamps is a mafia don, or something. Frankly I'm glad the lot of them have gone. Though I'm not sure even the mafia could cope with Martin and Gennie."

"We are also waiting for our eggs." Meyer's apologetic demand was greeted with a sigh from Richard and indifference from Valérie, though he was used to both.

"It says on your website that you provide your own eggs." He flourished one of Richard's fuzzily printed flyers, as if that were proof.

"Madame Tablier!" Richard shouted, losing any pretense at control of the situation. "Madame Tablier!"

"Yes," came the sullen reply from right behind him.

"Ah, I thought you were indoors. Could you please..."

"I agree with 'er." Madame Tablier nodded toward Valérie and gestured unnecessarily with her bucket. "Something's up." Valérie nodded in response, and Richard watched as a grudging mutual respect formed in front of him. He slumped again.

"My wife really wants an egg." Meyer was trying to sound forceful but was once again ignored. He slumped, too. Then he immediately stood up straight as he realized that the rest of the Meyer family were standing just behind him, each with the same disapproving look on their face.

"There is nothing going on!" Richard was adamant. "This is the Loire Valley. Nothing goes on in the Loire Valley." Suddenly he stopped and looked accusingly at Valérie. "How do you know the Rizzolis are at Martin and Gennie's?"

"Because I went there."

"You went there?"

"Yes. I went there. I knew you wouldn't come so I went on my own."

"And?"

"And they don't wear clothes; I found that out very quickly."

"The Rizzolis?"

"The Thompsons!"

"I could have told you that! They're bloody sex pests, the pair of them."

Madame Meyer tried to cover her daughters' ears while looking accusingly at her husband, who blurted out "eggs" as if that would help.

"I know that now. It doesn't bother me, they are adults; they can do what they like."

"And they do, believe me."

"And poor Monsieur Grandchamps stayed there."

"I knew it," Madame Tablier had put her bucket down and was fiddling with her cigarette, "something's going on."

"There's nothing going on!"

"We really would like some coffee, please."

"Yes, I heard you!" Richard found himself shouting at the wrong people.

"And he disappeared the same way. Blood, glasses, poof!" Valérie made a gesture like a cheap stage magician. "Into thin air."

Richard shook his head. "So what? I want nothing to do with it.

Knowing Martin and Gennie, they've probably got him locked up in one of their dungeons with a zip mask on."

Valérie's expression changed immediately. "Do you really think so?"

"No! No I bloody don't. I think he's a silly old man, playing silly games. Mafia silly games at that, and—and I want to make this absolutely clear—it has nothing whatsoever to do with me!"

"Eggs!" Monsieur Meyer finally snapped. "We want our eggs."

"Look." Richard had now lost control and pointed toward the chicken coop. "Go and get them your bloody self!"

The Meyer family all looked at the chicken coop not far away in the corner of the garden, shaded under a lime tree. The two little girls both screamed, and turned their heads into their mother's dress. The mother glowered at the father, the father looked stunned, and Richard, Valérie, and Madame Tablier all turned to look in the same direction. There, hanging from the coop, a wire noose around her neck, her eyes white with death, was a hen.

"The bastards," Richard said quietly. "They've killed Ava Gardner."

11

Wiping his brow, Richard leaned heavily on the spade. The late spring ground was dry and difficult to dig but he was determined to show Ava Gardner the same respect as he'd shown the others, and give her a grave and a dignified sendoff. There were at least eight hens buried behind the woodstore, their graves each marked with a stone to avoid being exhumed the next time a death occurred. He was working as fast as he could before Madame Tablier made off with Ava Gardner's tasty corpse. He'd already seen the woman eyeing up the dead bird, and while Richard was maybe no longer the boss in his own home, hopefully a temporary situation, he was not going to let Madame Tablier eat his beloved Ava Gardner.

"Do you bury all your hens?" Valérie had asked with the inevitable Passepartout in her arms and a hint of surprise in her voice.

"Yes," Richard had replied archly.

And that had been that, even Valérie showing some sensitivity for the moment and going back indoors. Richard went back to digging the hole and once he felt it was deep enough, he laid down some straw and placed the stiff bird gently in the ground and filled the hole back up.

"This is personal," he said to himself, sitting heavily on a nearby garden bench. "This is personal," he repeated. "The thing is," he began, "I don't even know what *this* is." He stared at the fresh earth on top of Ava Gardner's grave. "I don't get it, old girl. A bloke disappears, possibly violently and possibly more than once and it's you that gets it in the neck. That's not right, is it?" He paused. "You don't mess with a fellow's hens. Even if you are the mafia." *The mafia*, he thought, *that's obviously why Valérie is so convinced the Rizzoli couple are involved; there's no actual evidence, but easy national stereotyping is as good a place to start as any, one supposes. It's odd that she would go to the Thompsons' on her own, though.* He clenched his fist angrily; she goes running off and stirring up trouble and it's his hen that cops it.

"It's time I took back control, Ava, I think," he said, standing up stiffly. "I need to stop being pushed around. I won't let what's happened to you go unpunished. No." He picked up the spade as if it were a rifle. "A man's gotta do what a man's gotta do."

"Who are you talking to, Richard?" It was Valérie, for once Passepartout-less and thankfully treading gingerly around the hen cemetery.

He looked at her defiantly. "I am talking to myself, madame. It's the only way I can guarantee sensible conversation around here. Watch your step there, please, you nearly stepped on Katharine Hepburn."

"You were talking to the hen, weren't you?" She looked a little worried by the prospect.

"Yes. And?"

"Oh."

"Do you have a problem with that?"

"No, I think it's rather sweet."

"Oh, well." He didn't know what to say. "Thanks."

"And?"

"And what?"

"What did your hen have to say?"

Richard turned to Valérie to see if she was mocking him. She didn't look like she was and he suspected that she wouldn't be capable of hiding her emotions, even sarcastic ones.

"She didn't say a lot, funnily enough. Difficult to talk when someone breaks your neck. And her being a hen, obviously."

"So what have you decided?" She sat down on the bench and he sat back down next to her.

"I've decided that I don't like being pushed around."

"Who's pushing you around?"

"You are."

"I am not."

"Yes, you are." She looked hurt. "Look, it's not your fault, not really. I'm very easy to push around, but it's Ava Gardner down there who's paid the price."

"I don't think I've pushed you around at all."

"Oh you have, you and everyone else I know." He sighed wearily. "All I want is a quiet life, but what happens is you end up just being dragged along by other people's whims. I don't blame *you*, as such, but in a very short space of time, I've lost a guest, possibly murdered—in your opinion—possibly more than once, if what the Thompsons told you is correct. And two Italian killers—in your opinion—are now sending me hen-based mafia death warnings!"

"But..."

"Please don't interrupt. You see, I don't remember at any point signing up for all this and yet I appear to be at the very bloody center of it. I don't even know you; *you* might have killed Grandchamps for all I know! And poor Ava. You might be in cahoots with the Rizzolis, too."

"And why would I still be here, then, if it was me?"

"I don't know," he said tartly. "I've still got two hens left; maybe your work isn't finished."

She stood up. "You are being ridiculous."

"Yes, I know. I know I'm being ridiculous. This whole bloody thing is ridiculous. We've got an old man who detests his brother so much he needs to find him so he can keep annoying him, a policeman who doesn't seem to think Missing Persons is his job, a mysterious Italian couple now in the grip of two British perverts, you bossing me around like we're married, and a dead hen! I have a right to be ridiculous. I'm mad as hell and I'm not going to take it anymore." He looked at her to see if she recognized the film reference, which she obviously didn't. *Good God*, he thought, *has this woman never seen a film in her life at all?* "Well, I'm not going to be pushed around anymore. From now on we do things my way, OK?"

He looked at her; if he was expecting an argument, he was disappointed. Instead her face was a picture of innocence as if not recognizing one word of the damning picture he had just painted. "Of course," she said, patting his arm, "what do you suggest we do?"

Dammit, thought Richard, he should have seen that coming. It's all very well claiming control of a situation but you really should offer some sort of plan as well.

"Well, I've given this some thought," he said, not entirely with conviction.

"You and the hen?"

"The hen and I. And I think we get this policeman chap involved properly?" He heard Valérie make a noise under her breath that indicated very strongly that she didn't agree. "All we told him was that

Grandchamps had disappeared; we didn't tell him about the blood or the broken glasses. Surely he'd be more inclined to get involved if he knew the circumstances? Rather than fob it off on to us."

"But we have no proof that they ever existed. So we would only be reporting the same thing to him; also he would ask why we didn't tell him this in the first place."

"I wanted to!"

"But proof, Richard, the proof disappeared with the Rizzolis."

"What about the judge? Surely he must have some real concern for his brother; we could tell him about the missing evidence."

"Or"—she hesitated slightly—"we look for the evidence ourselves and *then* we go to the police."

He remained silent for a moment, weighing this up. "But you think the Rizzoli couple have the evidence?"

"I think so, yes."

"Which means searching the Rizzolis' rooms over at Martin and Gennie's?"

"Richard!" Valérie cried, jumping up off the bench. "That is a brilliant idea! We search the Rizzolis!"

"No, now hang on, I wasn't for one minute..."

"Really, you are very good at this. You are so right; from now on we do things your way."

"Eh? Now look, just wait..." He trailed off; he could feel his mouth moving but there was nothing coming out. He felt like an amateur chess player who had just come up against a grandmaster. So much for control.

"Hey, boss?" Madame Tablier appeared, a cigarette hanging from her lips, her eyes darting around to see if she was in time to grab the hen. "Boss?"

"Do you mean me?" Richard replied disconsolately.

"There's some guests arrived, asking for a room for a few nights. I said most people only stay the one these days, but they still want a room anyway. Shall I put them in the Germans' room? They've already cleared off."

The Meyers had left immediately after seeing the dead hen. Two traumatized little girls, a fearsome mother, and a father who knew it wasn't his fault but was racked with guilt anyway. They never had gotten their coffee. And they were probably forever turned off the idea of eggs.

"Yes," Richard said, "if it's ready."

"They barely stayed long enough to make a mess. It won't take long."

"What's the name?"

"Marie Gavinet, monsieur. My name is Marie Gavinet." The slight figure of Marie stepped out from behind Madame Tablier. "We have met. And, monsieur, madame"—she nodded toward Valérie—"I really need your help." She moved slightly to one side to reveal a young man standing behind her. "That is, *we* really need your help."

"Tch!" snapped a put-out Madame Tablier, trudging off. "And I suppose I'm just chopped liver around here."

12

It was hard not to stare at Melvil Sanspoil. For his part, Richard was only capable of framing the world through the parameters of old films—a gesture, a personality, looks, a situation, they were all categorized and judged according to how Hollywood had seen it. And to Richard, Melvil Sanspoil was Peter Lorre, the bug-eyed Hungarian émigré who had been Hollywood's go-to villain of choice for much of the 1940s: weak, impressionable, dangerous. He couldn't think of a modern equivalent and that, he decided, was exactly the problem with the modern world; there was no Peter Lorre in it.

There was something about Melvil Sanspoil, though, that was immediately likable. There was a tough vulnerability about him, an energetic fighting spirit that said, "Yes, thank you, I know exactly what I'm battling against, but I aim to win." It was clear too that Marie Gavinet loved him dearly and in that, young Sanspoil was a very lucky man indeed, and palpably, as Richard's dad used to say, "batting well above his average."

"He's a very odd-looking young man," Valérie whispered to him, "very odd. Yet she's very pretty." It was a relationship that was beyond Valérie's comprehension; beauty must be with beauty. The aesthetic lines should not be blurred, even for love. *Maybe that's the French in her*, thought Richard, and maybe his immediate rooting for the underdog was the Britishness in him.

"I like him," he said defensively. "I like them both."

"Monsieur, could I have some sugar please?" Melvil's voice was deeper than you'd imagine to look at him, a sonorous mellow voice that spoke of classical theater training, and with perfect enunciation.

"Of course." Richard put the sugar box in the middle of the table as he and Valérie sat down to join the young couple. Madame Tablier, chuntering away to herself and none too happy about being excluded from the conference, was clattering about upstairs preparing their room. Passepartout sat disinterestedly on the sofa, looking for all the world like a stuffed curiosity in an old-fashioned small-town museum.

There was silence while they all looked into their coffee cups, waiting for someone else to kick things off.

"This is very nice coffee," Marie said.

"Thank you." Richard was happy to start with neutral territory. "It's a funny thing, you know; I realized almost as soon as I started making breakfasts for people that everybody these days *thinks* they know about coffee, and nobody really does! Me included, I have to say."

"I have the same thing at Bruno's, people complain and then..."

"Why do you need our help?" The upper echelon of Valérie's beating about the bush tolerance level had been quickly breached. There was an awkward silence again. "Is it to do with poor Monsieur Grandchamps?" Richard couldn't help rolling his eyes at the "poor" sobriquet. "The missing one, I mean, not the judge."

The young lovers looked at each other quickly. "Both, really," was Marie's quiet response.

"I see." Valérie threw out a sudden and winning smile and everyone relaxed a little bit. "Why not start at the beginning then, my dear?"

The sudden warmth threw Richard slightly. *Hello*, he thought, *she's gone all Miss Marple*. He wasn't sure he liked the swift change either, suspecting he was about to be dragged in deeper.

"Thank you, madame." Melvil put his hand on Marie's as she began and she smiled at him warmly and gratefully. "I know we've met already, and when I saw you with Officer Bonneval, and later the judge, I wasn't sure about you. But the way that they talked about you both after you'd gone..."

"You eavesdropped?" Valérie's tone wasn't harsh, but she wanted to know the level of honesty.

"Oh yes," came the defiant reply.

"Good girl, carry on."

"What were they saying about us?"

"Oh Richard, that's really not that important at the minute."

"Sorry." He felt scolded, a Nigel Bruce Doctor Watson to her stern Basil Rathbone Holmes.

"Well, I used to work for the other Monsieur Grandchamps," Marie continued, "the one who's disappeared."

"The crook?" Richard was determined not to be left out of this.

"Apparently yes, monsieur. But he was such a sweet man. He was very good to me when my mother died; he always made sure I was OK."

"Not like monsieur *le juge*, then?"

"No, madame, the total opposite. That used to be the joke in town that the only way to tell the old Grandchamps twins apart..."

"I'd forgotten they were twins." Richard was thinking aloud, and Valérie gave him a look telling him to be quiet, making him feel like he'd be better off sitting on the sofa with Passepartout, another stuffed curiosity.

"What was the joke, Marie?" Valérie asked calmly.

"That the only way to tell the old Grandchamps twins apart was their personality." There was a brief silence.

"I don't get it?" Valérie said flatly.

"That one had a personality and that the other did not," Richard said as though throwing down a winning card hand. "I am right, aren't I?" he asked quickly and nervously.

"Yes, monsieur." Richard leaned back in his chair, a happier man.

"It's not very funny," Valérie said huffily. "So you used to work for Monsieur Grandchamps?"

"The crook," Richard said needlessly.

"Yes, but obviously when he disappeared there was nothing to do."

"And no one to pay your wages?"

"Exactly, madame."

"Can I ask"—Richard did all but put his hand up—"*when* do you think he disappeared?" Valérie gave him a look which, possibly for the first time, suggested that Richard may have contributed something relevant, and he basked briefly.

"At least a month, possibly more."

"Can you not be more certain than that?"

"No, I'm sorry. It wasn't unusual for monsieur not to be there when I came around to clean, but there would always be an envelope with money. On the Friday. It would be left on the dresser in the hall, if I hadn't seen him. And then they stopped."

"And what did you do?"

"On the second Friday without an envelope, the money, I told Officer Bonneval."

"And he did what?"

"Nothing. He said he was a silly old man who played games and that he wasn't going to waste valuable police time and resources..."

"Lunchtime and shoe leather," Melvil offered bitterly and Marie smiled at him.

"He said he would ask the judge what he wanted to do, and then a few days later Bonneval said that the judge needed some work doing around the house, cleaning and tidying and so on." She looked guilty. "I, we, need the money."

"Oh, that's completely understandable my dear." Valérie patted her hand. "Completely understandable."

"But I don't get it," asked Richard, with an apologetic look toward Valérie. "How can we help? What do you need help with exactly?"

Marie and Melvil looked at each other; there was a silent conversation going on as to who would do the explaining.

"I'm being followed," said Melvil with no hint of fear in his voice, more even that he was excited by the notion, and he lifted his chin like a ham actor.

"Followed, by whom?" Valérie asked, a spark in her eye which Richard, in the few days he'd known her, was already beginning to recognize as dangerous.

"A man and a woman, youngish."

Richard and Valérie looked at each other, their own silent conversation reaching the inevitable "Rizzoli" conclusion.

"Since when?" Richard had the weary air of a police desk sergeant nearing retirement.

"Well, it's funny," Marie interrupted. "I was cleaning at the judge's place—there's never much to do really—but I sent Melvil out to post a letter."

"Just the electricity bill," he added quickly.

"And when he came back I said to him that Wednesdays was always the day that my Monsieur Grandchamps would post *his* letters. Every Wednesday on the dot. The postbox is emptied at four forty-five. Monsieur would be there at four forty, whatever the weather, and hand his post to the postman. Unknowingly, Melvil had done exactly the same."

"I didn't notice these people beforehand, but as soon as the post went they followed me back to the judge's house, where I waited for Marie. Then this morning they were on the train to Tours and they followed me into work."

Richard looked stunned; he really had no idea how his life had become quite so cloak and dagger.

"And did you lose them?" Valérie was so excited she grabbed Melvil's hand on the table.

"Yes, madame," he said proudly and nodded toward a bag he had placed delicately on the table. He opened the bag carefully, like a magician with a slow reveal. In it was a life-size chicken costume, the "head" sitting proudly on top. There followed an awkward silence.

"You hid as a chicken," Richard said slowly, as if addressing the hard of hearing. "And this threw them off?" He hadn't meant to sound quite so skeptical but the whole thing was verging on the ridiculous.

"I am an actor, monsieur," Melvil said in the way that only actors can, with a mix of hubris and confrontation, causing Richard to nod knowingly; he'd guessed as much.

"As a chicken?" he asked, trying not to sound skeptical.

"I am between roles, but I do not rest!" Marie gripped his hand tighter. "I have a job at Monsieur Oeuf, in Tours," he added more sullenly. "I hand out flyers in the street."

"We need the money, monsieur," Marie said desperately.

"We need the money," Melvil repeated.

"Yes, yes." Richard was aware that Valérie was boiling like a kettle and didn't approve of this avian distraction. "But how did you lose the Rizz...this couple, this couple who were following you?"

Melvil regained his confidence quickly. "Well, I went into the restaurant, making sure they came in after me and went out the back to get changed into my costume. When I came out, I walked straight past them and I haven't seen them since." Marie squeezed his arm and smiled at him; Valérie was still clutching his hand while Richard had the image of Melvil in his head, being chased around the Gothic streets of Tours, dressed as an enormous chicken, and with the zither music of *The Third Man* soundtrack playing noisily over the scene. He smiled to himself, but dropped the thought immediately in case Valérie saw him.

"You are very lucky," Valérie said, "and well done." She turned his hand over, examining it a little too obviously. "Sorry," she said, "it's a hobby of mine. Were you a sickly child? Your lifeline is very weak."

"Yes, well done." Richard felt the situation needed rescuing as even the cool Melvil Sanspoil needed to recover his poise from that awkward line of questioning.

"I know that the judge wants you to find his brother..." Marie began.

"Yes, what did he say about us anyway?" Richard was still offended by the thought, though he had no idea why.

"I told you that doesn't matter. Carry on, my dear."

"Well, can Melvil stay here for a bit? I'm very worried about him and I think he'd be safer here with you."

"Really, why?" Richard couldn't help himself and, as he had singularly failed to safeguard his hens, he didn't feel up to the task of protecting Melvil.

"Of course." Valérie decided to answer for the both of them.

"We haven't got much money." Marie bit her lip as she spoke.

"That is not an issue at all," Valérie declared, standing up leaving Richard to ponder when it was he might actually regain control of the situation. "You two go upstairs and Madame Tablier will show you the room."

They picked up their small bags and the chicken costume, and, full of thank yous with Marie even kissing Richard on the cheek, went upstairs quietly.

"So, let me get this straight: not only am I investigating missing persons, I am now a bodyguard, is that right?"

"What would you prefer: to say no and leave him at the risk of the Rizzolis?"

"The Rizzolis might be a perfectly nice couple trying to see a bit of the Loire Valley!"

"The Rizzolis are everywhere, and I do not believe in coincidence." Valérie was emphatic and even Richard couldn't argue that they did seem to pop up an awful lot.

"What was all that stuff about palm reading again? If I'm going to bodyguard someone, I'd prefer you didn't tell him he hasn't got long left, you know. It doesn't inspire confidence."

"I wanted to see his hand, Richard. He is an actor; he could have been pretending to be Monsieur Grandchamps when he stayed here."

"Oh, right, do you really think so?"

"I wanted to be sure."

"And, are you?"

"Yes, Richard. Melvil Sanspoil was not the hand on your wall."

"So we still have a missing Monsieur Grandchamps, and now a little lost lamb, too, so to speak. Or chicken, to be more precise."

"Yes." Valérie scooped up Passepartout and from upstairs they both heard the happy humming of Marie Gavinet.

13

⟞⟝

I love you," Melvil said simply and earnestly, as they sat rigidly on the edge of the large double bed.

Marie smiled at him without breaking the tune she was humming. It wasn't that she didn't want to reply, but the presence in the corner of the room of Madame Tablier, dusting aggressively as if each particle were a personal insult, was enough to make even the most effusive lovebird slightly circumspect. Not that Madame Tablier had even acknowledged their presence, lost as she was in the world of Johnny Hallyday, *Dans la Chaleur de Bercy, 1979* to be exact, her orange headphones locking her in.

"I love you!" Melvil repeated more loudly, almost challengingly. Madame Tablier didn't flinch, turn round, or tut, and Marie stopped humming.

"I love you, too," she said, then went back to her tune.

"What is that you're humming today?"

Marie wasn't sure at all. Any tune she repeated was usually just the last thing she'd heard; it was as likely to be a TV advertising jingle as a complicated concerto. "I've no idea." She got up to open their small case. "Does it matter?"

"No, but I'd like to frame the moment, that's all. Give the full credits. It was a brilliant decision to come here."

Marie looked nervously at Madame Tablier, who had spotted a small cobweb in the beams that wasn't long for this world, and was still ignoring their presence.

"I think they can be a help to us." She sat down beside him and sighed heavily. She wasn't used to seeking help; her single-parent mother had taught her independence from an early age, but she also recognized when there was a need to do so and they were definitely in need. Melvil, being Melvil, was quite undaunted by the thought of being followed. He was self-aware enough to know he would never be leading-man material, and therefore an unlikely international spy, but when Marie had suggested that he may actually be in danger he had grown immediately into the role. The way he had managed to lose his pursuers was really quite bold.

But they wouldn't give up, she knew that. They were following her and Melvil. They were probably dangerous and she knew it was her fault. It had been her idea after all. It was she who had suggested that they keep up old Monsieur Grandchamps's postal routine. Every Wednesday, four forty in the afternoon, hand the envelope to the postman. The postman certainly wasn't suspicious. A young, lanky individual wearing headphones that bled sound so badly it sounded like the youth had a wasps' nest about his head. He would never even acknowledge Marie as she handed him an envelope, or maybe he did, but it was a nod of the head that went in time with the other nods of the head to the beat of his loud music. Just like Madame Tablier was doing now as she attacked the cobwebs, nodding her head to some musical beat, though her own headphones were doing a better job of keeping her music in.

Melvil and Marie sat next to each other on the end of the bed once more. She felt safer being here, though she knew she must go back to work later. She also knew that she didn't really need to go back to work. In the last month she had put aside more money than she could earn in years, but she was afraid to touch it. They could just use it to go far away but something stopped her. Was it that the money wasn't hers? Not really. If Monsieur Grandchamps was dead then he had no need for it. If he wasn't and he came back then she had it all, in used fifty-euro notes, a thousand of them, as they had been delivered and safely waiting for him.

If he came back. She had a feeling it was a big if.

She'd heard the old judge and Bonneval earlier and the judge was convinced that his villainous brother, as he'd called him, was still alive. "Still out there," he'd said, "up to no good." She wasn't so sure, though. He had left his envelopes to be posted on the bureau, all dated, all the same and all going to the same address in Trapani in Sicily. Plain, white envelopes, set out in date order and to her that suggested he'd had no plans to disappear, but that somebody else had planned for him to do so.

She sighed heavily and put her arm around Melvil. She had gotten them into this and it would be she who would get them out of it, but having the others, monsieur *et* madame downstairs, as cover, might send a message to the people following them. It might also put them in danger, too, but she quickly tried to dismiss the thought. She liked them both. Valérie was the kind of staunch woman that France produces on a machine conveyor belt, untroubled by any form of doubt whatsoever and with a determination to keep the world under their control. Richard looked a little lost, harassed even, like a driver who'd gone the wrong way up a one-way street but who couldn't get the car to reverse. Well, together they may not be the best security in the world, but they were all they had.

"It was very clever of you to say it was an electricity bill, my love." She hugged Melvil, seeing that Madame Tablier still had her back to them, still nodding her head to the silent beat.

"Yes, yes it was." He puffed out his chest. "Well, I couldn't very well say that all the envelope contained was grape seeds, could I?" Marie put her fingers to her lips quickly and nodded toward Madame Tablier. "Oh, she can't hear a thing!"

Madame Tablier kept nodding her head all the while and Marie and Melvil kissed soundlessly, their eyes closed in relief and passion. Madame Tablier, without turning round, knew what was going on and took the opportunity to stealthily reach into her pocket and press PLAY on her Walkman.

14

Brigadier-Chef Principal Philippe Bonneval put the desktop telephone gently back in its cradle, unfurling the twisted old cord as he did so. It was a constant niggle that he was so neglected, in what his superiors regarded as a backwater, that his office still didn't even have a cordless telephone.

He wore a contented if slightly harassed look about him, having just that minute joined the growing numbers of a club that might be called "That Valérie d'Orçay is a determined woman, isn't she? Club." She'd wanted to know how his investigation was going, to which his initial response, though he didn't actually say it, had been, "What investigation exactly?"

Philippe Bonneval had enough on his plate without getting involved in old men's games. He'd been at police conferences where his big city colleagues had mocked his supposed daily routine of missing cats, fallen trees and sheep rustling, but he knew the reality. He'd been up late just the previous night when a few of the lads from the travelers' camp—as he knew he was supposed to call it now—had been drinking tractor fuel again and had gone on a cow-tipping spree. Clément Roger, who owned a big farm out toward Saint-Sulpice, had called him late on, firstly complaining that two of his prize herd had been pushed over and then, unable to suppress his giggles, that the "silly sods" had tried to push over a bull.

"Is he injured?" Philippe asked, fearing a riot down at the camp if Roger had taken his gun to the proceedings.

"The bull? No, he's fine."

"The traveler lad, is *he* injured?"

"Difficult to say, Bonneval, he's still attached to the bull's head. Must be quite painful though with a bloody great horn stuck up yer arse!"

The lad hadn't been badly injured, embarrassed certainly, but Bonneval's relationship with the travelers was a good one and he was able to smooth things over. A few of the older travelers were going over to Roger's place later today to fix up an old bale wrapper as recompense. No, it wasn't big city violence or organized crime, but his skill and diplomacy meant that it was recorded as nothing more than high jinks. Philippe Bonneval ran a tight ship. The small town and *commune* of Vauchelles was immaculate, welcoming, and thriving, a marked change from when he had arrived at the place looking for lodgings twentysomething years earlier. He didn't care if the mayor took the credit for that; he and everyone else knew the real story. And Bonneval knew everyone and everyone knew him; there was virtually no crime in Vauchelles not because of where they were but because he could see it coming and stopped it in advance.

So what if Judge Grandchamps had lost his brother? He only wanted him back because he was a bit bored without him, without his nemesis. What a strange relationship that was. Bonneval genuinely missed his own brother. Older by some ten years, he had died on duty, a gunshot wound to the head killing him stone dead in one of the more dangerous estates of a notorious *banlieue* in Paris. "Death by Misadventure," the court had said, adding that he shouldn't have been showing off with an uncleaned weapon in the first place. "Let that be a lesson to all new recruits," the minister had intoned at a subsequent press conference, "keep your weapons clean, and don't, for God's sakes, put them in your mouth to show off."

Philippe Bonneval's brother, unrecognizable save for a small scar on his shoulder, might have been a first-class idiot, but Philippe still missed him. His framed picture hung on the wall, proud in his pristine uniform, wearing that mischievous grin he always had, like he may have stolen the uniform and was just wearing it for larks. Suddenly the picture reminded Bonneval that he'd promised Madame d'Orçay a picture of Monsieur Grandchamps—"Send me the email," she'd said, "and I'll pick it up on my phone." Bonneval stared at the office scanner, looking tired and neglected under a pile of hunting magazines. This might take a while, he thought, and Madame d'Orçay didn't strike him as the patient kind.

Of course any decently funded public defense service would have all files on record immediately, or at the very least a secretary to take care of the day-to-day administration, leaving law enforcement to those best suited to it. There must be a photo of old Grandchamps somewhere, he mused, as he made his way to the filing cabinet, though what she hoped to achieve by flashing it about he couldn't say. She had also asked for a list of other B&Bs where the old man had stayed recently, which was easy enough as the judge always rang up whenever a complaint had been made to him about his brother's nonpayment of bills and Bonneval had noted it down as the judge had asked him to.

"Had anyone suspicious been seen in Vauchelles in the past month?" she'd asked, too.

To which he'd replied confidently, "No, madame, I would have known." He might have pointed out that she could be put in that category.

"Yes, I think you would have," had been her considered reply.

The thing is, Bonneval was all too happy to accommodate public-spirited endeavors, especially if it stopped crime, but this just seemed like another game. The truth was that without the two old men living opposite each other, life was easier. On one occasion, the judge had literally taken a potshot with an old blunder-buster at his brother through the window. With one of them gone, life was quieter for everyone. Even Marie hadn't lost out as he'd persuaded the judge to take her on instead.

"I'm sure he'll turn up, madame, there's really no need for you to ruin your holiday in our peaceful valley." He'd meant it to sound like an oblique warning, just let it drop in other words, in which case she'd either not understood or just plain ignored him.

"You are aware of his criminal career, I suppose?"

"Yes, madame, his *former* criminal career, though. And there was a lot of boasting there; I'm not so sure he was as bad as he wanted people to think he was."

"His career may very well be *former*, Brigadier, but the price on his head is still very much current."

This was news to him. He had assumed that both the old man and the judge had exaggerated his history. Talk of mafia in the Val de Follet was like talking about FaceTime and artificial intelligence in the farmers' market: the two worlds were entirely separate.

"How do you know this, madame?" he'd asked, trying to make it sound like that was classified information that only he was party to and not a thundering surprise and a knock to his superiority.

"I have friends in the Interior Ministry. Now look, five hundred thousand euros is a lot of money and will attract some nasty people."

"Five hundred thousand euros?" he'd repeated.

"Dead or alive."

Bonneval had nearly dropped the phone. Five hundred thousand euros! You could buy a lot of cordless phones, scanners and secretaries for five hundred thousand euros. He thought of his own meager salary and pension, not that he was in the job for the money, thankfully, but it did seem unfair that those he was up against had far greater resources than he had.

He started putting together the list of places where Grandchamps had been spotted and dug out a picture of the old man. Five hundred thousand euros. He couldn't get the sum out of his head. What *had* the old man been doing? He cleared the magazines off the scanner and placed the photo on the glass. The image came up on his ancient computer. "What were you up to," he asked out loud, "that someone would see you dead for half a million euros?"

He emailed the documents to Valérie with a quick message about civic responsibility being all very well, but that personal safety and the safety of others are paramount and so on. He then put on his cap, smoothed down his shirt and made his way to the last place he'd seen half a million euros worth of old man Grandchamps. One thing was for sure, half a million euros would attract a lot of bad, greedy people to Vauchelles, desperadoes and lowlife looking for a big payout. Well, Philippe Bonneval wasn't going to sit back and let that happen, not on his watch.

15

The noise from Valérie's phone shook Richard from his reverie. Actually, calling it a reverie gave it a depth that was undeserved; it was more a vacant pondering. His face resembled a city office block at night: the lights were on but there was little or no activity. He'd tried his best, tried his best all his life in fact, but he simply couldn't work out how, in the space of less than forty-eight hours, he'd gone from slightly lovable (his description), occasionally sozzled film buff to mafia hunter and bodyguard. He felt like he should have a cape or something. Instead he wore a rather worn checked shirt, which his wife Clare had bought him years ago and which Valérie had already decreed that morning "did nothing for him." Once again overstepping a mark which seemed to move every day anyway.

How had it come to this? Richard Ainsworth, scourge of international organized crime and staunch defender of the victims of assassination? He wore his glasses on string around his neck, for God's sakes.

"Ah, that's our policeman friend." Valérie picked up her phone. "I have to say, he is very efficient."

"Sorry, what?"

"Please concentrate, Richard, lives depend on it now I think."
Richard shuddered. He would have whimpered but he guessed
that wasn't behavior characteristic of crime fighters. "I said, Officer
Bonneval has sent me a list of places where Monsieur Grandchamps
stayed and where he visited."

Richard sighed. "Right. How does he know where he visited?"

"Because apparently he always managed to either be thrown out
or receive complaints for his behavior."

"What an odd man."

"It sounds like he was trying deliberately to draw attention to
himself."

"Or to his brother."

"Exactly. Well done, Richard!"

"Why, though? It seems a peculiar way to carry on, a life of either
spite or boredom for both of them."

"They must really hate each other," she agreed. "Do you have a
brother or a sister?"

"Me? I have a brother but we don't really stay in touch. He lives in
London, works twenty-four hours a day to pay for two ex-wives and
grown-up children that he can't stand."

"That's quite sad."

"Yes and no. He's convinced himself that he's a vital cog in the
machinery of the world and that without him said world would cease
to function. He came out here once, hated it. Not noisy enough,
probably." He looked wistful. "Clare liked him." The thought seemed
to shake him. "You?"

"Some brothers." And she dismissed them all with a wave of her
hand as if there might just be the two or a whole legion. "Clare is your
wife?" she asked disinterestedly, scrolling through her phone screen.

"For now. How many brothers?"

They were both playing that game, that game that only adults play, of trying not to be interested in each other's background so as not to give anything away of their own. From Richard's point of view he reckoned he had pitifully little to hide anyway, but he was beginning to suspect that Valérie d'Orçay had far more going on than she was prepared to reveal. He hoped it was a temporary barrier; he had to admit she was rather exciting even if she had a rather blasé attitude toward poultrycide, if that was the right word. The upsetting image of Ava Gardner came back to him, and he shuddered again.

"Right then." He put his glasses on. "Where do we start?"

"Well, this list is quite long."

"So our policeman friend is more interested than he let on, you mean?"

"No, he says that the old judge has kept a file going, which would suit the legal profession, everything in writing, and Bonneval sent it to me. I only asked for it a few minutes ago. Like I said, he's very efficient."

Terrified more like, was Richard's conclusion. He suspected there was a long line of men suddenly terrified into action and "efficiency" by Valérie's call to arms. She handed him the phone to have a look at the list, which he did over the top of his glasses.

"Why do you do that?" she asked innocently.

"What? Why do I do what?" He turned to her self-consciously, again looking over the top of his glasses.

"Wear your glasses when you obviously have no need?"

He took them off. "They're more for driving."

"I think you like to look older than you are." There was a silence as Richard scrolled down the text on the phone. "Why is that?"

The bloody woman wasn't letting go.

"Do you know what strikes me about this list?" he said decisively, while simultaneously hoping he would come up with something when she asked, "What?"

"What?"

"Well..."

"'Ere, you two." It was Madame Tablier at the foot of the stairs.

"Not now, madame, Richard is on the verge of a discovery, I think."

Madame Tablier scoffed, muttered something about "not being good enough for the likes of yous" and disappeared outside.

"Well, you were saying?"

Suddenly something did strike Richard. He looked at Valérie but was almost too nervous to express it. "Well," he said again, "all of these places are the top destination in their, I don't know, field." She looked dubious. "No, really. There's one chateau, so it's Chambord. There's one *jardin*, it's Villandry. There's one vineyard, naturally it's in Sancerre, which is quite some distance from here, but it's the most famous. Actually, that's it; it's the most famous places he's visited. Personally I always preferred Chenonceau to Chambord."

"So?"

"Well, that's it really. It's just not very imaginative, that's all. If there's a church, it's Notre-Dame in Chartres. If there's an abbey, it's Fontevraud. It's like he's found a list of the most popular tourist destinations in the Loire Valley and is working through them."

She looked at him.

"Yes, well." He was losing confidence now. "I know it's not much."

"So he's going out of his way to be seen, is that what you mean?"

Richard wasn't entirely sure what he meant. "I guess so," he said like a reluctant pupil.

She typed something into her phone. "The Top Ten Tourist

Destinations in the Loire Valley," she said as she tapped in the letters. "Chambord, Villandry, Notre-Dame, Fontevraud...you may have something. He's even going through them in order! Richard! Brilliant. If he's used the same list, and they surely cannot be all that different, we can even see where he's going to go next!" She leaned over and hugged him, just as Madame Tablier came back into the room.

"Oh give it a rest!" she spat. "Honestly, everyone's at it." And then she left again, missing Richard's complete and utter inability to deal with what had just happened to him. He stood up, then sat back down immediately.

"So, well, it seems he's done all the major chateaux and we'll never find him just by taking a lucky guess at the hundreds of others. What do you think?"

Richard was trying to regain his composure by sitting completely still and staring at nothing in the distance.

"Are you OK, Richard?"

"What? Yes, yes, just thinking." He tried to look thoughtful. "Chateaux, you say?"

"Yes, chateaux. There are too many of them."

"That's the problem with those lists. It's the same for all of them; they talk about the chateaux and very little else."

"Is there anything else?"

"The zoo. The zoo dominates everything around here. It's seventy-five percent of my business, actually. It has its own TV series, rented pandas. It's huge and it never appears in those lists."

"And besides the zoo?"

Richard was disappointed. Whenever he mentioned that the zoo, at great expense, rented its pandas, that immediately became the talking point, and over time he'd developed some nice witty lines to accompany the conversation. Valérie obviously thought that pandas, rented or not, were superfluous to requirements.

"Besides the rented pandas?" He tried one more nudge and got nothing. "Well, there's the river itself. There's river cruises, canoeing and so on."

"Oh." Valérie looked disappointed.

"In fact, say what you like about the Rizzoli couple but they asked me to book them on a boat trip. It had to be done by phone because their French..."

"You booked them a boat trip?" Valérie was suddenly very animated.

"Yes, I just told you that. There's a few of them, I said they should choose one of the smaller ones, less crowded, but they had a specific one in..." He trailed off. "...mind."

Valérie was looking at him in a way that was not wholly encouraging, more like he'd been wasting her time. "Can you remember when you booked it for?"

"Erm, well yes"—he was trying to avoid her rather stern gaze—"it was for this afternoon, actually. It's not that far from here but we'll have to hurry. Do you want me to..."

"Yes, Richard, I do. We are going to be on that boat."

Madame Tablier came back through the double doors. "You two finished have you? Good, well, I've got some news, too."

"You can tell us later, madame, we need to leave quickly. Now, Passepartout doesn't like boats, he gets sick, so take good care of him please. He's already eaten." She handed an astonished Madame Tablier a mutually suspicious Passepartout and ran upstairs. "Take a hat and sunglasses, Richard, please, we should try not to be recognized," she called over her shoulder.

Richard looked at Madame Tablier, who was in a staring

competition with Passepartout that looked like it may go on for some time. "Anyway," Madame Tablier began, not blinking or taking her eyes off the dog for a second, "I've got something to tell you." Passepartout did that dog thing of licking his own snout, his concentrated gaze not wavering even for a second.

"Really?" Richard replied, fascinated by the confrontation.

"Yes, those two..." Richard's phone started to ring, the rather sad, tinkly rendition of "As Time Goes By" from *Casablanca*, which made him wince. It had seemed like a good idea at the time but it just seemed a little tragic now. He'd meant to change it but couldn't for the life of him remember how to do it. He picked the phone up; it was his daughter Alicia, and she was FaceTiming him, as she called it, which meant he not only had to sound interested in what she said, he had to look it, too. Telephones were much easier when it was just sound. He remembered an item on the French news when talking over the phone became a visual as well as an aural thing; a man had complained bitterly that it was an end to civilization as we know it. "Suppose my wife rings and I say I'm working late in the office?" He'd been really quite angry. "She can see that I'm not!" The reporter, not unreasonably, had asked where he might be then. "None of your business!" he'd said and scurried off, no doubt hoping his wife wasn't watching the news either.

"Alicia! How lovely to hear from you!"

"Hello, Daddy," was the echoing reply. She always sounded so disappointed in him, he thought.

"I can't talk long, darling, I need to go out quite urgently, are you OK?"

"It's Mummy, Daddy." The girl was twenty-seven and she still spoke like she did when she'd first started ballet classes at the age of four. "I really hope you two can work something out this weekend;

it's very stressful for all of us, you know?" Richard wondered if there was a statute of limitations where offspring could no longer blame their own inadequacies on their parents. Surely, when you become an adult yourself the scales should fall from your eyes and you can see that the vast majority of parents are as frightened and out of their depth as any newborn.

"I'm sorry, darling."

"You know that Sly and I are trying for a baby; this uncertainty really isn't helping us at all."

Richard had been blamed for a lot of things in his time; some of it was fair, some of it at best circumstantial, a good proportion he felt was absolute rot, but to have lack of progeny and fertility cycles laid at his door really was the end. Besides which he wasn't sure that anyone called Sly—an estate agent so Sly by name, sly by nature in Richard's ignored opinion—should be having children anyway. Certainly not ones related to Richard. He was a truly dreadful man. "Hi, Dick," he'd said at their first meeting, which was the wrong foot to get off on. "Of course, estate agency is just a stepping stone, I DJ at weekends." "DJ at weekends" to Richard was shorthand for playing away from home. He did admire Sly in one respect, though: he was an estate agent in booming, property-obsessed Central London and yet was singularly unsuccessful at it, to the point of embarrassment. Even Richard had to admit that that was some feat.

"I'm sorry, darling, try not to have me in mind when you're...try not to think about it, is what I'm saying. I'm sure we'll sort something out."

"I hope so, Daddy."

"So do I."

There was an awkward silence where Alicia twiddled with her

hair, as she'd always done as a child. "I think Mummy's hoping you'll get back together this weekend."

"Oh." Richard sat down. "Let's just take things slowly for now." He was surprised with Alicia's take on the situation, which seemed at odds with the facts as he saw them.

Alicia looked disappointed. "I see you put that awful film projector light at the bottom of the stairs again. Mummy won't like that."

"I like it." Richard turned his head to the stairs behind him just as Valérie came in to view. Elegant, refined, and looking absurdly glamorous in enormous sunglasses and a rather old-fashioned—and all the better for that, thought Richard—headscarf.

"If we have no luck today, Richard, I think we should try the zoo tomorrow," she said airily, disappearing from Alicia's FaceTime view almost as soon as she'd entered it. Richard turned back slowly to look at a now stunned Alicia.

"Oh, Daddy! How could you?" And with that, the screen went blank.

Yes, on the whole Richard preferred the old-fashioned type of telephone.

16

Driving slowly along the riverbank, past the crowded campsite, Valérie directed her sports car toward the car park beyond where the tour boats were moored. The sun shimmered on the still surface of the River Cher, broken by the occasional ripple or floating island of algae. The peace of the place was infectious, and Richard, who would normally rather beat himself with a stale baguette than stay at a campsite, felt a tinge of jealousy toward those who were occupying the leafy river edge sites on both banks. Being late spring and so not yet school holiday time, the campsites were full of the gray market, as they were known. Retired couples in pristine motor homes ambling around France before the big crowds hit the place. He sighed heavily.

"You're right!" Valérie suddenly said decisively, slamming on the brakes before reversing the car at some speed through the bus tour parties meandering along the narrow road. They jumped back and out of the way, surprisingly sprightly, as Valérie continued reversing into the coach car park before hiding the car behind two large blue coaches in the far corner.

She pushed the button to put the roof up while Richard sat stock still, scared to get out of the car in case he found a few of the pensioners knocked down like Skittles and the rest of the party brandishing torches and pitchforks. "Right about what?" he mustered.

"I thought you were sighing because parking in the main car park was a bad idea, that we might be spotted."

"Oh right, yes." Whereas treating a coach party of retirees like they were a tenpin bowling set was the height of discretion and disguise. Valérie adjusted her large sunglasses in the rearview mirror and tightened her headscarf. She looked like an off-duty movie star, at once trying to be incognito while at the same time making sure she was seen.

"Put your hat on, Richard, they are more likely to recognize you than me, I think."

Richard doubted that very much and had a lifetime of wallflowerism to prove it. Even on his own wedding day he'd spent most of the reception introducing himself to people, some of whom were his own family.

"I haven't got a hat, I'm afraid. I don't wear hats."

She looked at him aghast, like he'd just admitted to a life of delinquency and opium addiction.

"You don't wear hats? Why ever not?" She looked very disappointed in him, and he felt chided. "A man should wear a hat. He should at the very least own one."

"Well, my hair's too thick; they always leave a sort of rim around my head, just above the ear."

"A rim?" He noticed that when she struggled with English words she couldn't hide her irritation, but then Richard wondered if she'd ever tried to hide her irritation anyway.

"Yes," he said, switching back to French, "like a circle in my hair." She looked at him coldly. "Just above the ear," he added limply.

Again, he remembered his wedding day and the subsequent photos that were taken when he'd removed his top hat.

"Oh, darling!" Clare had snorted, opening the wedding album in the photographer's office a month later. "You look like you've been lobotomized!"

He hadn't worn a hat since.

"You have sunglasses, I suppose?"

Richard held up his glasses.

"Good. Well, I probably have a hat in the boot that you can use." She got out of the car, leaving Richard to ponder just exactly what kind of unisex headgear she had in mind. Apart from the dreaded, ubiquitous baseball cap, was there such a thing as a unisex hat? He couldn't think of one, and he had a vision of himself wearing a spare headscarf instead. He could always just tie a four-cornered hankie around his head...

His door opened. "Here." She thrust a perfectly reasonable man's panama hat at him. "Try this."

He looked at it suspiciously. "This is a man's hat," he said, trying not to sound surprised.

She looked at him oddly. "Would you prefer one of mine?"

"No, no. Of course not." There were so many questions he wanted to ask, none of which he felt were any of his business and besides which he was wearing another man's hat. It's difficult to be assertive in another man's hat.

"It's a little small, but it will have to do," she said, trying to adjust it to what might be called a jaunty angle to hide the fact that its small size made him look like a cartoon character. "Put your sunglasses on." He did so. "There," she said with a smile, "nobody will recognize you!"

Richard smiled wanly. *How unnecessary*, he thought, *nobody ever does.*

A few minutes later he was sitting on a stone bench in the sun just enjoying the calm of the river in front of him. Behind him there was a kind of grizzled pandemonium as the coach party were being unsuccessfully herded toward forming some kind of orderly line. The tour leader, a harassed-looking woman in her late twenties and in a blue uniform that had seen better days, was having difficulty directing them or making herself heard. The old folk repeatedly wandered off, making her job impossible, and she kept glancing back toward the iron gates on the sloped jetty, willing them to open so she could get the party on the boat and maybe then grab an hour to herself.

Valérie had gone off to buy tickets for her and Richard, though it looked like the boat was going to be quite full. Also, as yet, there was no sign of the Rizzolis. Richard had checked that this was the time he'd booked for them, but if they didn't turn up was that a sign of guilt or innocence? As far as he could tell, their guilt, as it were, was purely circumstantial. There was the Italian connection; that was all. There was nothing to tie them to the death of Ava Gardner or the disappearance of old Grandchamps, only that Marie and Melvil felt that they were following them. But then, why would they do that? Just for using a postbox? And anyway, if they were staying with Martin and Gennie, they might have already decided that the Loire Valley wasn't the place for them and gone back home to Trapani.

Valérie sat down next to him heavily. "There's only one ticket left." She kicked at the ground.

"I don't mind waiting here if you want to go." He felt like adding that he could stop them escaping, but he knew that was ridiculous in so many ways. Valérie looked behind them at the crowd starting to shuffle forward as the gates opened. She thrust the ticket at him. "See you on board," she said hurriedly, standing up, "but let's not sit together. You go to the viewing deck on the top, and I'll take a seat down below. And Richard, try not to look conspicuous!" With that she disappeared deep into the throng and he lost sight of her as the amorphous, gray-haired mass rolled down the gangplank and onto the boat.

Right, he thought, standing up himself, *try not to look conspicuous*, and he adjusted his small hat and queued up behind the tour parties, nervously whistling.

It was difficult not to look conspicuous, though, as he was the only one on the upstairs viewing deck; the rest were fighting for seats down below. But conspicuous or not, Richard quite enjoyed it. He felt like a captain looking down on galley slaves, and started tapping the wooden rail in front of him as though it was the rhythm drum for the oars. He then stopped as an old woman sidled up to him, one of the few who hadn't got a seat downstairs and had ventured to the top deck where there were some wooden benches.

"Excuse me, where are the toilets?" His slave-driver captain's image blown, he shook his head and his hat fell off.

Within a few minutes the large boat had slipped its moorings and was smoothly turning away from the weir to head downriver. There was the gentle hum of the engine matched by the equally gentle hum of quiet chatter as everybody, the stress of boarding behind them, settled down. The hostess tapped the microphone quietly as if not to awaken the sleeping river, and the quiet commentary, after the welcome, began.

Richard relaxed, enjoying the view, the spring smells coming from the riverbank, and the gentle breeze on his face. He hadn't done this for years, not since Alicia was small, when he and Clare had first started coming to this part of France. He smiled to himself. Those were good days and he had fond memories. Clare had put Alicia—was she five or six then?—in an enormous life jacket, with her tiny head just popping up out of the top. She'd looked like a cushion, and he'd pretended to keep sitting on her, which had made her laugh uncontrollably. He sighed again, though this time happily. *Better concentrate, though*, he decided. He hadn't seen the Rizzolis at all, though half of the lower deck was hidden from his view by the large, cream awning protecting the tourists from the sun. He could see Valérie, her headscarf billowing slightly with the breeze. She was trying to look like part of the tour group and had hidden well amongst them to get on the boat, but she stood out like a swan surrounded by mallards. Even sitting down her elegance and poise were obvious, her clothes not the kind you'd find on a bus tour, and even a nervous energy that she exuded was the opposite to the slumped, waterproof-wearing old folk alongside her. She looked up at him and shook her head. She hadn't seen the Rizzolis, either, seemed to be the signal.

He decided to relax and just enjoy the trip and the changing scenery as it glided past. The campsites were now well behind them, and each bank was now a mixture of woodland or vineyard; dragonflies hovered busily at the water's edge, and the odd heron stood sentry-like at regular intervals. The hazy tranquility was almost making him drowsy; then something caught his eye on the deck below as a few of the group around Valérie stood up to let someone sidle past them on the bench. And like Valérie, this some-one didn't look like he was part of the tour group.

The first thing you noticed about the man was his height. He must be well over six foot, Richard reckoned, and wiry with his arms looking slightly too long for his body. He was wearing jeans and a brown suede jacket with tassels hanging off each arm. Richard couldn't see his face, though, because what was most striking about the man was the enormous ten-gallon Stetson hat. He looked every inch the cowboy, totally at odds with the surroundings and obviously not bothered by that one bit. He was also, equally obviously, heading straight for Valérie.

Valérie noticed him coming along the bench toward her and Richard saw her stand up. Was she going to try to get away? Because apart from jumping ship and swimming to the bank, her options were limited. She looked more annoyed than frightened anyway, peeved, as if he'd just spoiled her plans rather than appearing threatening. She threw her arms out as if to admonish the man, and said something, though Richard obviously couldn't make out what. In response the man threw his own arms out in surprise greeting. Then Valérie sat down on the bench next to him as the two hugged and exchanged kisses. They sat down too with their backs to him, her headscarf hiding her neck and his ridiculous cowboy hat hiding nearly the entire lower deck. Well, the hat that Richard was wearing certainly didn't belong to this interloper, he brooded.

He watched as the man put his arm around Valérie's shoulder, and saw her stiffen at his touch. The man then removed his arm apologetically, and they both chatted stiffly for a bit. Richard felt a shadow fall on him, which initially and melodramatically he put down to the darkening of his mood, but which he soon realized was the looming renaissance beauty of the Château de Chenonceau blocking out the sun. People stood on the bridge and on the ramparts, waving needlessly as the boat slipped toward them. Why did people do that? He sulked, refusing to wave back.

He felt vindicated that not everyone standing at the chateau was indulging in this mindless frivolity, too; he wasn't the only one. Two people especially stood out in the middle of a large group of waving nincompoops, looking down intently at the boat, their arms still by their sides. Richard sat bolt upright as the boat slid under the chateau aqueducts. "The Rizzolis!" he ejaculated, and then heard his indiscretion echo half a dozen times off the stone arches. "The bloody Rizzolis!"

17

⚬─────⚬

They had been in the car for a good ten minutes and had barely said a word. Richard was angry, mainly with himself, and Valérie was obviously very frustrated though mainly with the tractor that was in front of them, blocking her path to the land speed record. In the end, and with a big sigh, she sat back in her seat and nestled at a safe distance behind the tractor, content for now just to let things take their course instead.

The silence stayed, however, and was verging on the uncomfortable.

"You're very quiet," they both said at exactly the same time.

"No, go on." Richard wasn't sure how to explain his reticence and was certainly interested in hearing the reason for Valérie's.

"Well," she began, her eyes darting all over the place as if there were cue cards scattered about to remind her what to say, "I'm not normally wrong about these things."

"These things?"

"Oh, you know."

"No, I don't actually."

"I was sure that they would be there. I was certain of it. And I'm not normally wrong!" she added, with all the confidence of someone who's seldom been told when they are.

Richard decided to keep his counsel. It was a rare thing for him to have the advantage, and it wasn't something he sought as a rule because advantages have a habit of being flipped over like beetles, but he knew that Valérie was holding out on him and if he were to do the same then they were evenly matched for now. And if she hadn't told him about the man on the boat, what else was she not telling him? Who else was she not telling him about, and why did all this matter to her so much anyway? And why did what mattered to her so much, matter to him so much? It was all very draining but it was also time to stop being her second Passepartout, he decided. It was time instead to exert himself. Subtly, obviously, nonchalantly even.

"Did you make any friends on the boat?" he asked, sounding about as nonchalant and subtle as a dentist's drill.

"Did I what?"

"I saw you speaking to a man. It looked like you knew him." He would make a rubbish poker player.

Valérie changed gear unnecessarily, causing the car to lurch slightly. "Oh, him," she said, changing the gear back. "Is that it?" It was obvious she didn't want to explain, but Richard had had enough. "You saw him then?"

"The six-foot-six beanpole with the ten-gallon cowboy hat? Yes, funnily enough I did notice him. And he clearly noticed you."

"Yes. I wasn't expecting to see him," she said airily.

"Know him well, do you?" Richard pretended to look at his fingernails.

"Not terribly well really, no." She seemed on surer footing now and Richard had no real reason to doubt her. "We were only married for six months, and we'd only known each other for a fortnight before that!"

Richard carried on staring at his fingernails, while inside his emotions lurched like slow-motion footage of a crash-test dummy. He wanted to speak, he wanted to laugh it off in a bohemian playboy kind of way, dismiss the information as though flicking dust from his shoulder.

"It was a whirlwind romance, and like all whirlwinds it blew itself out very quickly," Valérie said matter-of-factly, either unaware of the effect this information was having on her passenger, or enjoying it thoroughly. "You know how these things are," she added.

He had absolutely no idea how these things were at all. Whirlwind romances didn't happen in Woking when he was growing up; the closest you got was the occasional slight gust followed by a chill wind. "You were married, but you don't know him very well?" He couldn't hide his skepticism.

"Yes. It's entirely plausible, you know? It is possible to be intimate with someone and know absolutely nothing about them. Sometimes, I think, the problems start when you *do* find things out. The humdrum sets in and the mystery of the romance is pushed aside."

She spoke with confidence about a subject she clearly knew a great deal about and he thought about it. Was that the problem with Clare? That they just knew too much about each other now, that there was no mystery left? Possibly. Maybe that's why couples have children; they have nothing left to explore about each other so they introduce a new personality into the mix. *Anyway, enough of this*, he thought; he was supposed to be interrogating Valérie, not mooning over his own failing marriage.

"And you just happened to bump into your ex-husband on a boat in the Loire Valley? Just like that. A complete coincidence."

"Oh, it's not *that* much of a coincidence; he's a butcher from Tours."

"He looks American."

"Oh, I know! Such a silly man, with all those cowboy clothes—he even calls himself Tex! His real name is Pierre."

How disappointingly, reassuringly mundane, Richard thought. Just another deluded soul. "Hang on! You said your husband was dead, and that he was in pest control."

"That husband is and was."

"Right. Another whirlwind?"

"Oh no, we were married for over a year!"

Richard, not for the first time, had a feeling that his life had thus far been crushingly pedestrian. He'd had just the one marriage that had limped through to its silver anniversary—a length of time that Valérie would presumably regard as positively epic. "Is this his hat?" Richard fingered the brim of the panama gently as though he now mourned the owner.

"That? No, I can't remember where I got that."

Probably a marriage so brief it barely registered, he thought sourly.

"Richard." He felt her take her eyes off the road briefly, but he kept playing with the hat instead. "Are you jealous?" There was no mockery in her voice; she wasn't goading him. It was simply a straightforward question that demanded a straightforward answer.

"I saw them."

"Who?" she replied, though the excitement in her voice suggested that she already knew.

"The Rizzolis. I saw them."

"But they weren't on the boat, we would have seen them." She was very excited.

We? He let it go, for now. "They were on the bridge at the chateau watching the boats. It makes sense, really; why get on one boat when you can find a vantage point to see all of them?"

"But this is brilliant, Richard, we are on the right track." She paused. "I knew they would be there."

"Did you know Tex would be there?"

"I did not."

"You didn't look very pleased to see him."

"I wasn't. Is anyone pleased to see their ex? It's just one of those things." She was distracted, he could tell. "We must find out where they're going next," she said, back on track.

"The Rizzolis?" It was Richard's turn to be distracted. He wasn't convinced by the Tex coincidence at all; it just seemed too far-fetched to be believable, and he realized that he had a choice. He could say, "Enough is enough; I am a film historian with a sideline in hospitality, a failing marriage, and a disillusioned daughter," or he could admit that he hadn't felt quite as alive as this in years and, if not actually able to enjoy the ride, at least hold on to the safety rail while it threw him about a bit. He tossed the anonymous panama hat into the back seat. "We ask the Thompsons," he said decisively. "The Rizzolis have no level of French at all. I had to book them this trip, even though they didn't actually take the trip itself. Anyway, my point is that they're staying at Martin and Gennie's; my guess is that Martin and Gennie will have booked whatever itinerary they need."

"Of course. So we need to speak to Martin and Gennie," she repeated and without indicating or slowing down, pulled into a convenient shoulder, nearly knocking an old man over as he was relieving himself near a bin. Valérie pulled her phone out of her bag and the Thompsons' business card from her purse and dialed the number.

"Can you put it on speaker phone?" Richard whispered.

"Hello." It was Gennie who answered.

"Hello, Gennie? It's Valérie d'Orçay."

"Oh, Valérie, hello! Martin and I were just talking about you. And Richard."

Valérie widened her eyes at Richard, who rolled his.

"That's nice. We were wondering... Well, Richard felt a little left out about our evening together." Richard's face dropped, and he shook his head violently; surely there was another way of doing this? "And we were just wondering if you were in this evening?" She raised her hand as if to say, "What else do you want me to do?"

"Oh, how exciting!" Gennie could hardly contain herself, which left Richard regretting his decision to stay on the roller coaster. "We can't, though, this evening. How annoying. That lovely Italian couple..."

"The Rizzolis?"

"Yes, that's them. Well, they're rather interested in getting together with us this evening, if you follow me?" Richard managed to look dubious and nauseated at the same time. "Normally, more the merrier," Gennie continued, "but they're quite shy and have insisted on just the four of us for the evening. What a shame, I'm so terribly sorry."

"Yes, that is a shame." Valérie wasn't the least disappointed; quite the opposite, Richard noticed.

"Another time, perhaps, Valérie. We'd love to have you both."

"Yes, another time. Au revoir." She turned the phone off, cutting out Gennie's last sentence.

"Thank God for that!" Richard sat back. "So what do we do?"

"We go to the Thompsons', Richard." She had a twinkle in her eye that he didn't entirely like.

"But they'll all be...busy."

"Precisely." Her eyes widened again, a look of mischief joining the twinkle of excitement. "How are your pores, Richard?"

In his mind's eye Richard saw himself grip the safety rail as the roller coaster plunged downward. His knuckles were bone white.

18

Marie hummed quietly to herself and dusted under the hunting trophies on the hall sideboard, a large, ornate, dark—almost black—piece of wooden furniture that wouldn't have looked out of place in a horror film. It was almost like the judge himself, the judge as furniture. Dark, twisted and carrying the trophies of previous achievements. She dusted it some more, unnecessarily. She hadn't quite worked out why the old judge wanted her to come as often as she did; it wasn't like he had guests. In fact as far as she knew the only people who ever visited were herself and Bonneval, who was here now, bowing and scraping to the old crank.

Someone in Bonneval's position usually answered only to the mayor, but seeing as the mayor was only sober for about ten minutes after he woke up, usually early afternoon, he had trouble commanding respect. He was a prop, effectively appointed by the judge in bullied elections, and it was the judge who ran the town. Bonneval knew that, Marie knew that, Bruno knew that. Everyone in Vauchelles knew that. But recently the judge had stopped swanning around "his" town and stayed cooped up indoors, usually in his study, the shutters half closed. He sat there, a rug over his knees, peering through the gap in the shutters as though waiting for someone. She knew fear when she saw it, and through the study gloom she saw it in the once confident, blustering Judge Grandchamps.

Should she feel sorry for him? She did a little; even though he was a grouchy, bad-tempered old man, there was a vulnerability to him that someone of Marie's nature could sense that maybe others couldn't.

"Marie!" the judge shouted from the study. "Stop that bloody racket; we can't hear ourselves think in here!"

Marie knew very well how to deal with bullies and stopped humming immediately, replacing it with loud la-la-las instead, as if she were warming her voice up for a gala performance. She moved closer to the study door just to annoy him further, then went back to quiet humming so she could hear better.

"Damn girl!" she heard him say. "You can tell she worked for my brother; she's as insolent as he is."

"Or was," Bonneval said quietly, testing the waters.

"What are you talking about, man, 'was'?"

"I mean that your brother may be dead."

There was silence, and she tried to peer through the gap between the door and the frame, but the judge had his back to her. She wanted to see his face, to see if the thought of his brother's death caused him pain or relief. Or even happiness.

"What makes you think he's dead?" he asked quietly, but with no hint as to any emotion in his voice.

"I just think it is a possibility that we must consider." Bonneval seemed more confident than usual. "Something that we shouldn't rule out. You know there's a price on your brother's head?"

The judge waved an arthritic claw dismissively at Bonneval. "Of course I do. Serves him right. If you jump into bed with killers, as he did, then you pay a price. And somebody else always wants to cash you in."

"Five hundred thousand euros."

Again the judge stayed silent for a moment, and wheeled his chair closer to the window. "Five hundred thousand euros? How do you know?"

"I have a friend in the ministry. I've been making inquiries."

"Good for you, Bonneval." He sounded distant then, snapping back into himself. "There's more to you than I thought. Friends in the ministry, eh?"

Bonneval let the insult pass.

"That's a lot of money, five hundred thousand euros. They'd want proof of his death, though, somehow. Nobody, least of all the mafia, parts with good money without solid evidence."

Bonneval sat down at the table.

"Besides, he's not dead! Not yet anyway." He shoved some envelopes across the table, all opened, all official-looking. Bonneval picked them up. "They're speeding fines, public disorder notices, unpaid hotel bills and so on. The last speeding fine only dates from last weekend. Oh, he's not dead. He's living the high life."

"How did you get these?" Bonneval asked, surprised.

"I broke into his letterbox; how do you think? I can still get about if I need to. And before you drip on, Bonneval, yes, I know that's an offense."

The policeman flicked through the papers, shaking his head.

"And another thing, I had a call from a hotel, or a *chambre d'hôte* or some such yesterday. Apparently *I* had stayed at this place, run off without paying and had left my glasses behind. The man's alive and a menace, Bonneval, mark my words. And I want him found."

Bonneval stood up and placed the mail back on the table. "Where was this guest house?" he asked.

"Over in Saint-Sauveur. He seems to go there a lot."

"There are a lot of guest houses there."

"Well, this seemed more specialized than usual. They said I'd also left some 'material' lying around, and did I want it back?"

"Material?" Bonneval asked.

"Don't be naïve, man. Pornography. Ha! At my age!" He paused. "His age. Our age."

"Maybe I should go over and take a look?"

"Ha! That lonely, are you?" the judge sniped.

Marie thought she saw Bonneval blush. "I mean at the guest house. I have to go to Saint-Sauveur anyway. There's a missing person, Charles Paulin. The old soak has disappeared, and my colleague there wants me to pick up some pictures. My printer's broken again, and there aren't the funds..."

"Paulin? Yes, I remember him, useless man." He paused again, and spun round on the policeman. "Just find him, Bonneval, OK? Just find him. Maybe they've disappeared together."

"You remember Paulin?"

"I remember all my cases. I know my brother looked out for him, called him comrade even. But he was a halfwit before the drink, and a no-wit after." He smiled at his own joke. "A pathetic creature anyway. He fell apart after his wife had a breast reduction, would you believe? He started drinking heavily and tried to attack the doctor who'd recommended the specialist."

"I remember. I saw him often at your brother's house."

"Find my brother, Bonneval, never mind Paulin," the judge snarled. "Find him." He paused. "I might even give you a share of the reward." Bonneval stopped in his tracks and Marie moved away from the door, restarting the la-la-la-ing as she did so.

19

Richard sat stock still in the driver's seat, his hands gripping the steering wheel as though he were still driving. They had been parked for ten minutes now, and he was staring through the windscreen trying to ignore, or at least not to concentrate on what Valérie was doing in the passenger seat. She had produced some powder from her bag and had been mucking about with bowls and spatulas for a full five minutes now. He was fully prepared to admit that he had no idea what was going on in his life right now and was further dizzied by every new twist, which appeared to be occurring roughly every half hour, but drugs? No, he hadn't seen that coming. Not at all.

He had never been much of a user, if that was the word. He'd dabbled a bit at university, like almost everyone else, and then not bothered. The excuse he used when offered drugs was that "he would just go crazy, man," or something like that anyway. The truth was that he didn't care for them; any drugs he had taken had left him cold, bored even. And the effect they produced in others was to turn vaguely interesting people into crushing dullards. He certainly wasn't going to try them now, at his age. Hallucinations, should they occur, couldn't be more weird than his current reality, and the "brings life into focus" possibility of narcotics was the last thing he needed, quite frankly. It was however Valérie's choice, a grown adult, and if she needed the high, then so be it. It wasn't any of his business. He was, however, and though he tried not to be, hugely disappointed, disillusioned even.

"Here," Valérie said, offering him the bowl, which he didn't look at.

"I don't, thanks," he replied coldly.

"You don't, what?"

"I don't...I don't do that stuff."

"What do you mean?"

He turned to her. "I think one of us needs a clear head, don't you?"

"Richard, this is an expensive French clay face mask; it will camouflage us in the hedge."

Richard had spent the last five minutes moralizing and tutting inwardly like a Victorian father whose daughter had flashed her ankles, and he felt like a complete fool.

"I was joking," he said, breaking into an unconvincing smile, whereupon Valérie shook her head and started daubing her face with the gray-green clay. He tried not to watch her, but the same thought kept running through his head: *Why on earth do you, Valérie d'Orçay, think you need this stuff?*

"I am aware this stuff won't stop me aging, but it feels so lovely to have tingling skin occasionally. Tingles are important in life."

Richard, having taken the bowl and spatula, had absolutely no idea what she was talking about but smeared the stuff on anyway. It must be him, he thought; there were no tingles.

"You've put it too close to your lips Richard," she reprimanded. "Never mind. We have about twenty minutes before it dries, so let's hurry."

"Is there really a need for all of this?" he asked, deciding that one last plea for sanity, an appeal to Valérie's more sensible side, would be time well spent at this point, and not, as it actually was, like the last flappings of a fish on a beach.

"Of course it is." She was just applying the last bits of clay to her forehead. "Do you want to be recognized?"

"By whom?" would have been his first question, followed by the honest opinion that a bit of French mud was hardly going to render him invisible to the locals. It would mean only that he would be forever now known as "that English bloke who looked like he'd blacked up for a night with swingers." If his heart sank any further he'd be carrying it around in his back pocket. Not that he had any back pockets. He'd found some old black jogging pants, bought from the local supermarket and presumably purchased to herald the start of another short-lived fitness campaign, and a "Grumpy Old Git" black sweatshirt that Alicia had bought him for Father's Day and which was now worn inside out to hide the white lettering. He also wore a black bobble hat and felt less like a cat burglar and more like an escaped mental patient who'd found a spa.

Valérie, on the other hand, looked like she'd stepped straight off the set of *The Avengers*. She wore tight black leggings, a black roll neck, a black scarf, and knee-high black boots. He suspected that if Gennie and Martin found them lurking in the outbuildings they'd take one look at Valérie and have simultaneous heart attacks. A small part of Richard was even hoping that they would be found; that way he could gain some kudos from knocking about late at night with an Emma Peel lookalike. That sort of thing could do wonders for a man with, thus far, absolutely no reputation to speak of.

"OK," he said, opening the car door and stepping out as elegantly as a man of average size wearing a bobble hat can exit a 2CV. "Let's do this," he whispered fiercely, more to himself than to Valérie, who needed no encouragement. She carried an enormous torch which she turned on, testing it, and shone it in Richard's eyes.

"Bloody hell!" he hissed, reeling back and nearly falling in the ditch that he'd parked next to. "Did you steal that from a lighthouse?"

"Would you prefer no light?"

Again, the pure, immovable logic of her argument outweighed the ridiculousness of what she'd said. It was all or nothing with Valérie, no light or the surface of the sun, your choice, and absolutely nothing in between. Richard, however, with his pure English lineage, was always stuck somewhere in the middle, weighing up both sides. They walked cautiously toward the Thompsons' house, having parked discreetly a couple of hundred meters away, Valérie scouring the hedge for the wooden door, not wanting to fire up the torch unnecessarily.

"Here it is," she whispered and from nowhere produced what looked like a small black wallet but with an array of files and lock picks.

"You have a lock-picking set?"

"It is very useful," she replied as if he were an idiot. Again, the coldest logic. *Of course it's useful,* his mind was stamping the ground like a child having a tantrum, *it's useful for picking the locks. The point actually is...*

"Do you do this often?" He was finding it hard to be calm. The adrenaline of the situation together with the feeling that he was definitely working with a professional was becoming slightly too much for him.

She picked the lock with ease and gestured for him to go in first. He did so and found a shadow away from the yellow glare of an indoor house light. It was a discreet light, it had to be said, and didn't give off much of a wash. Valérie closed the gate behind them and stood next to him.

"That's the *chambre d'hôte* building over there." She indicated with the turned-off torch. "Like you they have a separate building, which makes things easier for us." Richard knew all this and was indeed very well aware of the Thompsons' layout but let Valérie direct as she pleased.

"OK," Richard said, "let's go." He scurried a few meters toward the white, pretty cottage, itself some twenty meters from the main house, and immediately a security light was triggered on the garden and he scurried back again. Valérie was no longer there.

"What *are* you doing?" The hissed question came from somewhere inside the hedge into which Valérie had sunk.

"Well, I am so sorry!" Richard panted. "My house-breaking skills are a little rusty."

Valérie reappeared smoothly at his side. "Follow me," she whispered, and moved off, staying close to the hedge as she did so, skirting the property before eventually coming up behind the cottage on the opposite side of the main house. She made her way to a back door and once again produced the wallet of picks.

Richard gently pushed past her, opening the door silently, "They never lock it," he said quietly, "and you really don't want to know why." Valérie nodded in a businesslike manner, causing him to wonder if what he'd said had registered with her at all.

They climbed the stairs as quietly as possible. "How will we know which room they're in?" Valérie for the first time showed an element of doubt in the operation.

"Easy," Richard said, "the Rizzolis are the only guests, so Martin will have put them in a room with large windows facing the house, is my guess. And of the four rooms there's only one that fits the bill."

In the moonlight glow through a skylight window, Valérie's eyes shone, as did her smile. "Brilliant!" she said, patting his chest. "Brilliant."

———

In the soft red glow of two dimmer-switched ceiling lamps, Gennie was equally effusive. "That's brilliant, Martin!" she said, patting his bare chest. "Just brilliant, everybody likes charades!"

The Rizzolis, sharing a look of utter bewilderment, didn't seem to agree with Gennie's enthusiasm for old-fashioned parlor games. Nor could they understand why Gennie was wearing a red basque with black lace trimmings, fishnet stockings and black stiletto shoes, or why Martin was in some form of rubber lederhosen. The look on Signora Rizzoli's face, in particular, was one of barely concealed disgust, while her husband shook his head almost imperceptibly, catching his wife's cold eye. "I have no idea what's going on," was the silent message. The Rizzolis considered themselves to be dynamic, young professionals, keen on getting things done without any fuss, generally quite unflappable. But for now this strange English couple had them stupefied into inaction, almost rigid with bafflement.

"OK, my dear, do you want to start?" Martin then pinged the braces loudly on his costume.

"Oh, OK. Let me see." Gennie fiddled with a black lace bow on her basque in thought, the very picture of saucy postcard cheek and suggestion. "Oh, I've got one!"

She bent forward toward the Rizzolis, who instinctively leaned back slightly before Martin settled clumsily in beside them, far too close to be polite.

Gennie looked like she was about to pray as she put her hands together, before opening them to make the international sign for a book. "*Libro!*" shouted Signor Rizzoli before shrinking under his wife's fierce gaze.

Gennie held up two fingers.

"Two words!" Martin was getting very excited.

Gennie held up one finger, then put two fingers on her arm before removing one of them.

"First word, two syllables, first syllable."

The Rizzolis shuffled along the sofa, trying to put some distance between themselves and Martin, who was concentrating hard so seemed not to notice. Gennie mimed holding a steering wheel.

"Driving?" Martin offered. Gennie shook her head. "Wheel, steering wheel, sounds like wheel...FEEL?" Gennie shook her head again.

"Auto." This time it was Signora Rizzoli, who had decided that the best way out of this nonsense was to win the game, get it over with.

Gennie pointed at her nose while pointing at the frankly stony-faced woman.

"Sounds like auto?" Martin mused and Gennie shook her head. "Oh, car! Of course, silly me." He patted Signora Rizzoli's knee, causing her back to arch as if shot from behind. Her husband gasped, expecting a response which didn't come.

Gennie indicated the second syllable and then pointed at herself.

"Wife! Woman! Lady! Car-lady! No, hang on!"

"*Madre.*" It was Signora Rizzoli again who got a nervous "well done" smile of encouragement from her husband, which was immediately smashed to bits on her rocky stare.

"Sexpot!" shouted Martin. "Car-sexpot!" Gennie shook her head and pointed at Signora Rizzoli again. "Madre?" Martin mused. "Mother? Mummy? Car-mummy? MA! I've got it, Car-ma! KARMA!" Gennie this time pointed at Martin and again at her nose. "Good luck, old girl."

Martin winked back. "This second word will be a test, I fancy..."

"What are we looking for exactly?" Richard stood quietly in the corner as Valérie expertly, noiselessly opened and shut drawers and delved into bags.

"I'm not sure at the moment," was the reply, which prompted Richard to wonder why they had broken into somebody's room if they had no real goal in mind. "They must be planning on staying for some time, though; from my experience nobody unpacks clothes into drawers, not in a *chambre d'hôte*."

"I have unpacked all of mine," Valérie said distractedly. "I don't know how long I will be staying." She opened another drawer and reached in under the clothes. "Ah! Richard!" She almost squealed. "I knew it!" She slowly removed her hand and, in the shadow of the oblique torch light, held a gun up at Richard.

"A gun," he said blankly, stunned and for a second worried that it was pointing in his direction.

"A gun, yes, a Beretta Pico .380 to be exact. It's a backup gun; there'll be others here, but that's all the proof that I needed." She laid it flat in the palm of her hand, weighing it. "It's loaded, too."

She tossed it to Richard who almost fumbled the catch, afraid it might go off, as she carried on her search in the drawer. "Ah!" She squealed again, and Richard, now sweating and holding the gun away from him as if it smelled rotten, dreaded what was to come out of the drawer next. A submachine gun, perhaps? A flamethrower? He was out of his depth, but what struck him, and he wondered why it hadn't struck him before, was that Valérie most definitely was not.

"A phone!" she said, and he was surprised she wasn't disappointed. "I'll take that."

"You can't just take it, that's stealing!" It was an odd moment to be trying to form an ethics and morality investigation, he realized that, even if he could feel the sweat mounting under his camouflaged face, about to burst forth like geysers. "Suppose they miss it and come back for another of my hens?"

Valérie thought about it for a moment as she tried to turn the phone on. "Hmm, it needs a PIN number... What did you say? Oh, OK. Well, I need time to work on it anyway, so you go down and keep guard for a few minutes just in case."

Reluctantly Richard trudged downstairs. He didn't mind being out of the room; he just didn't trust her not to ransack the place and take everything with her. It might all be perfectly innocent, and then the Rizzolis would turn up at his place with the police asking for their gun back. He looked at the gun. Nobody brings a gun to the Loire Valley, though, unless they're hunting, and this wasn't a hunting gun. Not for traditional prey at any rate. "*Chassé*," the old man had told Valérie. He stood back in the shadows, the gun hanging limply in his hand, when he saw the strange red light coming from the main house. *They are funny people, the Thompsons*, he thought. Each to their own and all that, but to Richard they had all the erotic allure of a Cornish pasty, and were just as English.

Then he started as he heard a crash coming from the lit room. Should he go? Should he leave his post? He knew Valérie would have already made the decision by now and he sprinted over to the main house and peered in the window, which surprisingly had no curtains or shutters. He did not like what he saw. Poor Martin and Gennie; they should have been warned...

20

Tiptoeing around to the back of the house, Richard was shaking his head as he did so, trying to dislodge the image now firmly imprinted on his brain. He tried not to crunch his footsteps on the gravel or set off any more security lights, and as he reached the back door he was quietly proud of his efforts. He reached the door and looked in through the window into the large kitchen. There was an empty bottle of local white wine on the table and a few plates with crumbs from the amuse-bouche that Gennie always hand-prepared for her soirées. He could see through the kitchen to the more dimly lit corridor and beyond that the subtle, if that was the right word, red glow of the living room farther on. It looked like someone had left the door open in a photographic dark room.

He hesitated before going any farther. What he'd seen was upsetting enough, especially with the thought that the Rizzolis might still be hovering about. What checked him was also his exact whereabouts: the Thompsons' back door. Martin's endless, dull repetition of his "tradesman's entrance" double entendre recalled to Richard innumerable evenings spent in their company wishing he could be anywhere else but there. *Martin is a crushing bore*, he thought, as he pulled his hand away from the door handle again, but one in trouble, too, he realized. He turned the handle slowly and walked softly into the kitchen, hiding to the right of the open door to the hall, listening for any movement. Satisfied that there was none, he tiptoed exaggeratedly down the hall toward the red light.

The living room door squeaked loudly as he pushed it open and he ducked back, just in case. When nothing happened he darted into the room. The view from this side of the window was no better than it had been from the outside. There, in the corner, were Martin and Gennie on the floor, sitting back to back and trussed up like Christmas turkeys. Their pale skin was goosebumped and the hair on their arms standing up as though they were being electrocuted. From where he stood he couldn't see Martin's face but he could see Gennie's. Her mouth was covered in what looked like pink cling film, and her eyes were wide open, not so much in pain or shock at seeing Richard, but in slight embarrassment at her predicament.

He crept in, still wary that the Rizzolis might be around, and signaled the question to Gennie for confirmation. She shook her head as best she could and he moved quickly over to the tethered pair. Martin had a look on his face about as far away from embarrassment as possible; his eyes were wide open, too, but with what was clearly excitement. His mouth was also covered, but by a small studded black belt strapped around his face and with what looked like a red ball between his lips. Continuing the meat theme, thought a blushing Richard, Martin looked like a suckling pig.

Martin flexed and moved his jaw like he was trying to unblock his ears and moved the ball down onto his chin. Richard watched with what he knew was a look of disgust on his face, but he was beyond caring about the social niceties of the situation. Martin sighed with success at removing the ball. "Richard," he said, looking him up and down, "what *do* you look like?"

Richard had always been careful to try and prepare for every eventuality. He wasn't necessarily given to spontaneity or living life by the seat of one's pants—it may even have contributed to the apparent terminal decline in his marriage—but literally nothing in his life had ever prepared him for this question and in these circumstances. It almost knocked him flying. He stood up, trying to compute Martin's question in some way, and as he did so he caught a glimpse of himself in the full-length mirror on the back of the door. Dressed all in black, topped off by a too-small bobble hat and his face smeared in mud, then yes, the casual observer may indeed have just cause for cross-examination. But for the love of God, it was a bit rich for one half of a pair of plump, tied-up rubber fetishists with bulldog clips on his nipples to question someone else's choice of evening attire. He was tempted to shove the red ball back in Martin's mouth.

"What happened?" Richard asked after some time, ignoring the question which he knew that, with many other things this evening, would haunt him forever.

"Sorry, Richard, what did you say?"

Richard realized with a dull sense of "bloody typical" that his clay mask had hardened and his lips were no longer capable of free movement and he sounded like a bad ventriloquist. He rolled his eyes, and splayed his arms.

"Wha...ha...ened?" he emphasized. "'orry, 'ennie." And he bent down to peel off her mouth tape.

"You'll have to rip it off forcefully, old man," Martin said over his shoulder, "that's how she likes it."

Richard looked away as he tore the tape off. Gennie squealed with delight and Richard couldn't help tutting, or at least trying.

"Told you," Martin said, as if he'd given functional instructions on how to change a car tire.

"We...wha...ha...ened?" Richard didn't try to hide his impatience.

"Well, we were having a lovely evening, weren't we, dear?"

"Lovely," replied Gennie, puckering her lips to free them up a bit.

"We were playing charades. It was Gennie's idea, a real corker. It was her turn, I mean the Rizzoli woman, and it was very easy, really. They'd kind of said they wanted to do it in French, so they could learn a bit of the lingo, but I mean, 'big field'? Well, like I say, that's just too easy. Big field? It's not even a book or anything?"

During this explanation, Richard had been moving his lips and chin, trying to free up his ability to talk. "Grandchamps," he said slowly and, thankfully, clearly.

Gennie went as though to try and point at her nose and at Richard, but her ropes wouldn't allow it. "Well, exactly, Richard! It was then that I remembered that Monsieur Grandchamps had booked to stay tonight again. He came by this afternoon, didn't he, dear?"

"Yes." Martin nodded, the red ball moving up and down his chin like an escaped Adam's apple. "Most odd, though. It was like he didn't remember being here before. When we checked him in, Gennie said, 'Don't you remember, you were here before, dear?' And that seemed to spook him for some reason. Poor old fellow, nobody likes to be reminded they're getting old. Anyway, he just left."

"But what happened with the Rizzolis?"

"Well, we were trying to explain all this, but we only got as far as him booking tonight, not that he'd run off. They got very excited, and erm, well, it's possible we misread the situation. Before you could spank a backside, to coin a phrase, we were like this. How you see us now. And they just buggered off!"

"How long ago?" Richard asked frantically.

"I don't know, not long. Ten minutes."

Richard stood up, and then kneeled down again to begin untying the Thompsons' bonds.

"Oh, don't worry, old man," Martin said, with at least the good grace to sound apologetic, "just pop the ball back in, and put some tape on Gennie, that'll do us for now."

"But..."

"Oh, don't worry about us," Gennie panted, "our cleaning lady comes very early. She's used to our little ways."

Richard did as he was told, stood up quickly and tried to imagine what Madame Tablier would do with such a scene at work first thing in the morning: carnage, in a word, carnage.

He made his way outside again and back around toward the annex, hiding in the shadows as much as he could. Once in sight of the Rizzolis' bedroom, he slunk back into the hedge. Their light was on and he could hear crashing about. His heart raced violently; what about Valérie? She must still be up there. He ran out of the shadows and immediately a security light lit him up on the lawn and he darted back where he'd come from, breathing heavily. He bent down and something stuck into his thigh as he did so. The gun. What was it Valérie had called it? A Beretta Pico? It struck him that she was remarkably well-informed about such things before he chastised himself for not concentrating. He took the gun out of his pocket and it glinted in the glow of the security light before the lawn went dark again.

He weighed it in his hand. He'd never used a gun before; he couldn't even remember holding one. Well, now was his opportunity, he thought and, gripping it tightly, he ran onto the lawn again. As soon as he did so, triggering the light, he lost his nerve and ran back. What the hell was he doing? *Is there a safety catch? And where?*

Was he really going to use it? "Stop it, man!" he hissed at himself. "She needs you now, so get a bloody move on!"

The light went dark again and he raced back out a third time. The light did its job once more so he turned and went back to his hiding place and continued his conversation. "Of course, this all just might be very innocent." He looked at the gun again. "Right, about as innocent as Jack the Ripper! Come on, man! Get a move on!" The light went out and this time Richard stood up. "A man's gotta do what a man's gotta do," he said, not bothering to whisper. He held the gun in front of him, just far enough to trigger the light, and he put one determined foot slowly forward.

"Slow down, cowboy," whispered Valérie, putting her hand on his shoulder. "Let's get back to the car and moisturize."

It was just about the sexiest thing he'd ever heard.

21

They fell in through Richard's door like drunk giggly teenagers, high on adventure. And like illicit teenagers they were met by the stern disapproval of the sensible adult, this time in the form of Passepartout, and he appeared to have his arms folded and a "what time do you call this?" look on his face.

"Oh my poor darling!" Valérie picked him up and cuddled him, kissing the top of his head. "You have been left here all alone in the dark, you poor thing. Did you miss Mummy?" She turned to Richard. "Madame Tablier must have left him here."

"Well, you can't expect her to stay all night waiting for us. She's a busy woman." Richard wondered just how true that might be. "Anyway, it's not totally dark; she left the television on as company, presumably." A violent, dubbed American cop show was showing in the background and he immediately switched it off. *No class*, he thought not for the first time, *no élan, no finesse*.

"Ah, Madame Tablier left a note." She put Passepartout back onto the sofa while Richard turned on some lights. "'Monsieur,'" read Valérie haughtily, "'I could not wait any longer. The dog has eaten'— oh my poor Passepartout, what has she been feeding you?—'and it likes *NCIS Detroit*. We must talk about that young couple.' What about the young couple, do you think?"

"Oh, probably sharing a room out of wedlock, I don't know. I need a drink." But rather than go and get one, he sat down heavily next to Passepartout. "They seem very sweet; the light was on in the salon when we got back, so they're obviously up. Maybe they like *NCIS Detroit* as well?"

"Well, I need a shower to get rid of the rest of this mask, but if they're up I cannot go through the salon like this."

It was a fair point, mused Richard, who, groaning with aches and pains, got up and went to the kitchen. "Would you like a drink?"

Valérie was once again standing with Passepartout in her arms and pondered the question as though it were of deep philosophical import. "Yes," she said eventually and in a way as to suggest life and all its myriad complexities were now solved. "I'd like a pale ale."

Richard began to wonder what parallel universe the woman operated in. How a woman of Valérie's grace, poise and what-everyoucallit—he had the words, but wasn't prepared to admit them to himself—would ever even come across a pale ale, was completely beyond him. It would be like watching Arthur Scargill order a pink gin.

"Of all the drinks, in all the world," he muttered, "why on earth would you ask for a pale ale?"

"I had one years ago, in England. I was on honeymoon, now when was it..."

Richard had no desire to hear more of Valérie's former husband, or husbands. "We have no pale ale, madame; we do have champagne."

"Oh yes, Richard!" she said triumphantly. "I think that we have earned that."

"Me, too." And he opened the large fridge. He heard her laughing and he popped his head back around the door. "What's so funny?" he asked self-consciously.

"Your description of Martin and Gennie!" She laughed again. "I wish I had seen them. You are very English; I can imagine you left out all of the juicy details."

"Believe me, I have merely reported the facts. It was most *un*-erotic, I can tell you." He popped the champagne cork. "I'll never see cling film or bulldog clips in quite the same way again." He handed her a glass. "*Santé*," he said, looking her in the eye.

"Bottoms up!" she replied and almost spat out her drink in the ensuing giggles.

"Yes, bottoms up indeed!"

It was a while before they calmed down, and Valérie sighed happily. "We did very well tonight, Richard, you and I."

"Yes, yes, I suppose we did. Well, we know that the Rizzolis are up to no good and that Grandchamps is, at the last count anyway, still alive."

"I wonder why he went back there, though. He has a *prime*."

"He's far from being in his 'preeme'!" Richard joked, exaggerating the French accent.

"It's just an expression," Valérie added hurriedly.

"Maybe, maybe after all this, he is just a bit, you know, senile?"

"I wonder..."

"The Rizzolis are certainly after him, though, so we must find him, I suppose. How did you get away from them anyway—the Rizzolis, I mean?"

Valérie turned to walk back to the sofa. "Well, after you had gone I realized how silly it was just to sit there and try to break into their phone, right there and then. They could come back at any moment, you know?"

"I do know, they did."

"Yes, well, I was already on my way out. I hid in the kitchen and they didn't see me. Then I found you in the hedge there—what *were* you up to? Running backward and forward like that. You looked very funny. I was watching you for a good long while."

Richard felt himself blushing again and was grateful he still had on the remnants of the face pack. He knew *High Noon* almost scene by scene, word for word, and he didn't remember the part where Grace Kelly, rather than implore Gary Cooper not to face the villains and his own destiny, breaks into a fit of giggles and says, "Oh, Marshal, you *do* look funny!"

"I thought they had you in there, so at first I was trying to cause a distraction," he began heroically, but then literally let the mask slip. "Then I realized I hadn't the faintest idea how to work a bloody gun. Sorry."

She walked slowly toward him. "And when I stopped you, you had decided to go in after me anyway?"

"Yes," he said, avoiding eye contact. She put her green-masked hand on his.

"Thank you," she said simply, and there was an awkward pause. "And now I would like another glass, please!"

He poured each of them another glass. "Are you hungry?"

"Oh no!" It was almost a rebuke. "We're drinking champagne; who needs food? Unless you have oysters, which are the *only* things I care to eat with champagne."

"Nope, sorry, fresh out of oysters." Richard wondered what she'd have asked for if he'd actually had pale ale in the larder; presumably he'd now be hunting around for some pork scratchings or a slice of black pudding. "So, where do we go from here, then? To the police, to Bonneval?"

"Not yet, no." She was very definite.

"Why not, why not yet?"

"Well, with what? A gun they may already have a license for? For doing something to the Thompsons that the Thompsons desperately wanted to happen in the first place? For following young Melvil? There is nothing there."

He saw her point. Apart from the fact that he was now convinced they'd done for poor Ava Gardner, what had they actually done besides? Was unauthorized use of bulldog clips a crime? Richard shuddered at the memory; *it should be*, he thought, *it really should be*.

"So, the aim is the same then: find our Monsieur Grandchamps?"

"Yes, exactly, Richard. Is there any more champagne? I'm feeling slightly drunk and I like it very much."

"Of course," he said, hoping that was the case. "I'll get some." He went off to root around in his *cave*, which was a walk-in cellar under the stairs. Valérie carried on talking as he did so.

"One way to do that, if their phone yields us nothing, is to follow the Rizzolis..."

"That may be more difficult after tonight, assuming they check out of Martin and Gennie's," he called up the stairs.

"We could set Melvil and Marie as bait?"

"That seems a bit harsh. I don't even know why they are bait. Ah!" He bent down and picked up a dusty bottle of champagne, a 1995 bottle of Heidsieck Blanc des Millénaires. He wiped the label. It had been a wedding present from a good friend, someone long since forgotten or, more likely, who had been put on the list of people "he no longer needed" post-marriage. Well, he definitely felt post-marriage now; best get it while it still fizzed.

"There must have been something in the envelope Melvil posted,"

Valérie continued. "He said it was just an electricity bill, but the Rizzolis obviously didn't think so."

Richard emerged from under the stairs and immediately opened the bottle. "So we go back to Vauchelles and see what happens at the postbox? Sorry," he apologized as the champagne fizzed over her glass slightly and onto her hand, which she rubbed.

"Oh look," she giggled, "your champagne cleans off the mud mask! Tonight I may bathe in champagne!"

Richard was becoming heady enough as it was without that kind of image rattling around his head like a pinball. "The thing is," he said, trying to stick to the subject, "we could wait there for days and nothing might happen."

They drank in silence for a while, and Valérie rested her head on the back of the sofa. "Of course"—she began talking to the ceiling—"we could go straight to the source."

"Meaning?" Fatigue and the champagne had hit Richard, too.

"We break into Monsieur Grandchamps's house."

Champagne definitely had a calming effect on Richard. He sat there, taking this in. Under normal circumstances he'd have been stomping around the room, decrying not just the illegality of the proposal but the not inconsiderable danger from assorted mafia assassins, police, and a very jittery, armed twin brother watching from across the road, but enough champagne was tantamount to creating your own locked-in syndrome and he was too tired to argue. "Shall we go now while we're still dressed for it?" he found himself saying.

"Oh no! I need a shower," Valérie replied, taking him seriously. "Do you think the young people have gone to bed yet?"

Richard got up and peered through the window toward the salon of the *chambre d'hôte*. "It doesn't look like it, no. The TV is still on over there."

"Can I shower here, Richard? Do you have any pajamas that I can borrow?"

Suddenly the room seemed to pull into sharp focus for him. "Of course." He tried to say it suavely, but he had the distinct impression he sounded like a teenager whose voice was breaking. "And there's Alicia's room made up already, if you want to stay..."

"Thank you," she said and downed what was left of her champagne. "Now, I will go and get these silly clothes off and wash off this paint." She got up unsteadily and went to the bathroom.

Richard sat stunned for a second and avoided the "prospective father-in-law" gaze from an unimpressed Passepartout. Then he shot into action. He quickly tidied Alicia's room, which was a large bedroom and very girly. He put on the light on the bedside table, turned down the covers and closed the shutters, noticing that Melvil and Marie were still up. *Good*, he thought.

Then he went to his own wardrobe on the landing and got out his best pair of dark-blue satin pajamas with white piping and monogrammed "RA" on the breast pocket. He took them downstairs and knocked on the bathroom door. Inside Valérie was singing to herself in the shower. In truth, she had an awful voice but that didn't bother him and he opened the door, making as much noise as possible, in case she thought he was sneaking about. He put the pajamas on the towel rail by the door.

"I've put the pajamas on the towel rail by the door!" he said loudly, though she didn't hear him over the shower and her singing.

On the floor were Valérie's clothes and her boots and on top of them was the gun, the Berëtta Pico. Instinctively he picked it up and put it in his own pocket. If asked he couldn't have said why; partly it was his natural inclination to tidy up—*I mean, who wants guns lying around the bathroom?* But also, it was just to be on the safe side. It had been a long day, and something about ill-fitting hats, Tex and pale ale was jangling some far-off alarm bells.

"I'll leave the pajamas on the rail here!" he shouted again.

"Thank you," she answered this time, and thankfully didn't continue with the singing.

He put the gun in his pocket, turned and left the bathroom and there, in the frame of the open front door across the hall, stood a fearsome, terrifying sight. Clare Ainsworth, née Randall, stood, feet apart, a small suitcase in each hand hanging by her side and a look on her face that would have had Medusa drummed out of the "turn to stone" club as a rank amateur.

"You were supposed to pick me up," she said, slowly and menacingly, her nurtured instinct for melodrama cranking itself into gear.

"I—I, er, sorry," he stammered.

"You were supposed to PICK ME UP!" She moved closer to him, her dramatic tendencies now mixed with her real and powerful emotions.

It flashed across his mind that frankly not picking Clare up was the least of his worries as he presently stood in his hallway in what was left of his camouflage gear, armed, and about to effect a presumably awkward introduction between a highly attractive French woman wearing his pajamas and his soon to be ex-wife. His guess was that the "soon to be" bit might be given a hearty shove; that's if she didn't keel over thanks to a surfeit of emotion first.

"Can I take your bags?"

She put them down and stepped away from them, sniffing the air, her eyes narrowing. Clare, a very handsome, attractive woman, dressed expensively and with the latest fashionable Home Counties blond bob was, nevertheless, when the mood took her—which was often in Richard's experience—quite simply terrifying.

"You were supposed to pick me up," she said in lieu of commentary as she moved through the rooms, and with each repetition the more menacing it became. She noticed Passepartout on the sofa but ignored him, sensing bigger quarry.

"Erm, good flight?" Richard had literally no idea what to do.

She turned toward him. "Why are you dressed like that?" It was as though she were only just seeing him, as the red mist of anger lifted.

"Oh, you know?"

"No."

"Well, it's been quite the evening." He affected a laugh. "Oh, I'm so pleased to see you." He moved toward her with his arms outstretched and then she noticed the bulge in his trouser pocket.

"So I see," she said caustically. "Got your old verve back, Richard?"

He looked down. "Oh, ha! No, I mean, yes, but no." And he clumsily pulled out the gun, just as Valérie appeared in his pajamas, a towel wrapped around her head and holding a glass of champagne.

Clare looked from Valérie to Richard to the gun, back to Valérie, to the gun and then settled on Richard. "You were supposed to pick me up," she said weakly, before fainting onto the sofa, narrowly missing Passepartout.

22

Richard walked slowly up the stairs, carrying the breakfast tray and taking care not to spill anything on it. He wanted no blemishes, no cause for complaint, though that wasn't the only reason for taking things slowly; he was dragging his feet, avoiding the confrontation. The very necessary and inevitable confrontation.

He stood outside the bedroom door and gathered himself; should he knock? It was his bedroom after all, their bedroom officially, though he'd slept on the sofa last night even after persuading Valérie that it was best if she stayed in the *chambre d'hôte*, and not in their daughter's room. The lights in the salon had eventually gone off so the coast, it was assumed, would be clear. Valérie, it has to be said, was more than happy to do so. He decided not to knock, but instead carefully maneuvered the door handle with his elbow and pushed the door with his foot.

If he was expecting a dark room and to have to wake Clare up with her morning tea, he was badly mistaken. The shutters were open, the room was bathed in morning sunlight and Clare was sitting upright in the middle of the bed, propped up by stacks of pillows. She had her arms folded and wore a look on her face that suggested, if not exactly Armageddon, then some serious heavy weather.

"I could hear you shuffling about outside," she said coldly.

"I didn't know whether you were awake or not," he replied, trying to sound cheerful. "I've brought you some tea and some juice. There are croissants, too, if you like."

He placed the tray in front of her and kissed her forehead. To his enormous surprise she didn't move out of the way.

"Thank you," she said simply.

"How are you feeling?" He sat down at the end of the bed.

"A little stunned, Richard, to be honest. Yes, that's the word, stunned."

"Yes," he mused, like a doctor weighing up a diagnosis, "I'm sorry about the airport, not picking you up. I don't know how it slipped my mind."

She pulled the end of a croissant, careful not to let crumbs fall onto the bed sheets. "I really think, Richard..." It looked like she was trying to stay calm, but the way she pulled at the other end of the croissant suggested to him that violence may be just around the corner if he wasn't careful. "I really think that you not being at the airport is some way down the list of discussion topics right now, don't you?" She looked him right in the eye, and he met the stare, determined not to give in. Well, not yet anyway.

"I suppose so."

"I don't even remember getting to bed. Did you put me here?"

"Yes, of course."

"And you put me in my night clothes?"

"Yes." There was a pause. "We are still married!" There was another pause.

"And that other woman..."

"A guest at the *chambre d'hôte*."

"But she wasn't here when…"

"Of course not. She went to bed and I carried you upstairs and—and—made you comfortable."

"Who is she?" Clare sounded vulnerable and he hadn't prepared for that.

"She's a guest at the…"

"A guest at the *chambre d'hôte*, yes, you said that. But *who* is she?"

"Her name is Valérie d'Orçay and she's in the area, house-hunting." It struck him that he had no idea why Valérie d'Orçay was in the area at all.

"And you two are…?" She left the question, loaded as it was, hanging.

"Nothing, just host and guest."

"Really? And do all your attractive female guests get to wear your monogrammed pajamas? Do they pay extra for that?"

"It's a long story," he said sullenly.

"I bought you those pajamas for Christmas," she added, a look of theatrical hurt on her face. It came back to him suddenly: that Christmas. They had made a conscious decision to try and be more physical as a couple, to rekindle some youthful passion amid the debris of middle-aged exhaustion and disappointment. She had bought him the silk pajamas, and he had bought her a long silk nightie. It was a classy thing to do, and they were pleased at how they looked and how mature they were. It was, though they'd left it unsaid, a million miles away from their friends, the Thompsons.

Somewhere in the evening the electricity between them grew, literally, and just as the spark of romance and sensuality should have burst forth, a static charge erupted between the two items of clothing, throwing Richard back on to the floor where he chipped a tooth, and giving Clare a migraine that didn't subside for a week. It was a disaster. In fact he hoped Valérie hadn't been cuddling Passepartout too rigorously while wearing those pajamas, or the poor creature would now look like an angry porcupine.

He shook his head; this was no time to be thinking of Valérie.

"And the gun?" Clare had obviously decided it was wise to let the silk pajama thing go, too.

"Again," he said, "it's a long story."

She sighed and laid the tray to one side before settling down into the covers. "Well, I've got the time to listen, Richard. So let's hear it: dressing up, guns, attractive women—it sounds like one of your films... I'm all ears."

He hated that phrase, "One of *your* films," like he was a child with a set of toys and that she was too grown up to possibly get involved. In a way, she had a point; it did sound like a plot for a classic film noir. Certainly the scene last night, the final tableau of a prostrate Clare lying across the sofa, while Valérie, wearing the hero's pajamas, stood over her and our hero held the gun. It was all very Raymond Chandler, all very Bogart and Bacall...

"Richard!" Clare snapped her fingers. "Where did you go? Film noir, was it? Try and stay in the present, dear, let's have it."

"Right then," he began, not really knowing where to go next and then suddenly deciding, somewhere inside, that honesty would be the best policy. Besides which, he knew he couldn't make anything else up that would even remotely fit the facts. "A few days ago a Monsieur Grandchamps checked in..."

She listened attentively for the next thirty minutes or so as Richard alternately sat and/or paced his way through his story. She asked the odd question but for the most part took it all in, nodded in all the right places, showed concern when it was merited, rolled her eyes at the antics of Gennie and Martin and in the end sat there mulling it all over.

"Be honest with me, Richard," she asked gently, like a parent hoping a child will own up to their crime. "Is that the plot of a film or the truth?"

"The truth."

"I can check, you know. I can cross-reference Google and IMDB and have the name of some 1940s B-movie in minutes, seconds probably."

He stood up again. She knew how to hurt him. IMDB dot com. The Internet Movie Database. His bête noire, his bugbear, his nemesis, and ultimately, his victorious opponent. Until IMDB came along with its search engine ferocity, it was experts like him, walking founts of film knowledge, armed perhaps with a *Halliwell's*, who had been held in high regard, keepers of the flame of cinematic history. Now, one click, and bang, you had Kirk Douglas's entire film career, marriages, photos, quotes and vital statistics in a flash, and none of Richard's ilk could compete with that. He stayed silent, brooding.

"I thought so." She cleared some imaginary crumbs from the bed and plumped her pillow. "I don't know what's got into you, Richard, I swear I don't. But I don't think telling the truth would hurt. You've hooked up with this Valérie woman—who I have no doubt is thoroughly charming—and now you're mixed up with Martin and Gennie and into all sorts of role-playing fantasy stuff." She sighed. "I suppose I should be happy for you. Isn't this what you wanted?"

"How do you mean?" He felt there was no point in arguing.

"This kind of sexual high life, isn't this exactly what you wanted?"

"I'm not leading a sexual high life."

"Oh, poor Richard. I remember distinctly you suggested to

me that we should consider an open marriage, so this is what you wanted. I hope you enjoy it, I really do."

Richard remembered the conversation vividly, too. Just out of work and depressed, he was desperate to inject some excitement or adventure into their lives, his life, really. Like any other tragic midlife crisis male, the first thought was sexual and he had indeed said they should maybe "loosen up a bit." Of course, when a wounded male says anything like that, it is a massive cry for help at which point said wounded male would be better off standing in a corner and crying "HELP!" massively. Not, as Richard had drunkenly done one evening, imply he was some kind of frustrated lothario with a string of offers so maybe Clare should watch out. Within six months Clare actually did have a string of offers, an open marriage and was having a whale of a time while Richard stayed at home and nursed his regrets.

"Why are you here, Clare?"

"I don't really know," she said softly. "I missed you. I wanted to make sure you were all right, and I'm pleased to see that you are. Whatever this game is, Richard, you look well on it. There's color in your cheeks and a spark in the eye and, you may not believe this, but that makes me very happy." He gripped her hand in return. "In truth, I think I'd hoped to come and find you moping about, a bit of a mess. I guess I had hoped you would need me."

He didn't know what to say; up until three days ago he had thought of little else and probably would have fitted that exact description. He still loved her; she obviously still loved him. But they both knew that sometimes, even after a lifetime, especially after a lifetime, that's just not enough.

By mid-afternoon they were standing under the departures screen at the central railway station in Tours. They'd had a pleasant lunch in the old town, discussed Alicia while avoiding anything that would involve practicalities of their own predicament. They both knew there was no hurry to dot the Is and cross the Ts, as she put it and, as things stood, no pressing need either. Richard had expected Clare to stay longer but they both knew that that wasn't practical. Clare instead was going to Bordeaux for a few days to stay with an "old friend." Richard didn't ask who, and Clare offered no further details.

"I'm glad I came, Richard," Clare said at the foot of the steep train steps.

"Me, too," he said and kissed her cheek gently. "'We'll always have Paris,'" he added and immediately regretted it.

She smiled at him. "'We lost it, until you came back to *Casablanca*. We got it back last night.' You see? I did pay attention some of the time." She climbed the steps, and he put the cases in the doorway next to her.

"I'll call you soon," he called up after her.

"OK, but Richard..."

"Yes?"

"Be careful with guns. They go off, you know?"

"I thought you didn't believe me!"

"Goodbye," she said and blew him a kiss.

Richard turned, as content as he reckoned he could be under the circumstances, and walked back through the large ticket hall with its high glass roof. He stopped as a tall figure passed in front of him. Yes, it was a large roof, but then it would have to be to house a Stetson cowboy hat like that.

23

He had seen hundreds of films where one man tails another, yet it was sadly, and very swiftly, clear to Richard that none of the finesse or techniques of such an enterprise had rubbed off on him. He turned quickly to face a shop window as Tex stopped to do the same thing farther down the street, albeit with less urgency. Richard immediately regretted his action as he came face to face with a young woman dressing a dummy on the other side of the glass. She was putting the finishing touches to a lingerie display and Richard's sudden attention clearly marked him out as suspicious. He apologized and turned away up the road and across the pedestrianized street, tapping his rolled-up newspaper innocently on his thigh as he did so.

What *was* he doing?

He really wasn't sure. The desire to follow Tex had been instinctive, but why? Tex was a butcher from Tours, so why follow him? Was it because he was Valérie's ex-husband—was jealousy the reason? Possibly. Was it the coincidence of his appearance on the boat trip? Again, possibly. But what did the two add up to? Well, to him that was obvious, and it didn't make him feel good about himself. The truth was that he didn't entirely trust Valérie.

There was a large part of him that wanted to trust her. She was a beautiful woman who, in the space of three or four days, he was beginning to lose track, had turned his world upside down and given him, though he wouldn't care to admit it, more excitement than he'd probably ever had. Certainly more than he ever thought he might have again. Even when he daydreamed and imagined that he was the gumshoe in one of "his" films, as Clare would have it, these things just didn't happen to Richard, or people like him. They happened in books, in scripts, on the screen, they were fiction. And that, he realized, was exactly why he didn't trust Valérie. It was because he was so unsure of himself, who he was and therefore wary of the world around him, to do so.

He turned around again, hoping that he hadn't lost Tex in the meantime. Then again, although Richard was hanging back at a discreet distance, it would have been extremely difficult to lose sight of the man. A beanpole of six-foot-six wearing an absurdly large cowboy hat and meandering through a French high street was about as conspicuous as it gets. He stood out like, well, like that ridiculous sculpture of a rhinoceros outside McDonald's near Central Tours station. Tex had even stopped to take a picture of it just like any other tourist would. Richard's eyes narrowed. Just like any other tourist would. Not, then, like a butcher in his hometown.

He saw Tex look at his watch and apparently come to a decision. He turned back toward where Richard was loitering, who again found himself being stared at by the same window dresser, though he held his nerve this time and allowed Tex to pass by behind him. He was no longer the wandering tourist; he strode with purpose and with somewhere to go.

Richard followed him for a few minutes, as Tex looked at his phone for directions as he stood outside the modern Vinci Center

International de Congrès. From there he turned left, back down the Heurteloup Boulevard, and waited by the bus stop. Richard's heart sank. If he got on a bus, could he follow him? The truth was that as far as he knew Tex didn't know him, but he couldn't risk it by sitting on the same bus. He could grab one of the many bicycles that litter cities these days and follow the bus...then he told himself to get a grip. The last thing he needed was a heart attack from sudden exercise. Tex looked at his phone again, turned away from the bus stop and into Les Jardins de la Préfecture. Here he slowed down and Richard assumed that he'd reached his destination—surely a meeting place. He gave Tex a few moments' grace and then scurried in, taking the opposite path, but keeping the cowboy mostly in view.

The tall man seemed quite taken with the place, as though city center greenery was new to him. The wide paths and the enormous, well-established plane trees meant peace and tranquility in a busy metropolis, and Tex had the air of a country bumpkin who had assumed that all towns were just concrete and noise. That he'd found a haven for himself. He kept looking at his watch, though. He was waiting for someone.

Richard found himself a bench as far away as possible from Tex's own bench while still being in view, but he spread his newspaper out as extra security. He'd bought *Le Monde* because it was an old-fashioned broadsheet size and he sat, as inconspicuous as possible, peering over the top. Tex himself was obviously quite jumpy, sitting down one minute then leaping up and walking around the bench the next, looking out for whoever was to come. He didn't have long to wait, though, and Richard nearly fell off his bench when he saw who it was.

Tex greeted the Rizzolis warmly as though they were old friends, shaking the young man's hand heartily and stooping to kiss Signora Rizzoli on both cheeks. They laughed and joked about something and then Tex looked at his watch again, explaining something else, certainly animatedly, and the Rizzolis sat down. Richard's heart was racing now and the newspaper shaking in his hands; deep down he knew who they were waiting for.

Valérie arrived carrying Passepartout and looking every inch the chic lady-about-town, dressed as elegantly as ever in yet another outfit. *She must have a suitcase the size of the* QE2 *in that bedroom,* thought Richard, trying to suppress how impressive he found her and concentrate on his rising anger instead. He felt used, mightily disappointed and betrayed. He also felt utterly clueless and couldn't for the life of him understand what the hell was going on. Tex greeted her effusively, as he seemed to greet everyone effusively—something which annoyed Richard immensely, though he noticed Valérie was a little stiff in response. The Rizzolis stood up and Tex appeared to make the introductions. The Rizzolis didn't smile and neither did Valérie as they all shook hands coldly. Tex sat down and Valérie put Passepartout next to him and between him and the Rizzolis, who resumed their seats, leaving Valérie to stand.

Richard wished he was in a position to hear what was going on, but thankfully Tex was like a bad film actor whose theater training was too ingrained for the cinema, his gestures and movements exaggerated and easy to read. Valérie and the Rizzolis weren't quite as obvious. Tex spread his arms wide in a "well, how do we do this?" kind of way, though Richard had no idea what "this" could possibly be. He hoped it was that Tex would get a slap in his permanently grinning face, but he doubted it. The big man left his outspread arm above Passepartout's bag, though, and the normally placid little animal leaped up and tried to take a lump out of his hand.

"Good for you!" Richard said to himself as Valérie patted the small dog's head, also congratulating him.

This was obviously a tense meeting.

Valérie was talking now and clearly referencing Tex himself, pointing at him while sweeping her arms toward the Italian couple. This went on for a few moments with Tex pretending to be hurt, though still grinning, and pointing at himself in mock innocence. The Rizzolis both turned to him at the same time, and the stupid, big, toothy smirk disappeared slowly. He frowned darkly before standing up and remonstrating about something or other. When he stopped it was clear that everyone was weighing up what he'd just said, like a jury deciding on the accused. The Rizzolis both shook their heads, and Valérie turned slowly toward him once more. Tex tipped the brow of his hat back and shook his own head slowly, then the wide grin returned and he laughed and slapped his thigh. *The man's ludicrous.* Richard shook his head, too. *It's cowboy by numbers,* and it reminded him not so much of John Wayne, which was surely the intention, but of Doris Day as Calamity Jane. He also knew defeat when he saw it, and so, obviously, did Tex. He spread his arms wide again, went to stroke Passepartout's head once more and got a snappy response for his troubles, did a kind of "so long" salute with the back of his hand and strode languidly out of the park.

Richard returned his watchful gaze to the three others; it felt like they were the remaining contestants in a game show. Signora Rizzoli had her hand out and was clearly asking for something, with Richard guessing it was their missing phone. Valérie, though, was shaking her head and ignoring the hand. She picked up Passepartout and held out her own hand to say goodbye. The meeting, conflab, showdown, whatever it was, was over. They all shook hands and Valérie left by the right-hand gate. A few seconds later the Rizzolis left by the left-hand gate. Richard folded his paper up and followed Valérie.

He was thankful that Passepartout was in a forward-facing bag, which meant that he wouldn't see Richard skulking about, thirty meters or so behind. Richard had no idea what the dog would have done had he spotted him; he'd hitherto shown absolutely no sign even of his existence, just a haughty air which was reserved for the masses, though not for Valérie, or Tex, but he wouldn't want to take the chance.

Valérie turned down the narrow Colbert Street and Richard tried to stick to the sides, which wasn't easy as there were so many restaurant tables in the way. He kept telling himself he was doing well, but he was also aware that he was spending an awful amount of time apologizing to people, and in a very English way emptying tables that he bumped into, and was leaving something like a trail of vexation in his wake. He saw Valérie turn down an even narrower side street and sped up to get closer. It was little more than an alleyway, two rows of ancient buildings leaning toward the slim thoroughfare, all at slightly different angles like teeth in a wonky smile. Valérie walked elegantly, the only person on the road, and Richard darted to a shaded doorway, watching her.

He leaned back on the door to catch his breath and felt it give way, revealing a startled Chinese woman whose broom gave him short shrift, so he ran down the road and ducked into an alcove. He was now out of breath and took a few moments to gather himself. He looked out again, slowly putting his head out of the shadows, and he didn't like what he saw.

About twenty yards down the road Valérie stood, feet apart. A few yards in front of her were the Rizzolis, slightly apart from each other and blocking her way. They stayed like that for a few moments, an angry triangle, before Valérie took Passepartout off her shoulder and placed his bag gently in a doorway. She then returned to her previous spot, feet apart, ready.

Signor Rizzoli advanced slowly, his hand outstretched, possibly one last entreaty for the return of their phone. Richard clenched his fists and told himself unconvincingly he was ready for action while bearing in mind what Valérie had said about the gun they'd found: "a back-up gun," she'd said, "there'll be others."

The man stopped directly in front of Valérie while Signora Rizzoli folded her arms in faux boredom. Suddenly, Richard noticed, they didn't look so young anymore. Passepartout gave out a shrill bark and the Italian turned to register a mocking grin at the attack dog. That was his first mistake. His second was trying to get up again a few seconds later having been poleaxed by a swift knee to the groin, and this time getting the same knee square on the chin and knocking him out cold. Signora Rizzoli looked unsurprised by her husband's inadequacy and advanced slowly, pulling a flick knife out of her pocket. Valérie advanced, too, stepping over Signor Rizzoli, confident enough that he was no longer an issue.

Richard felt sweat drip from his brow and his hands were trembling. He had been ready to spring, if spring was the right word, to Valérie's defense. To step in and do what he could to protect the lady. But it was now crystal clear that not only would he be in the way, but that she simply didn't need him.

Signora Rizzoli crouched, the knife in her right hand and her face in a mocking sneer. Valérie remained standing ramrod straight, tense but swaying slightly on her toes, like a king cobra, ready to strike. Then she suddenly broke out into a fit of giggling, putting her hand to her mouth to try and suppress the urge. Signora Rizzoli, now within knife-striking distance, looked momentarily confused and came out of her crouching stance. That was *her* first mistake. In a flash Valérie had grabbed her wrist and twisted her arm, spinning her to the ground where she dropped her knife. Her second mistake was trying to reach for the knife. She got an expensively leathered boot to the chin, sending her reeling again, arching backward in the air briefly before she landed softly across her prostrate husband. Valérie gave it a few seconds, making sure they were both out of action, and then picked up Passepartout, thanked him for his patience with a few kisses to the head and walked serenely away.

Richard put his glasses on for wont of something better to do and said quietly, "Bloody hellfire."

24

The scent of jasmine wafted on the gentle evening breeze as Marie sat on the top step by Judge Grandchamps's front door, inevitably humming to herself and almost gulping down the pleasant smell of spring. She was locked out. The judge hadn't told her he wouldn't be there, and he didn't trust her enough to give her a key, though she knew very well there was a spare under the bucket by the garden well. She would give him five more minutes and then go and sit by the river for a bit. Melvil was at work at Monsieur Oeuf, gearing up for a special evening meal promotion. He'd spent most of lunchtime practicing his clucking and talking about inspiration, and she didn't start back at Bruno's until seven. "Just in time for the evening rush," he always said, though it rarely materialized.

Bonneval arrived and parked his car directly in front of the narrow gate. He leaped out and helped the old judge out of the passenger door. For some reason, the judge looked even older than he had yesterday; his cheeks were sallow and there were dark patches under the eyes. He caught sight of Marie, and she saw immense sadness in his eyes; he was clearly in distress. Bonneval led him cautiously by the arm; he, too, looked upset. They had both obviously been shaken by something.

"It's OK, Marie," Bonneval said quietly, "I don't think monsieur *le juge* will need you today."

"Is everything OK?" She stood up to help with the judge's other arm on the steps.

"We, he, has had a bit of a shock. You can go, thank you."

"No, young lady," the judge said with his usual bitterness, "I'm not paying for her to be idle." And then more gently, "Would you make us a tisane? Please." He gave Bonneval the door key and they all went inside.

Marie went to the kitchen to prepare some tea while the two men went to the back study. "Are you sure you want her around? We have things to discuss, private things."

"Have we?" The judge sat heavily in his wheelchair. "Yes, I suppose we have, but I have nothing to hide and pretty soon the whole of Vauchelles will know anyway." Then he added forlornly, "What does it matter?"

"I still can't believe it." Bonneval sat presumptuously at the desk, his shock overriding his sense of propriety though he stood immediately as Marie came into the room carrying a tray.

"Can I help with anything?" She put the tray down on the desk and turned to the judge.

"No, child," the old man replied distractedly, "just your usual duties." She turned to go. "My brother is dead." It wasn't just a statement of fact; his voice was on the verge of breaking and the word "dead" came across almost as surprise. His piercing eyes bored into her, gauging every detail of her reaction.

Marie put her hand to her mouth and sat down; now the whole room was in shock. Each had assumed that the old man had been playing games, laughing at them all from a distance. "How?"

Bonneval turned to look out of the window, and away from the others. "He was shot, or at least died of gunshot wounds. We can't rule out an accident at this stage. We'll know more, obviously, in due course."

"Poor man," Marie murmured almost inaudibly, "poor, poor man."

"His face was clean blown away," Bonneval added unnecessarily, though no one else in the room was easily shocked.

"Then how..." She left the question, which seemed equally unnecessary, hanging.

"Monsieur *le juge* bravely identified his brother. The clothes he was wearing were a start; that's when I thought it might be Vincent. The judge confirmed it."

The judge broke away from staring into space for a second and said quietly, "He had his army number tattooed on his wrist in Algeria. He and his comrades all did. It was hidden under his watch strap." And he pointed at his own watch as illustration. "There's no doubt."

"Poor man," Marie whispered again.

"He had only been dead for a day or so." Bonneval felt the need to fill in the blanks. "So maybe he was playing his games as we thought. I don't know."

"With the wrong people," the judge added softly. "I think I'd like to be alone for a while please. You may both go." He sank back into the cushions on his chair, his face a tortured mask of grief and incomprehension, and the others quietly left.

Marie put on her seatbelt, having accepted Bonneval's offer of a lift for the short distance back into town. Somehow it didn't seem right to go and sit by the river. Her mind was full of horrible images and she would rather go straight to work instead; being active was a way to clear the mind, her mother had always said.

"It's just dreadful," she said as the policeman started the engine.

"Yes," was the terse reply.

"Do you know..."

"Like the judge said, he was playing with the wrong people. You know it was the mafia?"

"I had no idea," she lied. She'd overheard enough conversations and put enough two and twos together to know exactly what was going on. It also, thankfully, meant an end to her sending envelopes on the old man's behalf, which was a pity in some ways, but at least, now he was definitely dead, she wouldn't have to return the money she had collected. None of it. He didn't need it now, and nor did the judge, who would be unlikely to accept the "dirty" money anyway.

"Once there's a price on your head, and such a price..." He shook his head sadly.

"There was a price on his head?" she asked, the picture of innocence and ignorance.

"Only half a million euros!"

She thought about the stash she had already put away for them both; it was more money than she had ever seen in one place, but then Marie Gavinet had never seen €500,000 either, and that was ten times the amount.

"That's a lot of money," she said seriously, "a lot of money."

"It is, and that's the problem. Some people will stop at nothing for that."

There was a pause, and Marie started humming. "You could hardly blame them." She sighed and looked out of the window. "We could do an awful lot with half a million euros."

Very little escaped Brigadier-Chef Principal Philippe Bonneval, and he made a mental note of what Marie had said, smiling to himself as he did so.

25

I picked you for the job, not because I think you're so darn smart"—
the short, heavy-set man spat the words out through the smoke
of his cigar, and Richard sat back taking it all in—"but because
I thought you were a shade less dumb than the rest of the outfit.
Guess I was wrong." Richard turned his eyes downward; he knew the
man was right. "You're not smarter, Walter...you're just a little taller."
The short, heavy-set man was Edward G. Robinson and, with the
house shutters closed and the door locked, he was vicariously giving
Richard the dressing-down he needed in the darkened lounge.

Richard had never felt the need for psychoanalysis. The idea of
sitting back on a couch and spilling forth and being judged by someone else didn't fit his stilted, slightly mistrustful view of the world.
Clare had at one stage suggested marriage guidance for the pair
of them, but in Richard's view dirty laundry shouldn't be aired; it
must be washed on a higher temperature, that's all, tumble dried and
folded neatly away. He realized he was thinking nonsense, trying to
summarize life in a compact, neatly packaged epithet: solving life's
mysteries through snappy dialogue. In other words, fantasizing and
making his life out to be a film. Again.

Everything he needed by way of explanation, support, definition, and all-round rocket-up-the-backsidery had come from the cinema. And right now he felt let down and betrayed, and that called for film noir, specifically, in this case, *Double Indemnity*. Bleak, hardboiled, post-war cynicism as entertainment where dames came at you out of the shadows asking for a match, and the hero was a would-be tough guy, though hapless and with no idea of what was going on...and it was always the dame's fault. He'd read once that the trope of femme fatale, the dame, was both sexist and empowering and he'd had no idea what the author was on about, and as the author was a man essentially discussing feminism he suspected that the author had no idea what the author was on about either. He'd probably been put up to it by a dame wanting a match.

Where it didn't all fit, though, where Richard's theory that he was the sap being taken for a ride, Adam manipulated to his downfall by Eve, was that he wasn't offering anything in return. Traditionally the heroine with dubious morals uses sex, or at least hints that she's prepared to use sex, as a means to an end. She'll hold his match hand a little too long, a seductive look in her eye, and persuade the hood-winked rube to act on her behalf, either illegally or dangerously or both. Or she uses him as protection against other threats: he's an attack dog or a watchdog. Either way a low-down dirty mongrel who...he was getting carried away again.

It was obvious from what he'd seen in Tours that afternoon that, firstly, Valérie d'Orçay did not need his protection; far from it. And anything either illegal or dangerous—he regarded the breaking and entering into the bedroom of would-be mafia assassins as both illegal and dangerous—had been offered as a thrill, a ride, but no hint of sex lay behind it, unless he was missing something, which was entirely possible. He'd had a simple choice not to get involved and he'd

ignored it. He just didn't see where he fitted in, that was all. Nor did
he understand Valérie's role either, which at the moment was therefore easier to define through the two-dimensional stereotype of the
classic femme fatale. And, if he was honest, that made him a Bogart,
or a Burt Lancaster or, as in the case with *Double Indemnity*, a Fred
MacMurray, and in truth he rather liked that.

"We're both rotten," Barbara Stanwyck says.

"Only you're a little more rotten," MacMurray replies.

Yep, Richard thought while curling his lip Bogart-style, *I'm just
another gullible lummox, pushed and pulled around by a smart hustler
in heels who checked her honesty into Left Luggage along with a mink
bought by the last sap who fell for her.*

He admonished himself. Fantasy was all very well, but this wasn't
a film. An old man was still (probably) missing, his hen had been
killed, there was a gun in the kitchen drawer, and Martin really had
worn bulldog clips on his nipples. And anyway, what did honesty
have to do with it? He had decided some months ago that honesty,
as an idea, as a concept, certainly as a marital tool, was way, way over-
rated. A bear trap, the iced-over puddle on the doorstep. Why did he
want Valérie to be honest? There was a time he would have craved
the opposite in Clare, times when she had been too honest, too open.

That was a world away, though, almost a different life, so where
did Valérie's dishonesty end or begin? She was dragging him around,
looking for an old man who she might have disposed of herself, for
all he knew. She could have then destroyed the evidence. It might
have been her who did in poor Ava Gardner. It might even have been
her gun that she pretended to find in the Rizzolis' bedroom. She
could have placed and removed the bloodied handprint.

"What are you thinking, Richard?"

He nearly jumped out of his skin. Valérie stood in the lounge doorway, her shadow playing across the wall as the light from the film lit her at an odd angle, all very film noir indeed.

"How did you get in? I locked all the doors…"

She jangled her lock-picking set at him and stayed leaning on the door frame.

"I've been watching you for a few minutes. Do you have a problem with your lip?"

Richard stood up and walked into the kitchen. "I was thinking about honesty."

"Really?" She came into the room to take a look at the TV screen. "I think honesty can be a dangerous thing, more so than dishonesty sometimes."

He put the kettle on. A proper film noir patsy would have reached for a bourbon. He was aware of that, but being English to the core, Richard felt the need to put the kettle on, even if he didn't actually feel the need to drink a cup of tea.

"Has your wife gone?"

"Yes."

"I was worried."

"Really?"

"Yes. With the door locked and the shutters closed it meant one of two things. One, you were in danger, or two, you and your wife were making love and didn't want to be disturbed."

Richard couldn't remember the last time either of those things had happened.

"And in the end, you plumped for me being in danger?"

"It seemed the more likely."

"Thanks."

"Is that why you are thinking about honesty, because your wife was here?" She moved elegantly into the room.

"I suppose."

"She was too honest or too dishonest?"

"Honest, I suppose." He wished the kettle would get a move on.

"She told you of her lovers?"

"It was my own fault."

"You wanted to know?"

"That she had lovers. It was my fault that she had lovers."

"I don't understand."

"Me neither, to be honest." He paused. "There's that word again."

"You don't have to tell me." She moved closer, making it very clear that she really thought he must tell her. He had no intention of ever telling anyone, but there's something about an attractive woman making her way toward you in the shadows, and you knowing that a quick boot to the throat and she could break your neck, that brings out the confessional in a man. Besides, Fred MacMurray had gotten under his skin and he felt like being the wounded, flawed hero for a bit.

"Our marriage had been stale for a long time," he began. "Do you want tea?"

"No, thank you."

"It's one of the reasons we moved here when I was made redundant. Clare was bored, though, and pretty quickly. Not that she didn't try. But I knew that she missed her friends, her social group, her job in London, the UK, basically. I wanted to...I don't know. I knew *I* was boring her and wanted to look more exciting." He snorted in mock humor. "We had a drunken evening with Martin and Gennie, nothing happened, but for some reason when we got back here, I tried to be all 'man of the world.' I started saying that maybe we needed to freshen things up a bit, that we were obviously both just a bit...a bit bored."

"You mean to have affairs?" Valérie looked a bit bemused by the Englishness of it all, the heavy formality of it.

"Well, I'm not sure. In my head I sounded so grown up and sophisticated; an open marriage, I believe it's called. All very mature."

"And she didn't like the idea? That's why she left."

"Far from it. She bloody loved the idea!" He squeezed the teabag.

"So you both had affairs?" She said it in a "so what?" way.

"No. No, we didn't. I wasn't as successful as she was."

Valérie looked him square in the eye as he lifted his mug of tea up to his mouth. Then she looked away briefly as if trying to find the right words of sympathy. Then she burst out laughing, sudden, uncontrollable laughter that almost floored her to the point where she had to go and sit down. Richard stood there frozen, his mug halfway to his face.

"Oh, Richard!" she said through sobs. "That is so funny! You men!" Then she doubled up again. "You men are just so funny!"

Richard hadn't thought far enough ahead to consider the reaction to his confession. Some sympathy maybe, an element of anger at his presumption, silence at the sadness of it all? He really didn't know. To find out that it was funnier than all the Marx Brothers' films rolled into one wasn't on the menu, though, and he put his tea down, not a little hurt.

"I really don't see why that's so funny," he said simply, finally taking a gulp of his drink.

Valérie stopped laughing immediately and looked at him seriously. Then she couldn't help herself and started laughing again.

"I have been all around this world"—Valérie was struggling to speak—"and everywhere you go there are monuments, testaments and scars to man's dominance." She giggled again. "I just don't see how, as a sex, you managed to do it all!"

"Well, I..."

"What *did* you expect? Oh, Richard!"

He left it a while to give her time to calm down a bit, which took far longer than was polite in his opinion. "Why are you here anyway?" he asked fractiously.

"Oh, yes." She wiped her eyes and unsurprisingly her mascara didn't smudge at all. "Oh, it's poor Monsieur Grandchamps. They've found his body. I came to tell you."

It sounded final. It sounded like that was an end to it, whatever *it* was, and although half an hour ago he'd felt used and betrayed by the woman, and although she'd spent the last ten minutes letting him know, in no uncertain terms, what an idiot she thought he was, he now felt a feeling of loss as though this might just all be over. The end. *Fin.*

"How?" he asked sadly.

"They're saying it was a hunting accident, that he blew his face off with a gun. I haven't got all the details yet, and they're doing a postmortem tomorrow. These things are slow."

"Oh. So that's it then?"

"It looks like it, yes." Her face was still full of laughter despite the news.

The phone rang, and Richard was glad of the interruption as he picked it up. "Yes, that's me," he said dolefully, expecting another cold call offering him a chance to invest in renewable energy. Suddenly, he stood up straight as the voice on the other end spoke. "Sorry," he said, "could you repeat that?" He snapped his fingers to get Valérie's attention. "You're ringing from the Zoo de Beauval and you have a Monsieur Vincent Grandchamps there. He's in some distress and has asked for me?" Valérie stood up, too, as Richard looked at his watch. "We can be there in thirty minutes," he said and put the phone down.

"So it's not over then?" she said, a look of what was almost like hunger in her eyes.

"Apparently not." He still had a look of hurt on his face that he hadn't managed to dislodge.

"Oh, Richard," she said excitedly, and then burst into laughter again, "don't fret! You are still a man in your prime! I will go and change."

Ten minutes later she came down the stairs of the *chambre d'hôte*, and she looked stunningly beautiful, her hair up in a loose ponytail, and wearing a simple figure-hugging dress. She'd obviously spent time trying to make it look like it was an outfit just thrown together, and Richard couldn't take his eyes off her. She hesitated on the stairs, as if she may have forgotten something. What was it Fred MacMurray had said? "I was thinking about that dame upstairs, and the way she had looked at me, and I wanted to see her again, close, without that silly staircase between us."

After all, he was still in his prime, she'd said so herself, though he couldn't quite fathom why that bothered him so much.

26

They'd driven largely in silence; occasionally Valérie would fail to suppress a giggle, pretend it was a cough and apologize, but nothing had been said. Passepartout had sat on her lap in the passenger seat, a determined look on his face as though he were a canine GPS. Richard had questioned the need to bring the small dog at all, a futile argument, he knew, but one that he felt compelled to make even though there was no one to dog-sit if he didn't come, and the French, he knew from experience, took their small dogs everywhere, even to a zoo.

They were now at the entrance and things weren't going well.

"I'm sorry, madame." The young woman, still a teenager, in the ticket booth was having none of it. "I have no record of a phone call or a Richard Ainsworth or a Monsieur Grandchamps. Do you have the name of the person who called you?" The question was put in a way that suggested the young woman thought this was all a ruse to gain free entry.

Valérie turned to Richard. "Do you have the name of the person you spoke to, Richard?" He was hanging back a few yards, not really wanting to get involved and also holding Passepartout in a way that a new father holds his first offspring, awkwardly and with a look of "what on earth have I done?" on his face.

"Sorry, no," he said, apologetically. "Just a young man, he said he had our friend with him in the chimpanzee house."

Valérie tutted, which at least was a change from patronizing sniggering. The young woman's face turned even stonier. You're going to have to do better than that, it was saying.

"OK, forget it. Richard, pay la demoiselle, we cannot waste any more time. He might be dead!" She directed this at the young woman, letting her know that if that was indeed the case, she would be held responsible. The young woman, to her credit, thought Richard, rolled her eyes. She'd heard it all before.

"Two tickets, senior citizens?" she asked, overplaying her hand.

"Just two tickets, please." Richard fumbled for his wallet while trying not to drop Passepartout, before Valérie took him off his hands and went marching on.

"Can I interest you in a bag of popcorn for the goats?" The girl beamed at him.

"No," he said, "of course not." And he went hurrying after Valérie.

The sounds and the smells are what hit you first in a zoo, before the actual view of the beasts themselves. The distant sound of excited monkeys, the noise of the birds in their cages, the cloying odor of various types of dung. He had been here a lot and it had always struck him as an odd situation for the locals. The zoo had expanded massively in the time that they, he, had lived in the area, but it was still neighbored by small holdings and micro vineyards, and Richard had often wondered how odd it must be to be out in your garden pruning your roses, or putting the bins out at night and have rutting elephants, mischievous macaques, and permanently disgruntled parakeets as your aural backdrop.

A large group of flamingos stood elegantly by a lake, watched over by some bored lemurs on a separate island. Up ahead, Valérie was weaving in and out of slowly moving tourists like a speeding car on a motorway. It was as though she had completely forgotten that they'd come together. He caught up with her at a crossroads while she looked at a sign for directions.

"This way!" he said, affecting urgency and scooting past her. "The chimpanzee house is in the same building as the vivarium. Keep a good hold on Passepartout; those anacondas get quite peckish."

He had no idea what to expect when he got there or who to expect either. He didn't know Monsieur Vincent Grandchamps, and had obviously been very surprised to get a phone call effectively telling him he was responsible for the old man's welfare. He didn't know what Valérie expected either, but she was almost viciously excited by the prospect. Richard opened the heavy double door, holding it open for her to pass through, and the noise hit them immediately. To their right were smaller glass-paneled enclosures, each with trees in them and various small monkeys, nervously watching those who were watching them. Their quick, jerky movements and fearful eyes always made them look guilty like they knew they were up to no good, though they were probably just frightened and Richard felt sorry for them. Next were the orangutans, his favorite. The matriarch, Manis, sat slumped against the reinforced glass as she always did, a look of doleful serenity on her face as though it had become a chore to carry all of the world's wisdom on her mighty shoulders. When Clare had first left, Richard had spent hours sitting with Manis; just being in her presence had soothed him, though he couldn't have explained why.

He bent down to say hello; he always felt that she recognized him. Valérie bent down, too, and hissed at him, "What are you doing,

Richard? It's the chimpanzees we want." Richard looked into the eyes of Manis, who looked back at him, those deep, brown wells of sorrow again oddly comforting to him. Then the magnificent beast looked at Valérie and at Passepartout, and Richard swore that the old girl rolled her eyes at him in exasperation. "Come on!" Valérie said, and grabbed at his jacket sleeve.

The chimpanzees were strangely calm, as though they were tired post-exercise. The youngsters were playing; elsewhere some females were in a group in the corner; each male sat solitarily staring at their rivals while an older male chimp played with himself lazily, much to the delight of a large group of schoolchildren all recording the perversion on their phones. Behind the children was a bench, and on the bench sat a small, huddled figure leaning forward on a walking stick.

"That's him!" cried Richard, and made a move toward the bench.

"No, Richard, wait!" Valérie made a grab for his arm, but it was too late.

Richard reached the bench in a couple of bounds and put his hand on the figure's shoulder. "Monsieur!" he said excitedly. "Monsieur Grandchamps?"

An old face looked up at him, an old woman's face to be precise, and she didn't look best pleased at being referred to as "monsieur."

"Monsieur?" she said indignantly. "How dare you!" She stood up and hit Richard on the elbow with her walking stick.

Valérie arrived quickly and apologized on his behalf, ushering him away. "We need to find whoever rang you up, Richard, rather than just harangue every elderly person you meet, I think." He rubbed his arm. "It was a young man, you say?"

"Yes," he replied, cowed by the experience so far, "I couldn't get his name because of the noise in the background." Just then two male chimps started screaming at each other as if to prove his point, and Passepartout sensibly ducked his head into his protective bag.

"Excuse me!" Valérie collared a casually uniformed woman carrying a basket of dead, white rabbits toward the large snake tanks that Richard knew were around the corner. He liked the zoo a lot, and its conservation work was admirable, but it was also a brutal place, too; though the schoolchildren didn't mind and took pictures of the dead rabbits to go with their collection of onanistic chimpanzees. Valérie gave Passepartout gently back to Richard, to him a sign of trust, and went off to speak to the woman with the rabbits.

She came back a few moments later. "It was an Eric who called you, and he's feeding the tamarin monkeys back near the entrance." They hurried back past the school party, the chimpanzees, and Manis the orangutan, who in her wisdom had a look on her face that said she'd been expecting them, and there, in one of the smaller enclosures, stood a gangly youth covered in small monkeys. He had no name badge on, but if anyone ever looked like an Eric, Richard thought, it was this chap.

Tall and with an unruly mop of fierce orange hair and thick glasses, Eric looked like he was related to the small monkeys he was feeding. Golden lion tamarins, the information notice said, from the coasts of Brazil and endangered. They also had flame-red manes and though lithe and supple, their faces, even those of the babies clinging to their mothers, seemed old and slightly cross.

Valérie tapped on the window to get Eric's attention, and he turned round impatiently. He was used to telling children not to bang on the animals' windows, not middle-aged women who should know better. He gave her a hard stare, and his troop, of which he looked like a god, joined in a collective stare-out.

"I'm Richard Ainsworth," said Richard, getting his attention.

Young Eric turned his head slowly, leaving his eyes on Valérie as he did so. The small monkeys all did the same, and the effect was most disconcerting. "You rang me." Richard spoke slowly as if to someone hard of hearing and mimicked a phone. Eric looked confused, and mimicked the action of telephoning back to Richard. Disappointingly, the monkeys didn't follow suit.

Eric stared for a moment without focusing and then something approaching recognition hit his eyes. He nodded and the monkeys joined in, then he held up his hands to signal that they should wait two minutes and he'd be out.

"I'm not very hopeful," said Valérie, her face downcast in disappointment, making Richard somehow feel guilty like the monkeys surrounding them.

"*Bonjour*." Eric emerged. "I won't shake hands if that's OK." He wasn't as tall as he'd looked surrounded by his primate acolytes, but facially he was still very much one of them. "Is he not there? I left him on the bench." He started to walk back toward the chimpanzees.

"No, he had gone." Valérie sounded dubious.

"He said he felt faint, so I sat him down and he gave me a number to ring. He asked me to tell you to come immediately, which I did." Eric was clearly more used to dealing with animals than humans, and was already beginning to get quite touchy. "It's not my fault if he's not there! I've got mouths to feed, you know!"

"That was about an hour ago..." Valérie was thinking aloud.

"What did he look like?" Richard asked, causing Eric to look at him as if he were mad.

"You don't know what your own dad looks like?" He regarded Richard as if he were a monster, and some way below a golden lion tamarin monkey in familial sensitivity.

"I meant how did he look," Richard backtracked.

"Oh, well." Eric looked about him for inspiration. "A bit like old Titus there." He pointed at the elderly male chimpanzee. "A bit dazed and confused, a bit lost." There was a commotion back at the tamarins and Eric apologized, muttered something about having only one pair of hands and ran off.

"I don't get it," Richard mused, "what's all this about? Is he dead or isn't he?" He felt suddenly quite angry. "And where does he get off calling himself my dad anyway?"

Valérie, who had wandered off slightly, suddenly whirled round at him. "Oh, Richard." She put her hand to her forehead. "We've fallen for the oldest trick in the book! Come on! We must get back to your house quickly." She moved off smartly.

"Why?"

"The gun and the phone, that's why."

"The Rizzolis?" He couldn't hide his disbelief. "Look Valérie, I followed you. I saw you put them out of action."

She stopped and turned to him, then slowly and choosing her words carefully, asked, "Why didn't you say anything?"

"There hasn't been much chance. We got on to other subjects." She smirked again, which annoyed him intensely. "You lied to me." He raised his voice, setting the monkeys off. "You've strung me along, God knows why, but you've lied to me. I want to know why. And I'm not going anywhere until I do." He narrowly avoided stamping his foot.

Valérie walked toward him and looked him straight in the eye, her face serious and the smirk gone. "I don't know why, Richard. I'm not even sure what's going on myself yet. I haven't lied as such, just kept some things back from you, that's all."

"The meeting with Grandchamps where he apparently said, '*chassé*'?"

"OK, one lie…" He went to interrupt and she put her hand on his mouth. "But why did I involve you? Because you looked so unhappy, maybe that's why. You looked like you'd given up. Maybe I had a little, too, but you most definitely. You look less unhappy now, am I right? You can pretend you don't like all this as much as you want, but deep down I know you've rarely felt more alive."

Something inside burst, call it self-knowledge if you like, but the dam of awareness broke, came shattering down, and he knew, blast her, that she was right. He took her hand from his mouth, held it and said, "Come on then, what are we waiting around for?" And they dashed off.

Twenty-five minutes later they were in Richard's front room again, trying to placate a determined Madame Tablier, who held a pitchfork at neck height, pinioning two people into a corner. "I found these two skulking about," she said without taking her eyes off them. "I knew they were up to no good."

27

It was clear from the angry yet triumphant look on Madame Tablier's face that she regarded skulking in the same way that Richard had seen her regard other atrocities like veganism and public displays of affection. That is, modern inventions from a human race gone to seed and in need of a good old-fashioned, mob-heavy pitchforking.

She had pinned the couple into a corner under the stairs, though to give them their due they looked less frightened and more put out. Richard was also put out. He'd expected the Rizzolis. Some martial arts cuffing from Valérie, no matter how elegantly done, was never going to put off a pair of killers, if they were killers, that is; he still only had Valérie's word for that. He was somewhat surprised then that it was Marie and Melvil doing the skulking, though he couldn't work out for the life of him why or what for. Also, it was beginning to annoy him that people he was ostensibly "protecting" were biting the hand that fed them, so to speak.

"Well done, Madame Tablier!" Valérie said with a gravitas that suggested this was all part of their grand scheme. Madame Tablier, in return, snorted like a faithful watchdog. Richard felt, and not for the first time in his life, that he was out of the loop and in need of filling in.

"Yes, well done Madame Tablier. Just as I thought we might have guests that might stay for more than one night, you have them up against a wall with a sharp implement." Madame Tablier looked at him askance. "I mean, think of the stains." Her eyes narrowed and Richard made a mental note to file sarcasm in the veganism "do not touch" folder. "Will someone kindly tell me what's going on, please?" He wandered off into the kitchen in search of liquid refreshment.

"It's as I suspected," Valérie noted.

"Me, too," Madame Tablier confirmed.

"Good. That's good. Mind letting me in on the secret?" he shouted back over his shoulder, clattering about in the cupboards.

"Oh, Richard." Valérie had no patience for sarcasm either. "While you are in the kitchen, find a cloth and wipe that so silly look off your face." He re-emerged with a large whisky. "Our young lovers are looking for the same thing we are."

"Monsieur Grandchamps?"

"Yes." She moved closer to the young couple, who continued to look a bit bored, like scolded teenagers asked to tidy their room.

"But he's dead, isn't he?"

"Exactly."

Richard sighed. "No," he said, trying to show some patience, "I don't get it."

Madame Tablier tutted at his ignorance, though cocking her head waiting for an explanation, too.

"And why aren't you at work, Marie?" he asked, trying to regain a bit of presence via his only experience of these types of confrontation, by being parental.

"The brasserie is shut on a Sunday evening and a Monday lunchtime." Even the usually humming Marie was sulky.

"Let me explain," Valérie said, dismissing this irrelevance out of hand. "Monsieur Grandchamps *is* dead; what they are looking for is *proof.*"

"Sounds like a job for the proper authorities to me." Everybody else in the room rolled their eyes at Richard. "And anyway," he added hurriedly, feeling the pressure, "if Monsieur Grandchamps is dead, who was that at the zoo?"

Melvil turned a downcast eye to the ground. "That was me," he said, his deep, sonorous voice as always striking an odd chord coming as it did out of Melvil's peculiar shape. Marie stroked his shoulder, causing Madame Tablier to move the pitchfork menacingly closer to ward off the aforementioned "public display of affection."

"Oh, Melvil," Richard said disappointedly, "why? Whatever for?"

"So that you'd be out of the way!" Madame Tablier was beginning to lose patience herself with what looked like Richard's almost tectonic-plate slowness on the uptake.

Richard took a slug of whisky as he was back in film noir territory. "Why a slug?" was the question that briefly crossed his mind; what system of measurement was that anyway? He became conscious of people staring at him again. "Yes, thank you, Madame Tablier, I'm aware of that," he said, buying time, "but the question remains. Why? Why did he, presumably they, want me, presumably us"—he waved his glass blithely in Valérie's direction—"out of the way, exactly? Why? Answer me that?"

It was Valérie's turn to plug some gaps. "They wanted to see if we had proof of the poor man's murder?" She looked at the young couple, who nodded in acquiescence. "The handprint, the glasses and so on."

And so on, thought Richard as he began to walk in circles, while also tracing his finger around the rim of the whisky glass. "And so on," he repeated aloud. "I see." He paused. "Which brings us back to the question of"—he started raising his voice—"for the love of God, WHY?"

He rounded on them all, pointing an accusatory finger from the hand holding the glass. The response was immediate. Valérie, Marie and Melvil all started talking at once, looking at each other occasionally as they did so, waving their hands about. They were practically pleading with Richard, as if them all speaking at the same time was going to help. After a minute or two they stopped and Madame Tablier offered a "well everyone knows that!" to punctuate the thing, though her heart wasn't really in it; she'd just chosen a side, that was all.

Richard disappeared back to find his whisky bottle. *It really should be bourbon* was his overriding thought as he poured himself another slug. "One at a time, please," he said calmly.

"Two million euros," Valérie said slowly, and even Madame Tablier lowered the pitchfork a little, matching the trajectory of the dropping jaws of both Marie and Melvil. "You didn't know?" she added, casting an innocent glance at the stunned crowd.

"I was told it was five hundred thousand," Marie said, almost whispering.

"Who told you that?"

"Philippe. Officer Bonneval. He told me."

"Ah, I see. Well, that's my fault I think."

"How is it your fault?" Richard asked, sitting down.

"Because I told Officer Bonneval that the figure was five hundred thousand euros."

"Did you? Right-o." The whisky, which he never normally drank, was going to his head.

"So, it's two million then?" Melvil pushed Madame Tablier's pitchfork to one side, a brave move, but leaving Madame Tablier to pretend she was lowering it for good anyway. She leaned on it instead.

"Yes." Valérie looked at her nails as though she were talking about the price of baguettes. "It's two million euros."

Melvil whistled and Marie joined him at his side.

"Can I just ask?" Richard was feigning disinterest while inside he was raging like the Niagara Falls. "Two million for what?"

"That's the price on old Monsieur Grandchamps's head," Valérie said, avoiding his angry look.

"And you knew this?"

"Yes."

"Right-o," he repeated. "And you two were looking for proof so that you could claim the two million?"

"Yes." Melvil was unabashed.

"Only we thought it was five hundred thousand," Marie threw in.

"Which makes it OK?"

They both looked at the floor again.

"That's not all they're up to either." Madame Tablier strode forward, an "I'm about to play my trump card" look on her face. She leaned in close to the couple. "They've been posting grape seeds!" she said, almost shouting, in triumph. "I heard them. They thought I wasn't listening"—she turned on them again—"but I was!"

"Grape seeds?" Richard wondered if the old warrior had finally flipped, the smell of cleaning products having taken its inevitable toll on her mental capacities. "Why? Who to?"

Valérie nodded her head slowly. "That makes sense." She looked at the young couple. "It's a dangerous game you've been playing." They looked downcast. "Though I'd have done the same in your position," she added to cheer them up.

Richard swilled the remaining whisky around in his glass. "OK," he said, "seeing as no one is bothering to tell me anything and when they do it's a lie"—he looked from face to face, extracting what guilt he could—"I'm going to try and explain this myself." He stood up and began to pace, in his head channeling Spencer Tracy in his finest courtroom pomp. "Seeds, you say?" It wasn't the most confident start, and Madame Tablier tutted as though she'd been singled out for criticism. "Grape seeds." Richard put the arm of his glasses in his mouth as though pondering existence itself. "Our Monsieur Grandchamps sent grape seeds regularly... Where to?" He wheeled on Marie.

"An address in Sicily." She almost jumped back.

"Ha! Sicily. Grape seeds. A signal, then!" He looked triumphantly at Valérie, who nodded back, signaling encouragement. "And you two carried on this, this game—"

"I don't think it's a game, Richard," Valérie interrupted.

"Really? I think you people seem to be treating it like one!" In his head he'd hit a bullseye and he could hear a fairground bell ring out. "So, you two carry on this signal system, getting what in return, money?"

"Yes, money." Marie looked embarrassed. "But I've still got it. I saved it up to give back to him. If he came back."

"And you know now that he won't be coming back?" There was silence. "I see." He carried on pacing. "The Rizzolis, from Sicily, were, no doubt, sent because there was some suspicion of foul play, I suppose? Fraud? I'm no expert but I shouldn't imagine the mafia like to give money away for no reason."

"That's it, Richard, I hadn't thought..." Valérie seemed impressed, but impressed or not, Richard wasn't to be interrupted. He was on a roll.

"Do you mind?" She stopped talking. "Thank you. Presumably these signals you were sending to the mafia in Sicily weren't backed up with actual deliveries of...whatever...wine?"

"Yes. Cheap wine that they would put more expensive labels on. It's an old trick." He shot Valérie a look. "You would have got there, Richard, no doubt."

He ignored her. "The Rizzolis see Melvil post an envelope and suspect that Grandchamps is pulling a fast one..."

"A fast one? What does that mean?"

"A con, a swindle. The people in Sicily are informed, and a price is put on Monsieur Grandchamps's head. Monsieur Grandchamps, or someone pretending to be Monsieur Grandchamps, makes very public appearances before making it look like he's been done in. Bloody handprints, broken glasses and so on. But now he is dead, and you all want to be the first to prove it so you can get the loot!"

"Well done, Richard, bravo!"

"You're not even denying it!" He was still in victory pose.

"No. Why should I?"

"Do you not care who killed him? I do. You might have killed him!"

"Oh, don't be silly, Richard. If I had killed him I would have proof."

His victory cloud dispersed. "Damn it! Yes. Sorry."

"The police think Charles Paulin killed him." It was Madame Tablier who threw this in, and in a way that showed what she thought of the police and their suspicions.

"Charles Paulin. The old town drunk, really?"

"Yes. I had Madame Paulin on the phone earlier. They split up years ago, but she's still all he's got. He went missing, as he always does, a while back. On the drink no doubt. The police think he must have done it."

"But why?" Even Valérie didn't know the answer to that one.

"They're old friends. Soldiers together; Paulin was jealous, they think. I don't buy it. Grandchamps looked after Charles Paulin, put money in his pocket and clothes on his back. They were friends. Paulin didn't do it."

"That's true," said Marie, "monsieur gave lots of old clothes to Monsieur Paulin when he saw him. The poor man always looked like he slept outside."

"He slept where he fell down, usually!" Madame Tablier didn't care for sympathy.

"Anyway." Richard felt like he was losing his top billing in this scene, and wanted some of the limelight back. "That aside, you"—he pointed at Marie and Melvil—"decided to break into my house, presumably because you think we have proof." Again the pair put their eyes to the floor.

"The phone, the gun..." listed Valérie.

"The phone and the gun!" Richard added uselessly.

"The broken glasses, the bloody wallpaper."

"The broken glasses and the bloodied wallpaper!"

"And the severed hand," Marie said quietly.

"And the severed hand!" repeated Richard confidently. "Hang on! What severed hand?"

28

E ver since the demise of Ava Gardner, for which he still bore a very real grudge, Richard had been more attentive to the remaining hens. Checking on them whenever he could, making sure that Lana Turner and Joan Crawford were still in one piece. He'd thought about replacing Ava but it felt too soon, too flippant almost. Her death hadn't yet been avenged. *But is that what it's all about?* he thought, as he threw seed vaguely in the direction of the two surviving hens. *Revenge, is that what it's really all about? Is that why I'm involved in all this?*

He sighed heavily. In truth, and he recognized the tragic nature of this, yes, it was about revenge for Ava Gardner the hen. In some way she represented him and who he was. Plus she was a poor, defenseless hen, for crying out loud; why hurt her? There was more to it than that, though, obviously, and overnight he'd given it some thought. He'd decided, halfway through a bottle of cheap local wine, that middle age was about finding the right balance. The right balance between doing the things that you have to do and doing the things that you want to do, and too much of his life, for too long, had been an imbalance in favor of *must*, not *want*. This week, he had to admit, and thanks to Valérie, it had been very much the other way around. He distinctly remembered waking up one morning last week with the depressing knowledge that the only thing he was looking forward to that day, the only high point as he saw it, was his scheduled afternoon nap. He had been merely existing, whereas right now he was living.

He'd surprised himself, too. Outwardly he'd given a very good impression of a man somewhat out of his depth, dragged along by the force of nature that was Valérie. No more a part of the decision-making process than Passepartout even, probably less so if he was honest. But he had obviously been taking more in than he'd realized and had stunned everyone the night before with his detailed grasp of the situation as it stood. Himself included.

What next, though? Where to go from here? A man was dead and another man was being, in everyone's opinion, absurdly blamed for it. Richard knew Charles Paulin, and despite the almost aristo-cratic name, he was a pathetic, harmless creature. A town drunk who did no harm to anyone, a man driven potty by bizarre circumstances and pitied by all. The thought of him being a brutal, revenge-driven killer didn't square itself with the person Richard knew, who could barely stand upright after the noonday church bells had rung. But there definitely was a killer out there, and two million euros up for grabs for whoever could claim to have done it, or at least prove that it had been done. Hence the hand, and he shivered at the thought.

It was undoubtedly an ugly business, and he shook his head sadly at the state of the world and humanity's role in it. Still, the world going to hell in a handcart was one thing, but he, to put it callously, was having the time of his life.

"Your hens will get fat if you overfeed them." Valérie had once again appeared silently at his shoulder. "They are not geese; they will not produce foie gras."

"And I wouldn't eat them even if they did," he replied a trifle tartly.

"Are you still angry with me, Richard?" Honestly, what was it about French women? No preamble, no run-up, no small, warning jab, just an opening left hook, bang.

He sighed and threw a last handful of feed for the hens. "No," he admitted, "I'm not angry with you. I think you could have been a bit more open with me, but no, not angry."

"I thought that you weren't a fan of honesty anymore?"

"Ha! It depends if it's good news or bad news, I suppose."

They stood side by side watching the hens for a moment.

"I tried to contact Officer Bonneval last night, but his phone was off."

"He was probably out looking for a hand." Richard turned and made to walk back to the house. "I mean, do body parts often go missing from police custody? Seems a bit lax."

"I think that it's more the wrist that is the key," Valérie said, thinking aloud.

"The wrist, why?"

"Marie said that Monsieur Grandchamps identified his brother's body by an army number that he had tattooed to go under his watch strap."

"So whoever took the hand is the killer, do you think?"

"It doesn't necessarily follow. There might have been other motives to murder poor Monsieur Grandchamps, Vincent Grandchamps. The price on his head only appeared after he first went missing."

"And we still don't know when that was. How long has Melvil been impersonating the old man, do you think?"

"I don't know."

"And anyway, I thought you said that it couldn't have been Melvil who stayed here as Vincent Grandchamps; something about the lines on his hand."

"It was definitely not his handprint on the wall. I am certain of that."

Richard turned to look at her. "So there's somebody else impersonating Monsieur Grandchamps? This is getting out of hand." He stopped himself. "No pun intended."

"Or it really was Monsieur Grandchamps who stayed here."

Richard shook his head, hoping something would click into place. "It's all very confusing," he said, a touch defeated.

"Well, one thing is for sure." Valérie was more upbeat and hoping it would prove infectious. "Whoever has the hand is in prime position to get the money!"

Richard suddenly looked at her sharply. "What did you say?"

Valérie looked taken aback. "I said about the hand; whoever has it will get the money."

"No! That's not what you said, you said prime position, *prime* position. God, how stupid I've been!"

"Are you OK, Richard?"

"Ha! Prime! Ha! You must have thought I was a right dimwit."

"What are you talking about?" She was beginning to lose her temper.

"Prime! That's what I'm talking about, or more accurately *preeme*." He gave it an exaggerated French accent. "*Preeme*, or in English, bounty!"

"Yes, and..." Not for the first time Valérie was left nonplussed by the impenetrability of the English sense of humor.

"You are a bounty hunter! A *chasseur de primes*!" She gave him an odd look, her head tilted slightly to one side and suddenly the confidence left him briefly. "You are, aren't you?" he asked nervously.

"Yes." And with that she folded her arms in "so what?" fashion.

"Well I never!" He was aware that that was probably the most English thing he had ever said. "You could knock me down with a feather." No, *that* was the most English thing he'd ever said.

"Richard..."

"No, don't stop me. Your first husband, pest control you said, pest control! Rats and moles! Very clever." He looked worried all of a sudden. "He was a mafia hit man, wasn't he?" She shrugged and pursed her lips, which Richard knew was French woman shorthand for "busted." "And Tex? A butcher, you said, but not from Tours?"

"He is from Tours," she said confidently, then more quietly, "Tours in Texas."

"There's a Tours in Texas?"

"Yes."

"Good Lord. Hence, Tex."

"Hence Tex."

"Who's gone back to Texas? I'm assuming your conflab in French Tours was about territory, was it? Who gets 'the goods,' as it were."

"Tex said he was taking a plane yesterday evening. And you look very pleased with yourself, Richard. It doesn't suit you."

"And you don't look very pleased to have been found out." He pulled in his stomach and stood as tall as he could in triumph.

"I'm a little surprised."

"That I worked it out?"

"That it took so long."

"Oh." He deflated a little. "And the Rizzolis are colleagues, I suppose?"

"Rivals, Richard, the Rizzolis are rivals. And I've never met them before."

"Young upstarts?"

"Their methods are a little unethical, I would say that."

"There are ethics in the bounty hunter–hit man world? Really?"

"Of course!" She looked put out. "It's not lawless." Softening a little, she added, "Not completely lawless anyway."

He smiled at her, partly in warmth, which he certainly felt, but also looking a little for help. He was standing in his garden, apparently developing some form of "understanding" with a killer. He had never been more out of his depth, and he felt a little woozy. He tried to get a grip of himself, like a drunk attempting to look sober. "So, erm, so how does one become a bounty hunter then? Bounty huntress?" He was eager not to offend. "Bountress hunter."

"It's in the blood," she said calmly.

"Right." He nodded. "Is that a clue?"

"Do you do anagrams, Richard?"

"Not regularly, no."

"Do you know much about the French Revolution?"

"Only what I've..."

"Only what you've seen in films, yes, I thought as much. Look up Charlotte Corday."

"Charlotte Corday?" Having nothing else to draw on, Richard went skimming through the impressive Rolodex of film knowledge in his mind. French Revolution films were thin on the ground: *Les Misérables*, *A Tale of Two Cities*, *Scaramouche*, *The Scarlet Pimpernel*. "Glenda Jackson!" he said suddenly, very pleased with himself.

"What?"

"Glenda Jackson. The 1967 film *Marat/Sade*; Glenda Jackson played Charlotte Corday."

"And?" She had her arms folded again.

"And that's it really."

"Charlotte Corday was a figure in the Revolution, a very famous figure. Or infamous, depending on your point of view. She was guillotined for the assassination of Jean-Paul Marat, who was responsible for many deaths in The Terror. He was an evil man."

"So she was a good assassin, then?"

"Alphonse de Lamartine called her *l'ange de l'assassinat*, the angel of assassination. It's in the blood."

"Corday, d'Orçay. Right, I get it. Things don't necessarily follow, though; my great-great-grandad was a nob thatcher."

"A what?"

"A nob thatcher. He made wigs."

She gave him a look to suggest that he was rambling, "What are you talking about?"

"I don't know," he said with remarkable certainty. "Look, I don't think you killed Grandchamps. If you did you'd have proof, as you said, be two million euros richer, and not hanging around here with me and my hens. And I really don't know what all this is about, not really. But, I haven't enjoyed myself this much in years." He ran out of steam and looked a little dejected. "And some bastard killed Ava Gardner."

She put her hand on his arm and it felt electric. "You really haven't had this much fun in years? Really?"

"Yes," he said simply, "in a way you've saved me; you are my Clarence." She shook her head in confusion. "He was the angel in *It's a Wonderful Life*. James Stewart. *It's a Wonderful*...never mind."

"Shall I look him up?" She produced her phone from her pocket. "Will it be on IMDB dot com?"

He screwed his eyes up. "If you use IMDB dot com in my presence, Madame d'Orçay, you really will have a murder on your hands..."

29

Wearily pulling back the white sheet, Brigadier-Chef Principal Philippe Bonneval wondered how many times he had done this very action and always to reveal a faceless corpse. Maybe he would qualify for the *Guinness Book of World Records* and finally get the recognition he felt was his due. It was a sight that never got any easier, though, no matter how often you had to do it, and he made sure he had an eye on the well-dressed elderly woman standing on the other side of the tray.

Madame Paulin was a proud woman and carried herself that way. She had an idea what to expect, had maybe even been expecting it for a number of years, her estranged husband being what he was. But the way she gripped the handle tighter, her knuckles losing all sign of wrinkle or color, told its own story. It was a horrific sight. She looked at Bonneval and her face was almost apologetic; what was in front of her wasn't enough to give a definitive answer.

"Are there any distinguishing marks, madame? Anything else that could identify this person as your husband?"

"Ex-husband," she replied automatically, "yes. He had his army number tattooed on his wrist under his watch. Though he pawned his watch years ago."

"Right or left hand?" Bonneval asked, knowing the answer.

"Left, monsieur."

"Ah, in that case, are there any other marks that might identify him?" She looked at him in confusion. "I'm afraid to say that your husband's left hand has gone missing." He immediately regretted his choice of words. "That is to say..."

"Someone chopped off his left hand?"

"Yes," he said, then added inadequately, "I'm sorry." Nothing seemed to surprise Madame Paulin about her ex-husband and she had a look on her face that suggested the old soak had lost his hand in a card game or had pawned it with the watch. "Anything, madame? A birthmark, a scar?"

Her eyes dropped and she slowly walked around the tray to stand closer to Bonneval. It was clear she wanted to whisper something in his ear, and he bent down to accommodate her even though they were alone in the cold room.

"Really? But why? How would that happen?" he asked automatically in response to her quiet words.

"He regarded it as an act of self-harm," she said, shaking her head. "The same kind of 'self-harm' that I had done to myself." She continued to shake her head.

"You had a breast reduction, madame." He'd been trained to be noncommittal in these situations.

"For medical reasons, yes. He went quite out of his mind, you know. Anyway, there you have it."

Bonneval pulled the white sheet down farther, past the dead man's groin.

"Yes," she whispered, "that's the stupid old sod, all right," and turned away toward the door.

Next door in the waiting room, Madame Tablier sat with Richard and Valérie. Richard was stirring a tasteless, gray cup of coffee.

"I didn't know you rode a motorbike, madame." Valérie was obviously amused by the image of Madame Tablier astride a powerful, high-caliber motorbike.

"No reason why you should," was the frosty reply she got, then she softened as she addressed Richard. "I'm grateful for the lift, monsieur; it didn't seem right to bring Estelle, Madame Paulin, here on the back of my bike."

"Not at all," said Richard, "think nothing of it."

"Have you always ridden motorbikes, Madame Tablier?"

Madame Tablier was just about to respond when the door to the waiting room opened and Madame Paulin walked in quickly. "Yes, it's him, no doubt about it. No face, no left hand, but it's definitely him." Her matter-of-fact manner took them all by surprise, even the normally unflappable Madame Tablier. Madame Paulin sniffed, her one concession to public grief, and repeated herself. "Silly old sod," she said.

Bonneval came in quietly and closed the door behind him. "Thank you, Madame Paulin. I have some papers that I need you to sign before you go." He produced a briefcase and took out a sheaf of papers.

"To find one faceless corpse with its left hand missing"—Richard for some reason felt the situation needed levity—"could be regarded as a misfortune, to find two..." He stopped himself. "Sorry."

"There is just the one corpse, monsieur."

Richard and Valérie turned to look at each other.

"I don't understand, monsieur." Valérie understood very well. "Are you saying that Monsieur Grandchamps is not dead?"

"No, madame." Bonneval heaved his bulk onto a small chair while fishing for more documents. "I am not saying that at all."

Richard, Valérie and Madame Tablier all exchanged glances.

"What *are* you saying then?" Richard knew he was the only one amongst the three of them who would publicly admit to not knowing what was going on.

Bonneval exhaled deeply. "Monsieur Grandchamps may very well be dead, monsieur, that is what I'm saying. But what I am also saying is that the deceased in there"—he nodded to Madame Paulin—"is Monsieur Charles Paulin. Madame Paulin was in—ahem—in no doubt on the matter."

"Blimey," Richard said, aware that being constantly surrounded by French people was actually making him more English by the minute.

"There are quite a number of forms to fill in, madame," Bonneval addressed Madame Paulin apologetically. "Can I suggest we go somewhere more convivial? Bruno's, perhaps?"

"I am grateful, monsieur, thank you."

"I thought Bruno's was closed on a Monday lunchtime?" Valérie distinctly remembered Marie's words the night before.

"Usually, yes, madame, but I suspected that this might be a difficult morning and asked him to open just this once on a Monday."

"That's very good of you, and him."

"It certainly is." Richard stood up, rubbing his hands together. "I'm parched."

They trudged into the center of town looking like a bizarre tour group. Bonneval led the way, striding purposefully and then every so often stopping to let the others catch up with him. He had a worried look on his face. He didn't understand how the old judge could have misidentified his own brother, for a start.

Madame Tablier walked solidly besides the much taller Madame Paulin; together they were a force to be reckoned with and both wore an expression that said that the world was indeed a terrible place, and that yes, they'd bloody told you so a million times, but would you have it?

Richard, Valérie and Passepartout dawdled at the back of the group, with Richard and Valérie whispering conspiratorially.

"I really thought there were two bodies, you know?" Valérie shook her head.

"This is France; they've probably recycled."

"Richard, this is not the time for jokes." She stopped walking. "I suppose Madame Paulin couldn't be mistaken?"

"I doubt it. I don't think Madame Paulin, like Madame Tablier, has ever been mistaken about anything. Bonneval was fairly tight-lipped on the proof but no, I think it's Paulin, all right. I don't know where that leaves us, though?"

"Well, it leaves us still in the game, Richard." She was very serious.

"The game? I'm not sure I'd call it a game."

"Whatever it is," she said hurriedly, "whoever took the hand thought they were taking proof of Monsieur Grandchamps's death. But that is not so, so..."

"So the two million is still up for grabs, then, is what you mean."

"Exactly right. We need to find that corpse."

"If it is a corpse." They walked on a few meters in silence, before Richard stopped and was given a "now what?" look by Passepartout. "I mean it; what if he's not dead? Then what do we do?"

Valérie stopped, too, but without turning around said, "We can cross that bridge when we come to it." Then she carried on, leaving Richard wondering what on earth that meant.

A tired-looking Bruno was opening up the parasols on the *terrasse* when they arrived, yawning as he did so. Bonneval took Madame Paulin inside to conclude the filling in of forms while Madame Tablier sat at a table looking uncomfortable. She wasn't used to being waited on, and it clearly didn't fit well with her and where she saw herself in the great scheme of things. Richard and Valérie joined them and a surly Bruno took their order, with Richard careful to underline that he just wanted a beer, nothing local, just a beer.

"I don't like it," Madame Tablier growled.

"I admit it's very confusing," Valérie confessed.

"I mean, the man was an idiot, a solid gold idiot, but why kill him?"

"I would guess that whoever did kill him thought he was Monsieur Grandchamps. They were roughly the same age; he might even have been wearing some of his clothes."

"They might still think that, of course," Richard said after Bruno had delivered their drinks and moved away from the table. "It's also entirely possible that they would be believed, too. The mafia, or whoever adjudicates on these things, might make the same mistakes as Bonneval here."

"It was the judge who made the mistake and I don't see how that could happen."

"Well, he might have seen a number on the dead man's wrist and just assumed the worst. By all accounts he was pretty cut up. I wonder how he'll take this news?"

"That his brother is alive? Yes, I wonder. Someone must tell him."

Richard leaned back in his chair and closed his eyes for a moment, soaking up some of the sun. *Excitement is very tiring*, he thought, *really quite draining*. Suddenly he felt a hand grip his arm as Valérie sank her nails in.

"Ow! What are you doing?" he wailed.

"Look," she hissed, nodding toward the door of the brasserie, "look who it is!"

Richard turned his head, as did Madame Tablier, just as the Rizzolis walked into the sunlight. Signora Rizzoli put her large sunglasses on with a flourish, posing as if a photographer were there to capture the moment. Signor Rizzoli wore a panama hat, which he adjusted with equal aplomb.

"Well, I'll be..." Richard began and then found himself lost for words.

"It's the bloody Italians," Madame Tablier said without bothering to lower her voice.

The Rizzolis saw the group at their table and smiled, a hideous false bonhomie that gave Richard the shivers, more so when the couple walked toward them. As they got to the table they stopped briefly, and Signor Rizzoli bowed theatrically and removed his hat. "*Buon giorno*," he said, giving the phrase a menace that did nothing for Richard's shivers. He might have left it at that, but as he bent his arm as an invitation for his wife to hook it with her own, he said, very deliberately, and in English, "Until-a next-a time!" And with that they strode off in perfect synchronization.

"He's got some bloody nerve!" Richard said, not able to hide how impressed he was.

Madame Tablier snarled while Valérie watched them coolly as they disappeared around the corner. "How very interesting," she said.

"Well, that's an understatement. Why do you suppose they're here? Not a coincidence, surely?"

"Oh no, Richard, not a coincidence at all. They must know."

"Know?"

"That our body is not that of Monsieur Grandchamps."

"Well, they move quickly; we only found out ourselves ten minutes ago."

"I would say"—Valérie took a sip of her drink—"that they already knew."

Richard took a gulp of his own drink. "Bloody hell," he said, more to himself than for any effect, "bloody hell."

30

Richard spat a feather out of his mouth and with difficulty shook his head. He was, he realized belatedly, in something of a state of shock. He had found Valérie in a pensive mood the evening of the encounter with the Rizzolis, and he could see that she was fuming, sitting in the garden and holding a bottle of water, Passepartout inevitably by her side. He wasn't sure what kind of demarcation lines exist in the bounty hunter industry, but clearly there were some etiquette issues that the young upstart Rizzolis had trampled on, and Valérie looked like a wounded beast, and therefore dangerous.

"You've been quiet all day," he ventured tentatively. "Anything I can do?" It was a question he would come to regret.

"They're always one step ahead of us," she replied with a venom that suggested she wasn't going to take that anymore. "Now, obviously, they have a direct line to Sicily, I understand that."

"They certainly knew about the Grandchamps debacle pretty sharpish."

"Yes." She nodded. "That's because whoever took the hand, the hand we now know was Monsieur Paulin's, went to have it confirmed and found that it wasn't the right hand."

"The left hand, you mean?"

She gave him a look which said pretty clearly, once again, that this wasn't the time for jokes. "The correct hand."

Admonished, he fell silent, letting her stew on the problem before the heavy silence eventually became too much. "So, what are we going to do, then?"

She nodded her head again slowly, the decision made. "We need to take the Rizzolis out of the equation altogether. Even temporarily would do."

This was very much at odds with Richard's "may as well leave them to it" approach and his first sense was danger. "Well, that shouldn't be too difficult; I mean they're only mafia killers. It should be a cinch."

Valérie ignored the sarcasm, making him feel, once again, that he was either going to have to up his sarcasm game or knock it on the head altogether.

"We will set a trap."

Richard's heart sank. Excitement and living life were one thing, but he had a horrible feeling that this kind of talk could lead to it also being cruelly short-lived.

"A trap?" he said wearily.

"Yes, a trap. We need to talk to Melvil. Those two owe us a favor anyway, I think."

It seemed quite a big ask in Richard's opinion though.

"Absolutely not!" Marie said categorically when Valérie outlined her scheme to the young couple. "You are not using my Melvil as bait for killers, no. It's too dangerous." As usual Melvil had looked slightly detached from proceedings and said nothing.

"I see." Valérie knew stubborn French femininity when she saw it and began to think of a way round the Melvil issue. "Supposing then," she began slowly, "that Melvil is just the start and we take over long before any danger can arise?" She sensed that Marie was wavering. "All he needs to do is give an envelope to the postman and get a train to work; once he's at work we can take it from there, can't we, Richard?"

"Eh, what? Oh, probably."

"He will have to do nothing else? Just that."

"I promise." Valérie beamed, a maternal smile thrown swiftly in Marie's direction, though not in Richard's eyes with cast-iron sincerity. Melvil had accepted his role with a chin-in-the-air superiority which, considering his girlfriend had just negotiated him down to a bit part, was overdoing it somewhat. Richard also pondered the question of just how few details of the plan were being given to him, and he was fairly certain he would be involved and not just as a spectator.

Valérie and Richard were waiting for Melvil in the Monsieur Oeuf "restaurant" in Tours. It was an egg emporium; everything egg-related was there, and you could have them fried, poached, scrambled, raw, sunny-side up, down or sideways, hard boiled, soft-boiled, or pickled. It was a bit one-paced for Richard's tastes, and he'd noticed Valérie look at the menu with something approaching disgust and then pity as the server behind the counter wore a chicken hat, and did so quite obviously against their will.

"Just a coffee, please," Valérie had said.

"Make that two," Richard added.

They sat on specially designed chairs that looked like broken shells and which offered a similar level of comfort, waiting for news. Valérie's phone pinged. "Ah, that's Marie. They have taken the bait. Melvil and the Rizzolis are on the train to Tours. So, thirty minutes, possibly."

"Right. Fancy an egg while we're waiting?" He immediately regretted his flippancy.

"Don't be silly, Richard."

Almost exactly thirty minutes later Melvil came in through the doors, managing to look both flustered and calm at the same time, hurrying past their table and, without looking at them, said, "Quickly, follow me!" They followed him through a side door next to the serving counter and into the staff changing room.

The backstage, as it were, of fast-food restaurants, in fact all restaurants, should never be seen by a layman. They are grim, untidy, desolate places that match their catering staff users for a lack of hope and happiness. Everything seems suddenly tawdry and gray away from the expensive lighting of the restaurant side. The staff room at Monsieur Oeuf was no different.

"OK, we haven't much time," Melvil said, adopting suddenly a higher rank in the affair. "This is my locker." And he turned to open the metallic door, revealing his man-size chicken outfit. Richard distinctly remembered feeling sorry for Melvil at that point; *the poor man*, he'd thought, *the ignominy of it all*.

"He's right." Valérie had an excited, almost maniacal look on her face.

"It might be a bit tight, but there's quite a lot of give in it," he said and thrust the outfit at Richard.

"What? No way! Absolutely no way. I'm not wearing that!"

"There is no choice, Richard."

"There is," he wailed.

"What, what is the choice?" And she folded her arms.

"You wear it!" he said petulantly.

"OK, I'll wear it then."

"Good." And he thrust the costume back at her.

"So when I've lured the Rizzolis into a dark alley, how are you going to disable them?"

It was a fair question. Clare would have suggested that he bore them into submission with details of early Academy Award winners, but beyond that he had no specific mafia-killer disabling skills and reluctantly he began to change.

"The important thing to remember..." Melvil adopted the tone of an auteur; suddenly he was a giant of avant-garde French cinema giving directorial instructions to a callow, young actor. "In fact, it's vital to remember that at all times, think chicken."

The irony of that statement was not lost on him and even Valérie, all but lost in her own world, couldn't hide the smirk.

"Think chicken. Right."

———

He'd now been thinking chicken for a good thirty minutes, and he was a little bored with it all. The Rizzolis were nowhere to be seen and so he was reduced to reluctantly handing out restaurant flyers, though most people had the good sense to give him a wide berth. *What a soul-destroying job for a grown man*, he thought, yet Melvil treated it as though he were embarking on *Hamlet* at the Old Vic. What was the last thing he'd said to him? "I'll tell you what the manager told me, 'Concentrate at all times, and don't get cocky, kid, no one knows who's in the bird suit!'" Presumably this was supposed to aid him in his chicken-ness, but Richard had felt like pecking the younger man to death.

He paused in his duties for a moment, trying not to focus on the absurdity of it all. He had an itch somewhere in his chicken leg tights and wanted to address the issue but wondered if he was allowed to break character to do so. Then the itch moved. It moved down his leg and into his foot, that annoying itch you get when you're driving sometimes and no amount of contortion can help you get to it. He flapped his big, rubber chicken feet hoping to shake the annoyance but it wouldn't, and he noticed, after flapping about for a few minutes, that he was drawing a crowd. Specifically a party of schoolchildren, who didn't look all that impressed.

One of the party approached him menacingly, a look of pure nine-year-old mischief on his face. His spiky hair had lightning strikes shaved into it, and Richard foresaw a life of crime awaited the kid. And he didn't like the look on his face either. The kid kept coming until eventually he was standing on Richard's rubber chicken feet, pinning him down. The only way Richard could move would be to flip the kid over and he didn't see that going down well on a busy shopping street. Other, more wary members of the school party approached, making Richard feel like King Kong on top of the Empire State Building, flailing around before the inevitable demise. One of the kids kicked his shin.

"Ow!" cried Richard. "You little sod." Then he got another kick, all the while unable to go anywhere as more of the little sods stood on his large feet. This went on for a few minutes before finally the teacher, a starched, middle-aged woman who Richard, with his vision impaired inside the chicken head, hadn't noticed until now, said something to the children, who backed down and retreated immediately.

"*Merci!*" Richard said, not only grateful but jealous of the woman's powers.

"You should be ashamed of yourself!" said the woman, leaving a stunned and bruised Richard to his work. He shook his head again, and spat out another feather. That's when he saw them, the Rizzolis, and they were coming his way. *Thank God*, he thought, never thinking he'd be happy to see a pair of trained killers heading in his direction.

At first he pretended not to see them, as per Valérie's instructions, and then as they got closer he was to pretend to be spooked—like a chicken presumably—and lead them around the back of Monsieur Oeuf, where Valérie would take over. It was all very simple. They fell for it, possibly thinking that a man dressed as a chicken couldn't remotely be a threat to the mafia, and followed him into the shadows of the back alleyway. Richard turned quickly as he reached the dead end, and he saw Valérie waiting in the darkness. His adrenaline racing, he was looking forward to getting another ringside seat as Valérie, with balletic aplomb and grace, dispatched the pair once more. It would be as close as Richard had come to an erotic interlude in some time.

The Rizzolis slowly walked toward him, evil smiles on both their faces, and he saw Valérie spring into action. Valérie, though, wasn't living up to her graceful martial arts billing and in a second the Rizzolis were once again lying on top of each other, out cold.

"You carry a club?!" He was incredulous. It felt oddly like cheating, though he couldn't for the life of him think why. Surely nothing should surprise him anymore.

"I didn't want to take any chances, Richard, they are probably armed."

A quick search proved Valérie's assumption correct, and she bound their wrists and ankles together with practiced ease and with heavy-duty duct tape.

"What now?" Richard asked, still not in possession of the plan's details. Valérie looked around her, clearly not having considered what to do at this point either, before she hit on an idea.

"Bring one of those wheelie bins over here." She pointed at a large catering-style recycling bin.

"That's handy," Richard said, "then what? We wheel them back to my place? That's thirty-five kilometers."

"We take them to your car, and put a blanket over them."

"Yes, but then what?" Richard felt slightly let down that there seemed to be a distinct lack of planning from this point onward. "Do you know of a local dungeon where we can keep them for a while?"

She looked at him, not in anger at yet another attempt at sarcasm, but this time in sincere admiration. "Oh, Richard!" she said. "That's a brilliant idea!"

31

Despite them being in Richard's car, it was Valérie who insisted on driving them back to Saint-Sauveur. Richard sat in the passenger seat, ostensibly keeping guard over the trussed-up Italian couple wedged unceremoniously into the back of his 2CV. There wasn't much room and Richard's seat was as far forward as possible, leaving his face practically in contact with the windscreen. On his feathered lap was a loaded Beretta Pico and a watchful Passepartout. Richard wasn't sure which of the two put him more on edge.

He cast a nervous glance at the speedometer. It really wouldn't do to be pulled over for speeding at this point. He could well imagine some policeman's delight if he could add assault and kidnapping to a minor traffic infringement, and presumably there was also a law against being dressed as a chicken on French A-roads.

"I'm not speeding, Richard," Valérie said testily and without taking her eyes off the road. Once again leaving him wondering just how she did that.

"Just checking," was the attempt at a masterful reply. "By the way," he ventured, "while I'm naturally pleased with my brilliance, erm...

what did I say exactly?" One of the bodies in the back started to stir and Valérie put her foot down.

"The dungeon," she said as if all the explanation needed was contained in those two words.

"Right-o." There was a moment's silence while Richard tried to put into words that brilliant though he was, he was also none the wiser. "You know of a dungeon, do you? In Saint-Sauveur?"

"Nearby, yes. In Faurent."

Richard's heart sank. "Martin and Gennie! Oh no, must we? I'm not sure I can look either of them in the eye again after the last time." The thought also briefly occurred to him that they might still be tied up in their front room, semi-naked, bulldog clips and all. He shivered at the thought.

"They have a dungeon, Martin told me."

"I'll bet he did. Filthy old goat."

"He was very keen to show me."

"I'll bet that, too. But what makes you think that they'll want the thing occupied by a couple of murderous Italians?"

"We'll ask nicely."

Again one of the couple in the back seat groaned, and Valérie once more sped up.

The gate to the driveway was open when they reached Martin and Gennie's place, and the car crunched on the gravel as Valérie guided it to the back of the house. Martin and Gennie emerged from the kitchen, thankfully dressed.

"Hullo," Martin hailed enthusiastically.

"What a nice surprise," Gennie added.

Valérie opened the car door and, before stepping out, said, "We'd like to ask a favor."

"Ask away," Martin replied, practically dribbling at the possibilities sloshing around his dirty mind.

"Your dungeon?"

"Oh yes!" squealed Gennie.

"We'd like to borrow it."

There was a moment's silence.

"Borrow it, how do you mean?" Martin's eyes narrowed as the thought occurred to him that there was fun about to be had and he might not be included in it.

He looked across at Richard in the passenger seat and Richard raised a wing in reluctant greeting. Then he noticed the Rizzolis, bound and gagged on the back seat and beginning to come to.

Valérie noticed them, too. "We haven't much time," she said. "Can we use your dungeon, yes or no?"

"Yes, I suppose so." Martin looked at Gennie for confirmation, who nodded busily.

Richard emerged from the car, a five-foot-ten-inch chicken holding a gun and a chihuahua. "I know," he said wearily as Martin and Gennie stood, mouths agape, "but there really isn't the time to explain right now. Could you give us a hand?" Valérie gave the two stirring Italians another quick cuff with her cosh, which did nothing for Martin and Gennie's nerves, or Richard's.

"Sorry," he said, as if he'd just spilled coffee on a rug.

"I'll go and get the wheelbarrow." A nervous Martin wandered off, shaking his head as he did so.

It was some awkward time later that Gennie helped Valérie lock the last fur-covered handcuff to Signora Rizzoli, securing her to an iron ring on the wall. Her husband hung limply, chained as he was to two other rings hanging from the ceiling.

"Do you expect them to talk?" asked Martin.

"No, I expect them to die!" Richard said loudly, his nerves expressing themselves as only Richard knew how.

"Eh?" Martin looked startled. "Oh. Very good. *From Russia with Love?*"

"*Goldfinger.*"

"Right. I always get those two mixed up."

Richard shook his head in disgust.

Gennie stood up, pleased with her work. "OK," she said happily, "who'd like a cup of tea? Martin, you can give me a hand, please." And she guided her husband reluctantly out of the dungeon.

Richard had a look around the surprisingly well-lit room, while Valérie began to search their prisoners more thoroughly. It looked more like a workshop than a place of erotica; everything looked very functional and was arranged neatly like a pedant's tool shed. There was a large cross in the corner, like a large letter X, in beautiful, varnished mahogany and with a padded leather cushion in the middle. He shook his head. He knew he was old-fashioned, probably terminally unadventurous, too, but this was about as far from being his thing as it could be. And not for the first time, he just could not imagine Martin and Gennie using the stark equipment on display. The whips, the chains, the masks...it was all utterly beyond him. He tried to gather his thoughts and sat heavily on a wooden and red leather throne. It was more like a commode and had had part of the seat cut away. It left him utterly baffled.

His phone rang and he absentmindedly accepted the incoming video call, then practically screamed as the face of his daughter appeared on his screen.

"Alicia!"

"Daddy!"

"I'm a bit busy at the moment, darling." He sat up quickly and banged his head on some chains attached to the high back of the chair. He stood hurriedly before Alicia saw them. He immediately regretted the move.

"Daddy, what are you wearing?"

"Oh, ah, let me explain." And he spun round to take the chair away from the background, inadvertently revealing Valérie with her hand in the trouser pocket of a dangling Signor Rizzoli as he did so. He spun round again and Signora Rizzoli lay splayed on the floor, both arms attached to the wall.

"Oh, Daddy." Alicia's eyes darted all over the place, as though she were hallucinating. Then they focused solely on Richard. "What on earth has got into you lately?"

"Oh, darling. It's, erm, it's amateur dramatics. It's a play, *Chicken and Dungeons*, it's called. Marquis de Sade, unfinished work. I play..."

"I have a degree in French Literature." She looked awfully like her mother, Richard thought. "And that's pathetic." She sounded more and more like her, too.

The phone went dead and Richard stared at the thing, hoping that it might provide some explanation for just how crazy his life had become. How utterly out of control it was. He'd always quite fancied the idea of having a roguish reputation, but he had gone from naught to sixty, as it were, with lightning speed. His wife assumed he was having an affair, Martin and Gennie probably thought he was a murderous villain, and now his daughter, his only child, clearly was under the impression that he was a pervert with a chicken fetish. He whimpered at the silent phone.

"Ah-ha!" Valérie cried, her intimate search having produced the goods. "Door keys!" She held up a bunch of keys, a mixture of modern Yale and old-fashioned, large-size Chubbs. "And I have a very good idea where they are for." Richard said nothing and she shook the keys at him. "Are you feeling OK, Richard? You are very quiet."

He whimpered again. "I'd like to go home and get changed, please."

"Yes," she answered as if it were an odd request, "yes, of course. Anyway, you can't go dressed like that where we are going." Richard had no idea what or where she was talking about, and he shuffled passively to the mirrored door.

Martin and Gennie were waiting on the other side with Gennie holding a large wooden tray containing a fine china teapot and six delicate cups. The incongruity between the two rooms was almost too much for Richard and he whimpered again. Why hadn't Gennie's mise-en-scène been his background when Alicia called?

"Oh, are you going?" Gennie asked.

Valérie nodded. "Yes, Richard needs to change his clothes."

"I left my trousers at Monsieur Oeuf," he said blankly, unable to take his eyes off the shining innocence of the tea set.

"We've all been there, old fruit!" Martin received a sharp look from Gennie for his frivolity.

"What do we do with the erm, you know? The prisoners." She whispered the last word as if it might wake the Rizzolis up.

"Well, don't let them go." Valérie made a move for the back door. "They are dangerous. Feed them if they ask for food. I mean certainly don't let them starve, but don't release them. For your own sakes, don't release them."

Martin and Gennie looked at each other nervously, and Gennie backed away from the door while Martin closed it. "They've probably eaten anyway," Gennie said, "you know what these Italians are like..."

32

⊷

"Richard, you must keep up!" Valérie hissed at him through the darkness. He could just about make out her figure a few yards in front, though he tried not to concentrate on that.

"Sorry," he replied petulantly, "it's three days since I last did some breaking and entering, I must be out of practice." He heard her tut back at him. He was self-aware enough to know that he had gotten through life thus far without a great deal of poise, and if self-awareness hadn't been there, Clare had filled in any gaps. But he was about as far from poise now as it was possible for a sentient human being to be. He was tired, tiredness meant clumsiness and Valérie was to clumsiness what Richard was to poise and vice versa.

He had simply had the stuffing knocked out of him. That was all. There was no other explanation. It's not every day that a man on the cusp of divorce is caught by his, admittedly rather precious, daughter, dressed as a chicken in a sadomasochist dungeon trussing up a pair of mafia assassins. It was not, Clare's voice rang through his head, "Richard-type behavior."

It was Clare who had rung him late in the afternoon. "I've just had a rather disturbing conversation with Alicia," she had said, unable to hide the wide smile that was no doubt on her face. Richard, as was going to be his way from now on, had declined the invitation for a video call. "Richard, are you sure you know what you're getting into?"

The question came not with a wife's concern but a mother's. It was the maternal instinct in Clare, always strong anyway, but a clear sign of where their relationship now was. "I mean, do you even know anything about this Valérie?" Disappointingly, there wasn't the slightest hint of jealousy.

"Other than she's a hired killer, very little to be honest," he'd replied and Clare had laughed.

"Well, at least you still have your sense of humor." The word "your" grated.

He suddenly became aware that Valérie was right in front of him and looking up at him. She turned the torch on and shone it in his face. "This is no time for your jokes, Richard," she said menacingly, letting Richard know in no uncertain terms that he had abandoned one frying pan just for another frying pan.

Clare's last words had been, "At least you're enjoying yourself, Richard, that's the main thing." It was possibly the most patronizing thing that had ever been said to him, and what made it win out against some pretty heavy competition was the sound of a champagne cork being pulled in the background. He imagined an outrageously good-looking Latin lover in a monogrammed silk dressing gown, probably a racing driver, they usually were, and with the horsepower to boot. He wished he'd accepted the video call.

"Now, please concentrate, Richard." Valérie snapped him back into the here and now. "I really think lives depend on it."

"Yes, sorry. Whose lives?"

"Ours. Now follow me." It was not the answer he had been looking for.

They were in Vauchelles and had approached the small town from the opposite direction. They had parked Valérie's car some distance away and were now on the Jules Ferry Street, walking stealthily in the shadows toward the two imposing, very dark houses. It was two in the morning and the whole place was pitch black.

"How are we going to know where to go?" Richard asked, his mind now focused on the prospect of death.

"I am just guessing," Valérie said in a soft, barely audible voice, "but these old houses always have a back gate built into the wall. The male owners always insisted on it."

"What for?" he asked, and then realizing how slow he was being, just said, "Ah. I see."

They moved along the cold, high wall silently until they reached the back of the house, then Valérie suddenly grabbed his arm. "Richard, look!" She pointed at a very rusty, gray double gate built into the wall. A heavy-duty chain joined the two halves of the gate together, bound by an enormous padlock.

"I don't think that's been used in a while," he said disappointedly. "I'm not sure the keys will get it open."

She delved into her bag and produced the keys that she had wrapped in a paper towel to stop them jangling. It was obvious which key fitted the padlock and she turned it slowly; the padlock opened immediately, loosening the chain.

"I would say that it has been used quite recently." Her voice was still impossibly soft, but he noticed her accent was now thicker, something that came with the excitement, maybe. She unwrapped the heavy chain and laid it silently on the ground while Richard slowly turned the handle and pushed at the gate. He expected the thing to resist and squeak loudly but neither happened. He couldn't tell in this light but maybe it had been dressed to look old and unused.

Having learned his mistake last time, he followed Valérie closely around the inside wall. They assumed that the electricity would be turned off but it wasn't worth the risk of setting off the security lights, or even alarms. Once at the back door, Valérie took a look at the lock and immediately chose the right key from the set they'd taken from the Rizzolis. She pushed the door solidly and it swung open silently on smooth hinges. No alarm sounded and she stepped in gingerly; suddenly a cat jumped at her, nearly knocking her over in surprise before bolting out of the door through Richard's legs.

"That poor thing must be starving!" Richard said, a little too loudly.

"I don't like cats," a panting Valérie hissed back, "but it is good news."

"Good news? Was it a black cat?"

"No alarms, Richard, no alarms."

"Ah, yes."

Valérie turned her torch on and sprayed some light into the room.

"Is that wise?" Richard asked, slightly spooked by the cat himself.

"We have to take the risk, I think." Valérie was concentrating more on her surroundings. "We are at the back of the house and there are heavy shutters at the front." She opened a kitchen drawer. "We won't be able to find anything in the dark. That is for sure."

"What are we looking for?" Richard had brought a torch of his own and fired it up.

"I don't know." Valérie moved deeper into the room. "Something."

"Good. Well as long as we've got a plan, then."

She didn't deign to give a response and Richard wondered if Great Britain's position in the world had weakened around the same time as the decline of sarcasm. Sarcasm feels very British, but nobody else seemed to enjoy it at all. He winced as Valérie's torch shone on his face again and he realized he was just leaning on a large dresser, daydreaming.

"Are you going to do anything?" she asked, not unreasonably.

"Yes, of course, sorry." He shone his own torch around the kitchen and found it all rather surprising. It was so very modern. Not just the cupboards, which were all very stylish, with polished chrome handles and soft-closing hinges, but there was a large, central island with a marble top. Above it were chrome lights which matched the inset chrome sink and the tap with its black, extendable spiral hose. It was expensive, as were the appliances, the double oven, the latest coffee-making machine. Having briefly met the stooped and aged Monsieur Grandchamps, this was not the kitchen he would have expected.

The main living room was the same. Polished floors, leather and chrome sofas, and an enormous television screwed into the wall above the fireplace, which had a basket of lavender in the grate. There were some modern touches in the dining room, but not to the extent of the other rooms. It was the same upstairs. The main bedroom was very modern, but the others smelled a bit musty. One of the bathrooms looked like something from a billionaire's New York penthouse, the other from an abandoned farmhouse.

Richard sat on the stairs. He didn't know what they were looking for and therefore hadn't found it. Valérie joined him, clearly frustrated, but saying nothing.

"This is a very odd place, don't you think? It's like two different houses in one, some of it gleaming new, some of it as old as the place itself." He shone his torch on a light switch on the wall. It was modern, and the replastering around it didn't look that old either. "I think Monsieur Grandchamps was slowly having the place renovated, that's what it looks like."

Valérie sensed he was on to something. "To sell, you mean?"

"No, no it doesn't feel like that. If you were going to sell an old place like this, you'd get more if the original features were in it. Tarted up, obviously, but—what do they call it? 'Sympathetic to the period,' that's it, sympathetic to the period."

"It is spotless, too; Marie still comes in very regularly, that is clear."

"Yes, hoping he's come back or looking for more money, though?"

"I don't know. I would like to think it is that he might have come back."

"Yes, I know what you mean." They both fell silent again. "She does seem genuinely frightened to me, though. I know I'm an old romantic, and probably always hoping for the happy ending, but I think she wants him to come back. Maybe he's like a father figure to her, and she needs that. Apart from Melvil, she's very much alone."

Valérie flicked her torch on again and straight into Richard's eyes.

"Will you stop doing that! I'll be blind by the morning at this rate."

"But Richard! You have done it again. You really are brilliant at times!"

In truth he rather liked the idea of being a blundering genius, a sort of idiot savant but with less of the idiot, but once again he had no idea of what he had said. Worst of all, every time Valérie said he was brilliant, he had no idea why. He'd like to be deliberately brilliant for once; that would make him feel a whole lot better.

"OK," he said slowly, "explain it back to me so I know we both know what I'm talking about."

"A father figure. Monsieur Grandchamps is her father. It also explains this place, I think. It is being renovated for Marie."

"Really? I'd say the style was quite masculine, though."

"It is modern and expensive and youthful. It is for the two of them. Melvil's touch, I should say."

Richard nodded. "It would explain an awful lot, that's true." He shone his own torch around the hall again and stood up from the stairs. "Come on," he said, "let's not push our luck. We should go."

He stood up and as he did so he felt a cramp in his left leg. Instinctively he grabbed the back of his thigh with his free hand but felt himself slipping down the bottom few stairs. He let go of his leg and threw out his arm to grab hold of something to stop the fall; his hand wrapped itself around one of the staircase balustrades, but instead of steadying him it started to give way. It steadied him nonetheless, and on righting himself he could feel Valérie's disapproving stare on the back of his neck. Rather than turn around and face her, he pushed the balustrade back into place, and as he did so a panel door under the stairs swung outward.

Like the kitchen cupboards, the door was on soft hinges and silent as it swung open to reveal a narrow wooden staircase. They both looked at each other, with Richard trying to show that it had all been deliberate. He reached inside for a light switch, found one and turned it on. Somewhere below a light came on and Valérie darted down the rickety steps. Richard followed more cautiously.

They both stood under a bare light bulb in a cold, damp cellar, looking upon rack after rack of wine. Richard picked up a bottle and looked at the label. "I'm no great expert but even I've heard of Domaine Leroy. If they're all like this, this lot would be worth a fortune."

"Yes, but how do you know they are the real thing?"

"Good point. But you could say that about any wine. Hence the ease of Grandchamps's scam, I suppose." He walked around some of the racks, nearly tripping over a wire trailed over the cold, damp tiles. It was then he heard the low humming noise. "Can you hear that?" he whispered, suddenly aware of how vulnerable they were underground.

"Yes, I think it's rats."

For the first time he heard the shuffling sound, too.

"Well, if it's rats, you should have brought your ex-husband along." She ignored him. "No, there's another sound." He followed the wire to a corner where a large chiller stood, gently throbbing away.

"What have you found?" She arrived at his shoulder. The chiller was immense.

"It looks like an ordinary wine chiller," he said, needlessly pointing at the thing, which had a blanket draped over it, "but it's giving off a lot of heat. It's almost like it's working too hard."

Behind them the shuffling got louder, echoing off the walls. Valérie looked at Richard and suddenly pulled at the blanket, which dropped heavily to the floor. The chiller had a large glass-paneled door and there, sitting on a stool, a terrible grin on his face, was Vincent Grandchamps, an icicle hanging ignominiously off his frozen face, his beard frosted.

"So you've found him then. I must say it's about time." They both spun round just as a glint from the light bulb bounced back off the barrel of a small pistol and a voice from the shadows chuckled. Victor Grandchamps stepped forward. "Come on, you two, follow me." And with his gun he pointed to another door in a narrow recess. "Ladies first."

33

They moved slowly along the dank underground passage. Richard and Valérie shone their torches and tried to avoid banging their heads, while the judge held a gun and struggled to keep up. Richard had never been held at gunpoint before, but he felt pretty sure he wasn't supposed to keep stopping and waiting for his assailant to keep up. Eventually after thirty meters or so, they reached some stairs, the same kind they had come down, back at the other Grandchamps house.

An out-of-breath judge indicated for them to go up and they found themselves in the judge's dimly lit, imposing hallway. Valérie offered her hand to help the judge up the last few steps, which he took gratefully before ungratefully repointing the gun at them both when they were all in the hallway together.

"Into the study," he snapped, though without the usual authority in his voice. He sounded weak from the exertion. Once in the study he fell into his wheelchair, spent. For a few moments he gathered himself, closing his eyes and trying to regulate his breathing.

"Can I get you anything?" Richard asked. He was beginning to feel a little hard done by with his first gunpoint encounter.

"No. No, thank you." He opened his eyes again, and seemed a little startled by the gun in his hand. "I really don't need this at all," he said quietly, "I'm sorry." He put the gun down on the table. "I knew someone would come eventually, but I couldn't be sure who, friend or foe. As it's you…"

Richard had to stop himself from showing the indignation he felt. Not only had they had to help their would-be attacker in his frankly lackluster pursuit of them, but now Richard was considered so nonthreatening that the wheelchair-bound menace had put down his gun.

"Then I shall do the same, monsieur *le juge*," Valérie said gently and laid the ubiquitous Beretta next to the judge's gun.

"I knew I was right to trust you; I am still a very good judge of character," he said with a sense of superiority.

"How did you know we were there?" Richard put his torch next to the two guns, hopefully implying that unarmed combat was more his line.

The old man chuckled. "Ha! I rigged up a bell to the door over there. The door under the stairs. Very simple, very effective."

"And you were expecting us?" asked Valérie.

"I was expecting someone. It could have been any one of you, though; you've all been looking for him. I doubt you are the first to look there. You are the first to find the tunnel, though. Well done."

"That was me," Richard said, but was ignored.

"I didn't do it, you know," the judge said hurriedly, "I didn't kill him!" He caught his breath once more; he was obviously exhausted. "If you want to help yourself to a drink, do so. I'll have a whisky."

"So will I," said Richard, thinking that was more like it. "Valérie?"

"No, thank you."

"I found him like that. In the tunnel down there. Thank you," he said, as Richard handed him a tumbler of whisky. "A good portion, as it should be."

"And he was dead when you found him?"

"As good as. Heart attack; he'd been ill for a while so it wasn't unexpected. Luckily, he had it downstairs and I managed to get him into that chiller. I rigged that up," he added proudly. "It's not too difficult to change an ordinary refrigerator into a freezer, just a case of connecting a new thermostat to the compressor and the relay."

"But why?" Valérie asked, leaving Richard feeling grateful that he wasn't the only one who hadn't the foggiest idea of what was going on.

"Ah." The old man swilled the whisky in the glass, took a sip, smacked his lips in appreciation and then said triumphantly, "It was all part of the plan." He closed his eyes and for a moment Richard thought he might have dozed off, or worse. "Sorry," he said, suddenly opening his eyes, "I'm very tired."

"You were about to tell us the plan," Valérie prompted.

He smiled. "The plan was very simple." He looked slowly from one to the other. "The plan was to provide for Marie. My brother's death was earlier than expected, though; we weren't ready yet."

"Ready for what?" Richard asked.

"Ready to give it all up."

"Give what up?" He was now getting exasperated. Every answer seemed so deliberately vague and required more questions. It was like trying to do a cryptic crossword, and Richard couldn't abide cryptic crosswords.

"You worked with your brother?" Valérie asked quietly, as if a slow realization was taking hold.

"That's right, my dear," he chuckled. "The public face of my brother and I was of bitter enemies. I was implacably opposed to his illegal activities, and he despised the rule of law."

"Why? I mean, why bother?"

"That was his idea, too. 'They are dangerous people,' he said, 'why should we both be at risk if something goes wrong? Nobody retires from the mafia,' he used to say, 'the only way you leave is in a box.' So, although there were two of us, our Italian colleagues only ever saw one. 'Two brains, one face,' he used to say."

"And you had that tunnel constructed to meet in secret. That's quite a job." Richard was genuinely impressed. "How did you keep that quiet?"

"The lads from the travelers' camp. Hard workers, will do anything for money and"—he wagged his finger—"won't tell a soul as long as you're straight with them."

They sat silently for a few minutes, before Richard got up to pace around, trying to fit the pieces together. "I still don't get where Marie comes in," he said.

"You were both besotted by her." Valérie nodded in certainty.

"Besotted? Yes, though not in the way you mean, I think. We both loved her; I still do. I'm sure my brother still does, from wherever he is watching." And he raised his eyes to the heavens, which Richard thought was a touch theatrical considering he was underneath them in a converted wine chiller. "He thought he was Marie's father," the judge added simply.

Valérie pounced on the ambiguity. "Only thought?"

"Oh yes, thought. He wasn't her father at all, but it fitted our plans, so to speak."

"Because you are Marie's father, but your role meant that you couldn't show it."

"Precisely. You are a very smart woman." He smiled again and closed his eyes. "Her mother ran a guest house in town. She was like nature itself. Capable of both healing and destruction, of love and of spite. There was never a freer spirit in the world, and she would do anything to protect her daughter. As did we."

"Erm..." Richard was looking for the tactful way to ask the obvious. "What makes you so sure that you're Marie's father?"

The old man looked into the distance, misty-eyed. "Because she told me," he said simply. Richard and Valérie looked at each other dubiously.

"Marie told you?"

"No! Her mother, Antoinette, *she* told me. And Marie must *never* know! She made me promise that. And I know that she made my brother promise the same. She must never know!"

Standing behind Monsieur Grandchamps, Richard threw Valérie a look which in no doubt suggested that the old man may quite possibly be delusional. Valérie made no obvious movement, but her agreement was still clear.

"So the plan was to let Marie think that she was making money for herself, and not that your brother had left her anything."

Grandchamps nodded slowly. "I know what you are thinking, madame, that we are two old men, besotted, you say, by youth and beauty."

"Yes," Valérie said starkly, "yes, I do think that."

He chuckled again. "Perhaps. I left half a dozen or so envelopes for Marie. I knew that her loyalty to my brother, her curiosity, would mean that she would post them and, in return, the money would arrive for her in the usual way, bottles of wine filled with fifty-euro notes." His face darkened suddenly. "Her beauty and her curiosity were all inherited from Antoinette. Along with her greed."

"You hadn't banked on her making more envelopes for herself and sending them off?"

"Precisely, monsieur. She has enough money now to be

comfortable, and the house is in her name; my brother told her it was a tax scam. But, like her mother, she wanted more. And when Bonneval mentioned there were some unsavory people in town, Italians, and not relatives of Bruno..."

Richard and Valérie looked at each other again and Richard mouthed "Bruno?" at her.

"...I knew I had to stop it somehow. I had to stop her getting in too deep."

"Your dead brother had to die, you mean?" Valérie stood now and took a sip from Richard's whisky. The old man nodded. "But first you had to bring him back to life, so that Marie wouldn't be suspected."

He smiled at her, clearly impressed again with her intuition. "But someone else had the same idea. Someone else was pretending to be my brother at the same time as I was!" He seemed outraged by the notion.

"Did you stay at my place?" Richard asked, hoping he didn't sound like he was asking for the return of his expensive patch of wallpaper or his €85. "That wallpaper wasn't cheap, you know," he muttered.

"Possibly, I lost track. Wherever I stayed I left a kind of calling card."

"A bloody handprint?"

"Yes, or some variation. I wanted the Italians to think I'd been taken by a rival. I'd hoped it would dissuade them, tell them they were too late." He chuckled to himself. "My brother would have laughed at my naivete."

They sat in silence for a moment.

"But you did succeed in laying a trail, hoping that people would come back to the source."

"That was a fortunate side effect, madame, yes. I've been waiting.

And as I said, I did not know who to expect. It could have been any one of half a dozen people. I am pleased it was you, madame."

Richard felt he wasn't getting the credit he deserved here. "I guess the death of Monsieur Paulin slowed everything down; people stopped looking for your brother, dead or alive."

"Poor Charles. That upset me greatly. We were all in the army together, we grew up together. I hadn't spoken to him in years, obviously, but my brother would tell me often what a simple soul he had become. Addled by drink, of course, but harmless."

"Yes, that's how I remember him, too."

"I saw poor Charles as a way out. Somebody had blown his face clean off, he was wearing my brother's clothes..."

"But you forgot about the number?"

"I didn't forget about it, my dear, I just didn't think the Italians would be that thorough or even know about it. I underestimated them. Someone took the man's hand, had it verified, and proved it wasn't my brother at all. I feel for Charles; my brother loved him, took care of him. He wouldn't have wanted him killed to protect our business."

"But back to square one all the same."

"Yes. In order for this to stop, I need my brother found. Again."

"And killed. Again."

"Yes, my dear." He looked at the two of them with a slight hint of desperation. "And of course, the money will be yours," he added. "Five hundred thousand euros." Richard looked sharply at Valérie, who wore a picture of innocence. "You don't have to, of course, it's up to you, but I'd be grateful if you could give some of that to Marie..."

"I don't think she'd object..."

"But what if Marie killed Charles Paulin?" Valérie tried to ask the question delicately, and just about got away with it. "She was certainly impersonating your brother."

"Really?" Richard was agog.

"Oh yes, look at her hands."

The old man looked very sad. "The thought had occurred to me, and I don't want whoever murdered Charles to get my brother's bounty." He shook his head; tears were welling up in his eyes. "What will you do?" he asked, his voice breaking up.

Not much later, Richard and Valérie made their way back along the passage to cover up their tracks, stopping briefly to replace the blanket on the chiller and cover Vincent Grandchamps's cold smile.

"So they both thought they were the father?" Richard was shaking his head, trying to jolt a silent Valérie into conversation. It worked.

"Obviously they were both meant to," Valérie snorted, clearly angry. "Vanity is so easy to manipulate. Especially in men of a certain age." And she moved off ahead of him toward the stairs.

"I guess so, but it's the classic *cherchez la femme*..." he answered, trying to even up the score.

Valérie nodded slowly, her eyes widening, and very quietly, out of Richard's earshot, she whispered the word, "Brilliant!"

34

He'd always hankered for the quiet life. Get up, potter about, do a bit of research, write a few hundred words; a late morning *apéritif* followed by a spot of lunch was Richard's ideal start to the day. And that's exactly how the day had gone thus far, so in theory he should have been far more content than he actually was. He broodily poured himself another glass of white wine to compensate, but it did nothing to shift the overriding question that was ricocheting around his mind like a balloon released before it's been tied, noisy and aimless.

What was she up to?

He was well aware that as far as planning goes he wasn't on the committee, as it were, that was made up of two as far as he could tell, Valérie and Passepartout. But they had come this far together, shared so much, he felt anyway, that he was surely entitled to be in on things, and he was a little hurt to discover that he was now, apparently, surplus to requirements. Valérie had been pretty quiet over breakfast, concentrating on her phone mostly, then she'd retired to her room to "make some calls" and then an hour later he'd heard her drive off at the usual Mach 3 pace and that was it.

The thought crossed his mind that he should actually be concerned for her, but he couldn't imagine a scenario in which she'd be in trouble. The Rizzolis were out of action; only the two of them knew of Grandchamps in the wine chiller... On the face of it, everything seemed under control.

So, what was she up to?

Well, sod this for a game of soldiers, he thought, downing the wine in one go, *I may as well do some work,* and he wandered over to his shelves to choose a film to watch. He ran his finger along the top of the DVDs, arranged by genre, alphabetized within a complicated date and studio structure. He eventually stopped at comedy, 1945, Paramount, *Road to Utopia. Enough of this playing the sap in film noir; let's have some laughs.*

He put the film on to play, settled briefly in his favorite chair, before getting up again, reclaiming the bottle of wine and sitting back down. The shutters were closed and his phone was off; the perfect afternoon awaited.

"I thought I would find you in here." Valérie strode in, Passepartout in her arms. She flicked the lights on before opening the windows and throwing open the shutters. Richard didn't move, his wineglass halfway to his face. She put Passepartout on his lap—the small dog at least had the good grace to look apologetic—took the glass from his hand, had a sip of it herself and placed it on the table, out of his grasp. He looked at it longingly.

"Can I help, madame?" he asked stiffly.

"Of course you can help!" she cried. "I can't do this without you, Richard."

His face went through the task of trying to show the full range of emotions that he was now processing. First he smiled, before a distrustful look came into his eye, followed by an indignant pursing of the lips and a flaring of the nostrils, and then an eyebrow arched in suspicion. He looked like he'd entered a gurning contest. "Really?" he asked, the voice agreeing with the eyebrow.

"Really," she said, definitively.

"So where have you been all morning?"

"I had a few things I wanted to check—our friends the Rizzolis, for instance. They're fine, a little sore, but fine. Just some errands really." She sounded suddenly coy.

"And what do you want me to do?" He was still not yet prepared to let go of his suspicions.

"I want you to take me out to dinner," she replied, in a way that implied he should have known that.

"OK." He decided to just go with it. "Shall I book a table?"

"I've already done it," she said, scooping up Passepartout.

"And where am I taking you?"

"Chez Bruno." She had a mischievous look in her eye. "It's more of a party really."

"A party?" He wished, just once, that she would give him the information he needed all in one go, rather than making him feel like a dolt all the time.

"Yes, everyone will be there, Marie, Melvil, Juge Grandchamps, Bruno, obviously. The two of us, everyone."

Richard's eyes narrowed. "You're up to something, and I wish you'd tell me what it is."

"I know who killed Monsieur Paulin," she said earnestly, and he went to interrupt her. "Well, actually, I *think* I know who killed Monsieur Paulin, and I need your help to prove it."

"Who?"

"I don't want to say until we know."

"But then you won't have to say."

"Yes, and you'll know."

"Yes, but can't I know now? I mean, if you want my help and all."

She started to pace the room nervously. "Richard, you are a lovely man, and I really think we are a good team, yes?"

"Ye-es." It seemed like he'd had this type of conversation before, many times. It always ended with him being the stoic after being called the "brotherly" type.

"But you are just too honest. If I told you now you would not be able to hide it." He pursed his lips again. "You watch actors"—she pointed at the screen still playing *Road to Utopia*—"but you aren't one."

He couldn't help being slightly hurt but also he couldn't help realizing that she had a point. He and Clare had joined a bridge club once—it had been her boss's idea—but after only a few hands Clare refused to be his partner. "Your face isn't just an open book, Richard; it's a bloody great shop window!"

"Well, I can't say I'm not hurt by that." He tried to sound wounded.

"I'm sorry, but if who I think it is has the least idea that they are suspected, it could be very dangerous."

He sighed. "OK, but in that case, we don't do it alone..."

"But..."

"I insist. Bonneval must be there, the police must be there. This isn't the Wild West; we must do this properly, Valérie." She turned away. "Please," he added.

She gave a deep breath. "Oh, OK. If you insist." And with that, she left the room.

Richard took a deep breath himself and turned to the screen for inspiration. "I ain't looking for trouble, pardner," Bob Hope was saying, "but if trouble comes looking for me, I'm gonna be mighty hard to find."

Hope always did have impeccable timing, thought Richard.

35

What's up with him?" Juge Grandchamps asked as Richard pushed his wheelchair toward the town center. "He's got a face like a squashed pumpkin."

"I think he's being English, monsieur *le juge*," Valérie replied while digging Richard in the ribs. "He is wearing his stiff upper lip."

Richard, still unsure of his role, childishly parroted her.

"Well, he'd best lose it before dinner, or it'll be like eating soup after visiting the dentist." The old man chuckled to himself. He was wearing a big Homburg hat that hid most of his face and that somehow made him all the more intimidating. He must have been horrible to come across in court, thought Richard.

The late evening sun bathed the square in an almost orange glow, and a gentle breeze stopped it from being too warm. It was the perfect spring evening and the bird chatter added to the idyllic setting. Bruno, once more impeccable in his white shirt and black trousers, greeted them with a low nod of the head. "*Bonsoir*, madame, monsieur, and monsieur *le juge*." He looked edgy. "I wasn't aware that our esteemed judge would be our guest this evening; I am most honored."

"Ha! I imagine you are, Signor Frascatti," snarled the old man. He was certainly aiming to keep up appearances.

Bruno ignored the greeting. "I have your table ready," he said quietly, bowing again.

"Bruno's family are from Italy," said the judge, "but that's all in the past, though, eh, Bruno?" He cackled again.

Richard caught Valérie's eye and she winked at him, a slight smile playing briefly on her lips.

Bruno had prepared a table for four on the terrace just by the window, with a pristine white tablecloth and dark-green napkins folded into the wineglasses. Marie was there, humming something as always, and just arranging the last of the cutlery. Melvil sat at a table the other side of the door, sipping a Coca-Cola and holding a cigarette, every inch the wannabe matinee idol. He nodded to them, his dark glasses hiding his eyes, too cool to break his pose.

"*Bonsoir.*" Marie greeted them all at the table, and after the formality of kissing, they sat down as Bruno removed a chair and positioned the judge's wheelchair at the table. Valérie sat with her back to the window, next to the judge, and with Richard opposite.

"I'm sorry I'm late." Officer Bonneval hurried onto the terrace, slightly out of breath. "Someone has vandalized the speed camera on the D72, not strictly my jurisdiction but someone has to mop up."

"Did you catch who did it?" Valérie asked, standing and offering her cheek.

"No," he replied, "we never do."

"Good, those things are a menace."

"I agree, madame, that's why we never catch who did it. I didn't say that I didn't know who did it!" They both laughed.

"The law's the law," spat the judge, "speeding, vandalism"—he paused—"murder."

"Can I get some drinks?" Marie stood smiling at the head of the table, pen and pad in hand.

"Good evening, Marie." Bonneval stood, towering above her, and then bent awkwardly to kiss her cheeks. It would have been easier if he'd stayed seated.

If Richard had thought that the judge having broken the ice with his talk of murder might hurry things along, he was wrong. Small talk was made all the way through the meal. Bonneval was good company, Valérie in sparkling form, and the judge happy to throw in the odd barb, while Melvil looked on from a distance, Marie worked hard, and Bruno apparently sulked inside, nipping out to have the odd cigarette with Melvil.

It was all very convivial, and therefore not at all why they were there, in his opinion.

Toward dessert it was clear that the judge was getting tired, his erratic, poisonous interruptions all but dried up, and he nodded off quietly.

"I suppose we should take him home," Valérie said to Richard, a hint of disappointment in her voice, her plans for the evening ruined.

"So soon?" Bonneval said. "That's such a shame. It is still early."

"Unless, Richard..." Valérie looked at him pleadingly. "Would you drop the judge at home? It's only a short walk. It seems a shame to break up the party."

Richard looked at her incredulously, and then at Bonneval, before sighing heavily and muttering "typical" under his breath. "Yes, OK then," he chuntered, "come on, Judge, bedtime!" The judge's head was slumped forward; only the top of his hat showed.

"So are you still just a 'guest,' madame?" he heard Bonneval ask before wheeling the judge away, muttering as he did so. *He didn't waste much time*, he thought.

Richard returned ten minutes later looking very sheepish indeed.

"Erm, do you have the key?" he asked Valérie.

"I thought you had it!"

"No, I..."

"But I gave it to you." She sounded angry.

"Yes, that may be, but I don't have it."

Bonneval laughed. "Poor Richard, I do this all the time, but I do not get henpecked for it by a 'guest.' Sit down, Richard, sit down. Monsieur *le juge* is fine where he is for now. It is still light and warm yet. Have another drink."

Richard was grateful for Bonneval's friendliness and he put the judge's chair back in place and sat down. "Thank you," he said, trying to avoid eye contact with Valérie.

"OK, we are all here again." Bonneval leaned in conspiratorially. "I must ask why. This is very pleasant, it happens so rarely, but why, madame? Do you have information?"

Valérie leaned in. "Yes," she said simply, "it was Marie."

Bonneval's face went dark. "What was Marie?" he asked, making sure she wasn't nearby. "Marie did not kill Vincent Grandchamps."

"Oh, I know that!" she said and Bonneval leaned back, a look of relief on his face. "Vincent Grandchamps isn't dead."

He leaned forward again. "What makes you so sure, madame?"

"Because he's over there, look!" She pointed to the other side of the square, where an old man stood, stooped. Richard's jaw dropped, and he spun round to watch Valérie closely. In the bar doorway, Bruno crossed himself and Marie dropped some plates. Even Melvil looked shocked. Bonneval stood up quickly, but the old man disappeared around a corner before the policeman could give chase. He tried anyway and returned to the stunned terrace a few minutes later.

"We must all have been mistaken," he said, out of breath again and unconvinced. He sat down and had a drink. "Probably old man Levreux, they always did look alike." Slowly but silently, the brasserie got back to business and Richard filled his glass.

"It was Marie," Valérie repeated deliberately.

"Madame...with all due..."

"She is her mother's daughter, is she not?"

Bonneval caught sight of Marie in the doorway again and he smiled. "She is," he said slowly, "she is."

"Yes, beautiful, vivacious..."

"All of those things..."

"Disloyal, manipulative, greedy..."

Bonneval turned back to Valérie, and Richard could feel the big man tense up next to him.

"She killed Paulin."

"She couldn't have," Bonneval hissed. "Why would she?"

"That is obvious, monsieur. Money. She had been making money from Grandchamps's activity since he vanished."

"I knew that; I was keeping an eye out for her, though. Making sure she didn't go too far."

"She did, though, didn't she? She did go too far."

"That doesn't mean she would have killed Paulin; why would she anyway? She had made enough." The man was talking quietly, and through gritted teeth, not in a threatening way but as someone desperately trying to stay in control.

"If she is her mother's daughter, there is never enough; you know that." Bonneval went to say something else, but Valérie wouldn't let him. "How long have you known that she was your daughter, monsieur?"

Bonneval closed his eyes, then put his head back and looked into the night sky.

"I don't believe it; there he is again!" Richard spat out his drink as he saw in the reflection of the window Vincent Grandchamps, but this time running across the square. Once he reached the other side, another Vincent Grandchamps ran in the opposite direction. Bonneval stood up quickly this time and his hand reached for his gun. It was too late, though, as both Grandchamps were out of sight before he could react, but also his attention was diverted as a watching Marie fainted and fell into Melvil's arms.

Richard grabbed the *pichet* of wine that was still on the table and poured himself a large glass of red. He hadn't the slightest notion of what was going on.

Bonneval seated Marie gently in a chair inside, pushing Melvil aside as he did so. "She is in shock," he said angrily as he returned to the table without sitting down. "I don't know what game you are playing, madame, but it's not amusing."

"Monsieur, this is no game. I shall ask again, how long have you known that Marie was your daughter?"

Bonneval leaned in over the table after looking at the door and making sure Marie was out of earshot. "Just before Antoinette died, she told me. Before that I had always suspected something, but I couldn't be sure. I see now the resemblance." Richard glanced over at the recovering Marie, then discreetly back at the behemoth next to him. He didn't see it himself. "Antoinette made me promise to look after her, make sure that nothing happened to her, and to make sure that she shouldn't know."

"But?" Valérie asked softly.

"But I cannot be everywhere at once!" He was angry, not with Valérie but with the situation. "I realized too late that she was playing a game with the mafia, Grandchamps's game." He spat the name. "I had always turned a blind eye to Grandchamps, because the judge asked me to; he said it would ruin him if I exposed his brother, so I left it. When he went missing I admit I was relieved, until I found out what Marie was doing. I can't take on the mafia, madame; with my resources I can barely cope with..."

"But then she killed Paulin, and that was an end to it."

"She did not kill anyone, madame; she is not capable of doing so." He spoke deliberately, trying to maintain his calm.

"And even if she did, she couldn't claim the two million euros. Wrong man," Richard said.

"Two million?" Bonneval turned on him.

"You didn't know?" Richard sank back in his seat, cradling his glass of wine.

"It's no surprise the child has lost her senses!" Bonneval was furious. "And tonight, this charade. You will drive her to her limit; she will try and kill Grandchamps if she finds him."

He stood up, ready to restart the search right there and then for the old man, or men, Richard still wasn't sure.

"I don't think so, monsieur." Valérie was calmness personified.

"And what makes you so sure?" Bonneval leaned over her threateningly, but she didn't flinch.

"Because he is her father."

"That's a lie!" he rasped. "That lowlife, that scum, he could never be the father of my Marie!" His face was now inches from an unflinching Valérie's. "I'd kill him myself if he were here!"

"Do so," Valérie said and flipped the Homburg hat off the sleeping judge, but instead revealing a hideously grinning Vincent Grandchamps, looking unrepentant to the end. Bonneval stood back and fired three shots into the man's chest. The body barely moved. He fired three more with the same effect. Stunned, he bent forward, long enough for Signor Rizzoli to step out of the shadows and club him to the ground, while Signora took some pictures of the doubly deceased Vincent Grandchamps.

Richard took another full glass from his *pichet* of wine just as Martin and Gennie Thompson arrived, each dressed as Vincent Grandchamps. "I don't suppose there's any more of that knocking about, is there, old man?" Martin gasped.

"I've not run around like that in years," said a red-faced Gennie. "How exciting."

Richard poured them all a drink. If he hadn't, he may have fainted himself.

36

So who was the father then?" Madame Tablier asked, trying to appear aloof.

"I don't know," Richard said, "there are rather a large number of candidates. Even Bruno, apparently."

"Men!" she spat, leaving Richard slightly confused with her interpretation of events.

It had been a week since Bonneval's confession. As soon as the Rizzolis had disappeared with their proof of Grandchamps's death, thankfully not the entire wrist and hand, but enough, they felt, to satisfy their superiors, the authorities had been called. Everyone had their stories straight: Valérie, Judge Grandchamps, Bruno, Marie, and Melvil; all had been prepped brilliantly. Martin and Gennie got away quickly and were not part of the cleaning up, and Richard's role as the slightly drunk innocent who just happened to be caught up in the whole thing was a masterful performance, mainly because that's exactly what he was. He had been in on the switch between the judge and his defrosting brother, but nothing else, and he hadn't hidden his subsequent disappointment well.

"You really felt you couldn't tell me anything, then, nothing at all?" he'd quietly asked Valérie in the car home much later that night. He was genuinely hurt.

"But Richard, it was you who solved it all in the first place!" Valérie had gushed.

"Was it?" he'd said sulkily, and then waking up to what she was saying, followed it up with a puppy-like, "Really? Did I?"

"Yes! You said, '*cherchez la femme*...'"

"Meaning Marie?"

"Meaning Antoinette."

"Antoinette, of course." He still wasn't sure.

"She managed to build up a formidable team of protectors for the daughter she knew she was leaving behind, and how did she do that? By convincing them all that they were her father."

"But that means..."

"Yes, Richard."

"I'm not sure whether that's terrific parenting or among the worst I've ever heard." They drove on in silence for a while.

"So it wasn't Marie who killed Paulin, then?"

"No, that was Bonneval. When he found out about Marie and the envelopes, he knew he had to do something to protect her, and when he found out about the price on Grandchamps's head he saw the way out. And, also, a way to give Marie the money she would need to start a new life, money he knew he could never provide himself."

"He really loved her," he said quietly.

"Yes, he did. My guess is that he stumbled upon Paulin, thinking he was Grandchamps, and killed him without really thinking about it. You saw how emotional, how out of control he was." Richard shuddered. "Only then," she continued, "he realized he had the wrong man. That's when he shot the poor man's face off."

"I expect he couldn't believe it when the judge identified him as his brother, then?"

"Yes, though it was convenient for both. In fact, in the end everybody got what they wanted."

"But what about the Rizzolis? How did you get them on your side?"

"I think they felt like they had no choice in the end." She was trying to be dismissive.

"You made them an offer they couldn't refuse?" He could barely contain himself, but still nothing from Valérie on the film front, nothing at all.

"Precisely. I told them they could either go home with nothing, or help us out and pay me a finder's fee out of their bounty. No money or a lot of money, it was an easy choice."

"And, er, how much is a finder's fee out of two million?" He almost dared not ask. He couldn't vouch for Valérie's motives, but the money never really occurred to him.

"After your cut? Not all that much." She looked tired and for once was driving at a conservative rate.

"My cut? Just buy me a new hen."

They'd spent the rest of the journey in silence, exhausted, and had then said their awkward good nights. The next morning, she was gone.

And here he was a week later, and if it hadn't been for Madame Tablier's inexhaustible curiosity, he couldn't, with any degree of certainty, say that it had actually all happened. Clichéd or not, it all seemed like a dream. What was it that Valérie had said? "In the end, everybody got what they wanted." Not everyone, he thought sadly; he was still a hen down and feeling sorry for himself, too. The prospect of the busy high season to come did nothing to lift his spirits.

"Monsieur?" The first of that busy season was lifting up his wife's coffee cup to show that she wanted a refill. *More newlyweds*, he mused, recalling the Rizzolis, another one playing the attentive husband. His phone pinged, distracting him from the coffee pot. "New booking," it said, but Richard decided to save it for later. A minute after, his phone pinged again: *NEW MESSAGE FROM CLIENT D'ORÇAY.*

He spilled the coffee and nearly dropped his phone. He read the message.

Dear Richard, I have reserved a room for Passepartout and myself, from tomorrow. I have come into some money and have decided to buy something in the Val de Follet. Please leave a bowl of water in the room.

Love Valérie x

P.S. I can't give you a departure date—can we leave it open for now?

His heart started pounding; even his eyes seemed to lose focus on the message.

"Monsieur!" said the young husband. "My wife is without coffee!"

Richard raised his head slowly, an enormous grin breaking out on his face. "Frankly, my dear," he said, "I don't give a damn!"

Acknowledgments

It's been a lot of fun writing the first in the Follet Valley series. I wanted to write something that I would like to read, so having gotten this far, I hope you liked it, too. If you did, my first thanks go to you!

I'd also like to thank my agent, Bill Goodall. Any writer will tell you that to have an agent who believes in you and encourages you is vital to the process, and Bill has done that since day one. Pete Duncan and the whole team at Farrago Books have been the same, and their aim of publishing books that "put a smile on your face" is something the world needs more of.

The publishing industry's brilliant Abbie Headon was vital in kickstarting the idea for Follet Valley, and also with early suggestions. Julia Chapman, Caimh McDonnell, and Maureen Younger, all excellent writers themselves, were always on hand with tips or support, as has Mark Billingham from day one of my writing career. The French used in the book is as close to French as the French will allow you to get as, in my experience, nobody ever agrees on the rules of French, and when they do, they change them! My French adjudicator in this then is the *formidable* Christelle Couchoux.

I must also thank my wife and family for putting up with me, not just while writing but all the time; and lastly, my gratitude goes to my adopted home of France and the Loire Valley for providing endless inspiration, comfort, and good wine.

About the Author

Credit: © Richard Wood

Bestselling author Ian Moore is also a stand-up comedian and conference host in the UK, and husband, father of three boys, farmhand, chutney-maker, and Basil Fawlty impersonator in France. Since doing less stand-up, he has stopped taking himself so seriously.

Death and Fromage

A FOLLET VALLEY MYSTERY 2

Scandal erupts in the small French town of Saint-Sauveur when its famous restaurant is downgraded from three Michelin stars to two. The restaurant is shamed, the local cheese producers are shamed, the town is shamed, and the leading goat's cheese supplier drowns himself in one of his own pasteurization tanks.

Or does he?

Valérie d'Orçay, staying once again at Richard Ainsworth's B&B while house-hunting in the area, isn't convinced that it's suicide. Despite his misgivings, Richard is drawn into Valérie's investigation and finds himself becoming a major player...

COMING SOON